I0748395

THE SHITHEAD

ALSO BY TIM GRAHL

Your First 1000 Copies

Book Launch Blueprint

Running Down a Dream

The Writers' Common Language

The Threshing

THE SHITHEAD

A NOVEL IN FIFTY SONGS

TIM GRAHL

Edited by
SHAWN COYNE

STORY GRID PUBLISHING

Story Grid Publishing LLC

Nashville, TN.

Cover Design by Timothy Hsu

Edited by Shawn Coyne

First Story Grid Publishing Paperback Edition

September 2024

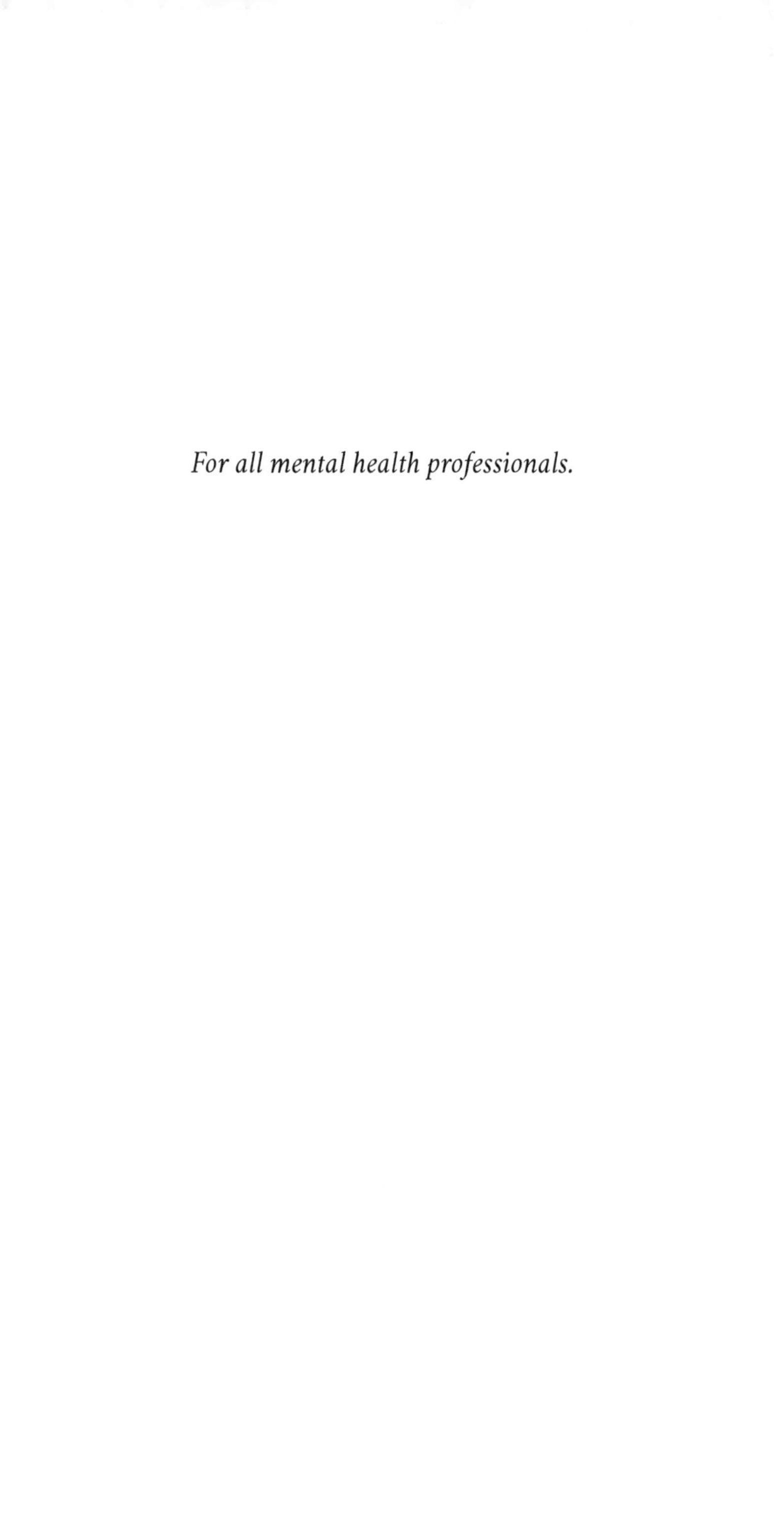

For all mental health professionals.

To the Boo-Hoo Crew!

Facing the end, Shakespeare's Macbeth said this,

> "Life's but a walking shadow, a poor player,
> That struts and frets his hour upon the stage,
> And then is heard no more.
> It is a tale told by an idiot, full of sound and fury,
> Signifying nothing."

I don't agree. So, indulge me, and allow this idiot tell his tale. You can be the judge of its significance.

Love,

Me

Son, Husband, Father, and Friend.

1

CAN'T YOU HEAR ME KNOCKING

"Have you ever had *Sundaynightis?*"

Faye raises her eyebrows.

"The sickness that hits you at the end of the weekend. You know... you begin to dread going to work the next day even though there's no real reason to. Just the thought of it makes you queasy."

She smiles and nods, so I continue.

It's Sunday, one of those slate-gray, way-past-the-holidays, beginning-of-yet-another-year versions. January 28. David is a week from turning nine, which makes Matthew five. Marie has run to Costco to pick up a roasted chicken for dinner. I've got the Premier League on. Even though I've got my red stocking and scarf on and my miniature cannon perched on the arm of the couch pointed northeast towards London, where they are playing at home, Man City is crushing my beloved Arsenal.

I'm willing them to victory.

"Bark! Bark!" Matthew yells, jumping up and down on the couch. David howls, "Good boy!"

"Quiet!" I yell at them as the ball advances across midfield. "Watch the game!"

Matthew attempts to lick David, to which David screams and lurches away, bumping me hard. My shoulder hits the cannon, and it skitters across the floor. Man City blocks the goal attempt.

Fuck.

"Guys!" I'm on my feet now, "Can't you sit still for two—"

Then the scraping of the screen door's hinges reminds me I forgot to WD-40 them yet again. Seconds later, the rustle of the same plastic bags Marie has been recycling since August announces her arrival.

Like a Pavlovian dog, I call out, "Hey, hon, need any help?" but my eyes remain glued to the television.

"What's this?" Marie asks.

I pause the playback and turn to find a thick white envelope with a red stripe down the center inches from my face, the Internal Revenue Service logo emblazoned on the front. The blood drains from my head as I suddenly stand and drop the remote on the cushion to accept the envelope from Marie, all in one rapid motion. I stop myself, careful not to snatch at it, before clearing my throat and then trying to take it from her nonchalantly.

"It looks serious," she says. She shifts the bags in her arms, waiting for a response.

"Where was this?" I change the subject. "The mail doesn't come on Sundays."

"I got it on my way out on Friday and forgot to bring it in from the car."

"Marie, I've asked you a thousand times not to do that."

"It's from the IRS," she says, eyeing the envelope again.

"It's nothing. I get stuff from the IRS all the time," quickly adding, "because of the business."

"Do you owe them anything?"

I force out a dismissive *pfft* and try to laugh it off. "Of course I do! I'm a small business owner. There's never a time you don't owe taxes. Do you have any idea how much shit I have to manage with all of the forms and reports and just total bullshit?" I'm starting to believe it myself.

"So, everything is okay?"

"Yeah! Of course!" I slink over to the nook by the front door and slip the envelope into the old dive bag I use as my briefcase. "I'll take care of it tomorrow."

"Can I help with anything? I can take over paying

the bills again. I know you have so much on your plate."

There it is again. Her mistrust of me is constantly oozing into every comment.

"It's no big deal. Really," I say, waving her off. Marie holds my eyes for a moment longer than necessary, like she does to let me know she's not entirely buying it. Still, she knows she doesn't have enough evidence to really rake me over the coals, so she carries the groceries through the living room and then the dining room into the kitchen and plops everything down on the counter. I retrieve the remote and hit play.

"Did you get a chance to order the cake for David's party?"

She's got me now. "Oh, no, I'm sorry. Completely slipped my mind."

"Eric..." It's never good when she uses my first name. "There will be seventy people at our house at this exact time..." She points to her watch for dramatic effect. "Next week. It was you who insisted on it being a big party. Ordering the cake is the one and only thing I asked you to do... If I can't depend..."

I try to return to the game, but it's useless. The boys' volume continues ratcheting up as Man City widens their lead to three goals. It's all a dull roar underneath the envelope, screaming curses at me from the depths of my bag.

Dinner, dishes, and Sunday family board games

follow. I wrestle the kids into bed. Then I watch two reruns of New Girl as Marie drifts off to sleep. As I begin to fade into the darkness, I dream of a black snake with a red stripe painted down its back, slithering through the house, calling my name.

2

THE PROMISED LAND

"That doesn't sound like Marie," interrupts Faye.

"I can only tell you what she sounded like to me," I offer.

She still looks at me circumspectly.

"That's fair. Right? It's kinda my story, and I need to tell it from my point of view. Don't I?" I reply.

"Go on," she says with a frown.

I jolt awake at exactly 4:38 a.m., sweating from surviving the usual hand claws from the dark and accusations from the deep nightmares.

4:38 is what I call "Fuck. You. Shithead" time.

Let me explain. I remember reading in some magazine that when Mr. Rogers was alive, you know *Mister Rogers' Neighborhood,* he used to weigh himself every day. His preferred weight was 143 pounds, which he translated into "I" for one, "Love" for four, and "You" for three. You see where this is going. My numeric translation isn't as nice as Mr. Rogers', but it feels just as accurate. At least I don't weigh 438 pounds.

I try to go back to sleep, but every time I reenter the twilight between "here" and "not here," the nightmares roar back. The only way to get rest is to be so exhausted at the end of the day that even my inner tormentors need a few hours to reenergize. Like clockwork, though, they push me back to the real world at 4:38.

No matter what.

So, I'm up for good now and working through my morning prework work routine on my laptop in the living room, but I can't stop thinking about the dive bag in the entryway. I alternately think it's just one of those "here's a written confirmation that your address is the same that it has always been" letters or a "you have been designated for termination without prejudice" notice. But I don't go near it because, if I do, I know I'll give away just how terrible it is on my face. Marie knows me too well, and I can't risk it. I need hours to process stuff to hide what's eating me up. I resolve to open the letter when I'm really alone. At work.

At last, the time has come to get David up and moving—a welcome distraction. This usually takes a good five minutes of cajoling. Then, back downstairs, seven minutes to brush my teeth, comb my hair, and dress. My daily uniform consists of three parts: a pair of faded blue jeans, one of seven plain Old Navy T-shirts differentiated only by color, and one of five variations of New Balance sneakers.

Two minutes to make the bed—Marie's been up since 5:30—five to mix my morning smoothie filled with all of the roughage, protein, and vitamins I never get a chance to eat during the day, and then ten minutes of free time to finish up any other to-dos before it's time to leave.

But David is always the wild card. I am still working on getting him to adhere to a reliable schedule. Anything can distract that child from doing what he needs to do to leave on time.

"You don't have to tell me," Faye breaks in.

I don't say anything but pause and drink a glug of lukewarm coffee until she indicates it's okay to continue.

Finally, I'm out the door at 7:34 a.m., dropping David off at the Music City Montessori School just before the 7:55 a.m. "last call" door closes. Then, depending on

Nashville traffic and weather, I expect to arrive at my office around 8:15, the usual time.

Today, though, the fog is hanging low and heavy, slowing traffic and empowering my insides to churn over that letter. For now, I run the business out of a coworking space buried in the bowels of a nondescript building in downtown Nashville off 9th Avenue. I have two offices next door to each other.

I use one, and my employees, Andre and Bethany, share the other. Besides us, the additional offices are filled with one-man law firms, insurance salesmen, and a handful of therapists. After getting my coffee from the shared kitchen, I pop into Andre and Bethany's office to check in.

Andre is the only full-time employee, only a few years out of college. He's a tall, lanky fellow, who even in the midst of a brutal Nashville summer, commonly arrives at work in a Rage Against the Machine concert hoodie. The company's copywriter, front-end web developer, and overall tinkerer, he's a bit like me, only younger and more intelligent.

Bethany is more competent than Andre and me combined. She works about thirty hours a week—at least that's what I agreed to pay her for—half of them from home. As the sole provider for three kids under seven, she still holds down a second-shift telemarketer job even after I hired her as our project manager. She refused to take the position without me knowing she'd be coming and going as she pleased.

Long ago, I surrendered to her incredible systems-oriented mind. I don't care how long it takes her to do her work because I could never do what she does if I worked twenty-four hours a day.

She handles the delivery of all our proposals and the important invoicing that accompany each one. Bethany tells me never to send a proposal without the attached invoice. The last thing you want to do is make a client ask for a bill after they've already verbally agreed to hire you. Plus, I used to inevitably forget the details of the deals I'd made only minutes prior and have to bug the clients to tell me what they'd already accepted. My sieve of a mind drove her crazy, so she got some doohickey off Amazon to record my business calls in the office and an app for my cellphone. Now she transcribes the calls, emails them to me, and then incorporates them into a business proposal template she constantly updates to make better and better and better.

This morning, Andre and I spitball a book launch project, which will need a landing page that, as clients inevitably say, "pops!" Whatever that means.

Satisfied, he says, "Cool," and then slips his headphones on and returns to his monitor.

I stay in the doorway, tapping the side of my Harry Potter Cauldron coffee cup with my finger, unable to move. Work has slowed considerably over the past six months. Looking at the back of Andre's head makes me realize I've been coasting way too long on a tiny bit of bonus buffer I got for a project that went to number one on the *New York Times* bestseller list.

Now, I realize that success is fading fast in the rearview mirror, and the company is, yet again, running on fumes. Payroll is due at the end of the week, and it will be tight to ensure Andre and Bethany get paid on time. When you work hard, and something comes of it, it's hard not to take a breath and relax for a little while. At least, that's what I tell myself. Apparently, my *little while* went too long. Again.

Andre, obviously feeling my laser stare on his back, turns back to me and pulls back one side of the headphones.

"Need something else?"

I shake my head and scurry back to my office.

It's time.

After I decide there is no getting around a form of suffering—I'm a "pull the Band-Aid off as fast as you can" person—I seize the envelope from my dive bag, tear it open, and unfold the stack of paper. My eyes dart around the first page, ignoring everything else until I find the total. They always put the full amount owed somewhere on the first page.

The IRS hasn't broken protocol.

Yep.

There it is.

I feel nothing. It can't be because I'm Zen. I don't even know what that is.

For some reason, though, I start to laugh.

$83,262.58

3

CALLING IT QUITS

It might as well be a million. Or ten million. Or some other astronomical amount that is hopeless for me to pay.

The truth is that I've known this moment would come. For years, I've been struggling to build my little marketing agency. I've had a good run, and I stupidly hired more employees in anticipation of more work, which always seems to slip through my fingers at the last minute when some competitor undercuts my pricing. Then I'm stuck scrounging up enough cash to meet payroll or provide severance for those I have to lay off.

All the while, I still have to cover my own expenses, the office lease, computers, and the never-ending onslaught of utility, grocery, tuition, car, mortgage, legal, accountant, and emergency bills. Plus, it's really not that easy to pay taxes.

Figuring out the estimates, submitting the quarterly forms, and writing the checks was a pain before the software came along to do it all "for you." Back then, though, at least it was at the front of my mind. I would write all the checks simultaneously and then physically hand them to my employees on "Payday." Then I'd drop the other checks in the mail to the IRS, the state, the city, the county, and all of the other governmental agencies that get a piece of every dollar of every business.

Now that everything has switched to direct deposit to the employee, I can easily not go into the old QuickBooks file and wire the money to the tax authorities. The payments and the forms just sit in a different software tab, and you can pretend they're not there.

Quarters pass, then years, and I'm not getting in trouble. Nothing other than the occasional questioning or warning letter from the Internal Revenue Service arrives. I'm so full of other shit that I simply don't respond, and the more time passes and the more nothing happens, the more I put it out of my mind. You'd be surprised how easy it is not to think about it.

Another fire always burns closer and hotter that needs putting out. The car breaks down. The kids need new school clothes. The internet in the office is too slow, so I have to upgrade the service.

"I'm sorry," Faye interrupts, "but why were you using desktop QuickBooks accounting instead of a third-party payroll service?"

"Um, because they didn't exist then...and even if they did, I wouldn't have been able to use them because I was always robbing Peter to pay Paul, and you can't do that with those services. You must transfer the payroll and the tax payments in one fell swoop. And also because I'm a shithead?"

"Gotcha!" Faye laughs a little. "So what did you do?"

I force my eyes back to the top of the page of the notice and start to read through it. I flip to page two. Then three.

That's when I see it.

A date. A time. A place. An address.

This Friday, February 2, 10:00 a.m. Nashville Internal Revenue Service Taxpayer Assistance Center located at 801 Broadway.

It's less than a mile away from my office on Tenth Avenue. Jesus, it's a fifteen-minute walk!

There's even a name.

I'm to see an agent named Mason.

This is new.

I have never been summoned before. I keep reading and find the warnings. If I don't show up for the meeting, a subpoena will follow. Then they'll seize my bank account and garnish my cash. Because I had to use Marie and my personal assets to secure my business's bank account and credit line, they'll put a lien on our house, too.

I know at a certain point if you can't pay, they'll even cart you off to jail. Four days to come up with over eighty grand…

Or spill my guts to Marie, which will result in her calling her father crying. He'll either convince her to finally dump my sorry ass, take the kids, and move back in to her perfect childhood home, or worse, he'll "rescue" us with some kind of castrating lecture that ends up with some sort of loan at some kind of "market appropriate" interest rate that will enslave me to pay in blood money every month for the rest of my life to that miserable prick whose wife left him years ago because he was such an asshole.

So, basically, jail or jail.

I meticulously order and refold the papers before placing them back into their lovely red-banded envelope. Then I slump forward and rest the right side of my face on the pleasingly AC-cold laminate of my $69.99 Lagkapten Ikea desktop.

Naturally, I decide to contemplate and count the ways that Agent Mason at the IRS is a complete asshole. I'm betting he's some sixty-two-year-old career bureaucrat, fat and bald, thriving in this job where he has the full backing of the federal government to come into people's lives like a wrecking ball.

I tick off my current debt-to-debt ratio. I owe forty thousand on my Tesla and fifty and a half for Marie's Navigator. Both credit cards—the one Marie knows about and the one she doesn't—are always hovering within a few hundred dollars of their nineteen thousand and ten thousand maxes. I still owe this month's twelve-hundred-dollar payment for David's school. We have a three-hundred-and-ninety-thousand-dollar mortgage on the house we bought just last year. And another forty grand in student loans.

Whaddya know. My phone buzzes.

It's Calvert Struthers.

He is tall, in his mid-fifties with perfect salt-and-pepper hair, just the right cowlick, and a permanent smile framing alabaster teeth. Harrison Ford would play him in the movie.

I met him at a conference two years prior, and we hit it off. He runs in wealthier circles than me, so I rarely see him even though we both live in Nashville. But we've been staying in touch, and he's been referring me for a couple of smaller projects. It feels like I'm auditioning to be his friend, and while it gives me the heebie-jeebies, the truth is the guy has been helpful and never asked for anything in return.

I can't turn on my happy talk right now, so I send

him to voicemail and nestle my cheek back on the desk. The phone buzzes again.

He's texted me, "Call me ASAP."

I shrug off my sorrow and ring him back.

"Eric!" he picks up before I hear it ring.

"What's up, bro?" I answer, forcing buoyancy into my voice while I dig my nails into my thigh.

"I've got a big one for you, man. Are you free today?"

"Sure. What do you need?"

"I've got a buddy from the Pinnacle League"—the rich boys' club he's a member of—"flying through Nashville, and you need to meet with him."

"Okay—"

"His name's Tyson Banks. Ty. He's a major whale and has some kind of marketing gig he's looking for someone to manage."

"What is it?"

"I don't know. He didn't spill, but if he's attached to it, it's big. I floated your name, and he's interested. Can you meet him at the international terminal in half an hour? He's only got an hour between flights, so you'll need to meet him in the American Airlines Admirals Club lounge."

"Lounge? They're not going to let me through security."

"Yeah." After a pause, he starts talking to me like I'm a four-year-old. "Um. You'll have to buy a ticket? If it were me, I'd buy the cheapest flight I could find and then, you know, not get on the plane?"

"Got it. Sorry, sometimes I'm a shithead."

Cal rattles off Banks' flight information and signs off with, "This is the big one, Eric. You're going to owe me big time!"

4

STEAM

The last-minute, one-way price for a ticket from Nashville to Atlanta is $285. I split the cost between maxing out the business credit card and using some of our grocery money on the family card. I print out the boarding pass in case my phone crashes and head to the Tesla.

A wreck has traffic snarled, so I've already burned through the first ten minutes of Ty's layover by the time I've made it to security. I try not to check my watch every thirty seconds to indicate to those around me that I am luggage-less and obviously in a hurry, hoping someone will care and let me cut in front of them. No such luck.

I finally make it through the TSA line and, like a freak, start running down Concourse A to the Admirals Club, telling myself I'm governing my pace just right so I won't arrive sweating and panting. The twenty-something at reception stops me and asks for my club card. I explain that I have a meeting. She checks her guest list but my name isn't on it.

I can still access the club with a hundred-and-ten-dollar fee. That also goes on the debit card, wiping out what is left of the week's grocery money. Thankfully, Marie won't need to go shopping until Thursday at the earliest.

Deep breath. I force a nonchalant pace as I enter the lounge and scan for Ty. Only two others are in here. A woman in a business suit sits hunched over as she furiously pokes at a laptop. An SAE tank-topped college frat boy is sleeping next to five empty beer cans.

No whale.

I double-tap Bethany's recording app and replay Cal's call. I have likely fucked up the specifics of the meeting somehow. BNA airport, 11:00 a.m., Admirals Club on Concourse A. Nope, this is right. Maybe he has missed his flight?

"Eric?"

I startle like a baby's Moro reflex at the volume and closeness of the announcement of my name. I turn to find a large, red-faced man with a shaggy mop of dark graying hair. He reminds me of Dick Cheney but is more formidable. His business suit looks like it has been lived in, and his tie hangs loose like a noose around his neck. However, his watch has got to be worth at least a hundred grand. He's three inches taller than me and must outweigh me by one hundred pounds. Not fat, exactly, but significant. He's what my grandmother would call "a man in full."

He holds an open can of Guinness in his left hand as his right swallows mine while shaking it.

"Hi, Mr. Banks, nice to meet you." I give him as firm a handshake as I can, trying not to wince from his.

"Bah," he says, waving me off. "Call me Ty. Let's sit down. Do you want a beer? Don't cost nothing."

I decline and follow him to the booth he's taken over. His briefcase sits on the table, revealing stacks of various-sized papers with dozens of multicolored Post-its floating among the mess with illegible scrawls on each. Two empty Guinness cans are perched next to the briefcase.

"Glad you could make it down here today. When I called Cal for a suggestion, yours was the only name he would give me. Said you're the guy for the job."

"I'll have to thank Mr. Struthers for his trust and confidence," I fumble like I'm talking to the queen of England. I am kind of losing it, what with the IRS news and all. I should have had that beer. I sound like a real sap but press forward. "He didn't say much about the position's requirements, though.

"Right, right." He waves me off like I don't have to be so fancy with my words. "Hang on a sec."

Ty takes a massive gulp from the Guinness and bangs it down on the table hard enough that foam fizzes out of the top and runs down the side as he shoots me a wink. He then slides his briefcase over and rifles through the papers until he finds what he's looking for. He pulls out a sheaf, turns to the last page, folds it back, and then hands it to me with a pen.

"NDA bullshit," he says. "Anything we talk about I need to keep under wraps for now."

I nod like I always sign these kinds of things. "Of course." I turn back to page one and start to read through it.

"Pretty standard stuff," Ty says, glancing at his Patek Philippe.

"Sure," I say and then pretend to skim through the rest of the legalese before signing my name on the last page.

Ty grabs it the second my pen leaves the paper and tosses it into his briefcase without a look.

"So, here's the deal, Eric. Have you heard of Ricky Bryant?"

"The congressman?"

"That's the one. What do you know about him?"

I hesitate.

"Not much," I say, stopping before I add, "that I respect." Out of the four hundred and something congressmen, I can name a half-dozen. Bryant is one of them, both because he always appears as one of those blustering talking heads on various news shows and because of the obnoxious memes I have seen of him. My favorite is a bumper sticker I saw with Bryant's face on it that said, "Ricky Bryant ate my baby."

"Doesn't matter. What you need to know is that Bryant will be announcing his bid for the presidency in six weeks."

"What about..."

He cuts me off quickly. "No way. She's cuckoo bananas, and the party will get her out of the picture in, you guessed it, about six weeks. He is on the shortlist to get the nomination, and from there, it is a flip of the coin to the White House."

At this point, I have no idea what is going on. My little marketing agency is running online launch campaigns for square-foot gardening how-tos and Amish paranormal fiction far more than the flashy business books that make the bestseller lists and deceive me into thinking I'm good at what I do. While we get the occasional music album or online course, we're talking seven-figure businesses, not seven-trillion-dollar governments.

I assume whoever Ty is, he has some big book contract that he wants me to help him promote for my modest five-figure fee. I can't wrap my head around why he is bringing up a political candidate.

So, I stare slack-jawed at Ty, unsure of what to say.

"You know what a super PAC is, Eric?" Ty seems to get why I'm befuddled and has decided to take pity on me.

Not really. "It's a campaign finance thing, right?"

"That's right!" Another snap on a fresh new can of Guinness. "It is basically a way to pull together a big pile of money from donors and spend it however the leadership of said super PAC wants to get someone elected."

I nod like I understand.

"Ricky's campaign manager is an old friend of mine. I've helped him now and again as he has worked his way through and to the top of DC. Not that bullshit you see on Fox or CNN or the internet but the real DC. Now, he has tapped me, yours truly." Ty taps his chest like the Matthew McConaughey character in *The Wolf of Wall Street*. "To run this super PAC, which means I need to have an online marketing plan. Only problem? I don't know shit about online marketing."

He is now pointing at me and practically poking my sternum. "That's where you come in. Cal tells me you have pulled off some outrageous launches for the campaigns you have worked on."

"Well, I'm mainly a guy who pulls the most obvious levers to grab people's attention."

Ty barks out a laugh. "Cal told me you'd say some bullshit like that. How many books have you put on the *New York Times* list?"

"A couple dozen, but—"

"All doing online marketing on a shoestring budget for a product no one wants to buy. Seriously, like, who the fuck wants to read a book? Am I right?"

I can't help but nod. It really is brutal trying to get someone to pay enough attention to a book to buy it, let alone read it.

"What could you do with a real budget and a list of connections that owe a lot of favors?"

I hesitate, but it's hard not to open myself up to the possibilities. "It's hard to say. I'd have to take a look at the budget, the platform, and who these people are before I could really give a projection."

"Right, right, but your gut? What's it saying?"

I'm too excited to answer, and he senses this, so he answers for me.

"I'll tell you what it's saying. It is saying you could knock it out of the fucking park. I trust Cal implicitly, and yours is the only name he offered. I'm no douche, so a bit of Googling and a follow-up call here and there, and I confirmed that what he was telling me was one hundred percent correct."

I ask for clarification, "So you want me to help with some of the marketing for the campaign?"

"No, Eric, I want you to run the whole fucking, goddamned super PAC with me. You will have an eight-figure budget and carte blanche to do whatever is necessary to get our congressman the nomination and then run it all the way to the White House."

"Wait, what? Like, head it up? This would be a full-time thing?"

Ty is nodding.

"So, you are offering me a job, not just a project?"

Ty chugs his Guinness in three big glottal contractions while simultaneously giving me a thumbs up.

"Okay, I'd have to—" I am pausing as the list of responsibilities that must be resolved before I can even consider this crazy opportunity organizes in my head. I have Andre and Bethany to think about. Not to mention the half-dozen retainer clients I am carrying along with several open projects I am in the middle of. What would I do with all of those? Cal didn't mention this being a job offer, and God knows I've had jobs before that pushed me to the brink of my sanity, so I vowed never to have another.

"I'm sorry, Mr. Banks, I don't know if this is a good fit for me. I have employees and clients and—" Jesus, there is no way. "Yeah, and I have never worked on a political campaign before. I have no idea where I would even start."

Ty laughs my protestations off. "These are all just details. Look, Eric, how much are you pulling down a year after you pay those employees and all your expenses? Just a tad over six figures?"

I don't say anything, but he's remarkably accurate as if he's been reading my mail.

"Doesn't go very far in Nashville," he continues. "So, you are always hawking for new clients and hoping they pay on time so you can make payroll." He's on a roll now. "Is this really the life you imagined when you struck out alone? How long have you been running your business?"

I think back to when David was born. Three months later, with Marie's support and a downgrade to our living standards, I quit my job. I was spending fifteen hours a day commuting and doing a job I hated, and I never got to hang with the two most important people in the world to me. I started my own thing.

"Answer me, son!" Ty puts on a Foghorn Leghorn voice to snap me back to reality.

"Almost nine years."

"No offense, but shouldn't it be getting easier by now? Isn't that Malcolm Gladwell's thing? By ten years, you should be world-class at something? I bet you have put in way more than ten thousand hours. And here you are still running a podunk little marketing agency that is no different from a thousand other guys who are always teetering on the edge of losing their business. Aren't you ready for a change? Don't you think it's time for you to level up?"

He stops talking and lets his argument sit on that cheap Admirals Club tabletop like the glowing, precious escape hatch I've been looking for.

I lose all ability to respond, but as they say, the ball is in my hands. The man has seen right through me. Not two weeks earlier, I was bitching to my buddy Aneel over beers about this very thing. "Shouldn't this be getting easier?" I asked.

I graduated from the University of Tennessee in 2003 with a double major in marketing and business management. Aneel had dropped out of the same program in the first year and, instead of attending expensive classes, spent his days at Barnes and Noble sipping coffee and teaching himself programming and online marketing. He didn't even pay for the books!

Fast forward fifteen years. I run a struggling agency and am still paying off my school loans. At the same time, Aneel is the most sought-after marketing consultant in Nashville, New York, Chicago, and Los Angeles. We never talk specifics, but I know he is making some several multiples of six figures with just a part-time remote assistant and a home office.

Aneel has offered me praise and "go get 'em, tiger" platitudes, which I should take as his genuinely caring about me, but it really irritates me. He is always getting invited on cool trips and traveling with powerful people. Meanwhile, I'm stuck unclogging Marie's hair from the shower drain.

Just the week before, Aneel found himself in the desert outside of Phoenix with the CEO of a tech startup shooting various semi-legal semiautomatics. Not that shooting guns in the desert is my dream, but you get the point.

"What's the salary?"

Ty slaps the table, knocking over the empty cans, and the business lady a few tables away jumps, shooting a perturbed look at the back of his large head.

"Now you are asking the right questions! It's a hundred and eighty a year to start with and then thick bonuses when our boy gets nominated and elected... and a hundred grand signing bonus."

Ty's form splits into two and then four. Stars swim

into my vision, and I can barely grip the table's edge with both hands to keep me from sliding out of the booth and puddling on the floor. A hundred thousand! One-zero-zero fucking thousand! IRS debt? Gone. Like that! And I would have enough left over to make some room on the credit cards, plus a salary big enough to pay them off in less than a year. I open my mouth to answer, but I can only gape like a fish.

Ty blurts out a laugh. "I am taking it you are in?"

5

WE ARE THE CHAMPIONS

I wander around the airport in a daze, trying to find my way out but unable to focus enough to follow the signage.

I keep spending and then re-spending the hundred grand in my head, but figuring out how the money would shake out was pretty easy.

The one hundred and eighty thousand a year salary comes to fifteen thousand a month. Minus forty percent to cover all the tax, social security, and health insurance deductions leaves me nine thousand a month to cover the family nut. I would only have a little extra buffer, but at least it wasn't negative.

Plus, I'll have an expense account, so I'll be able to eat most of my food out during business, which will reduce our grocery bill. I am kind of a pig when it comes to eating. With the one-time hundred-thousand-dollar bonus, which I'll also have to pay about fifteen thousand up front to the IRS—a prepay is definitely the way to go, so I don't spend money that isn't mine—I can cover all the back tax debt immediately and even have a few thousand dollars left. A fresh start is a fresh start, even if the reality of the offer isn't as great as I thought it would be. And Ty said I had a possibility of getting a bonus, too, if it all worked out the way they wanted.

No two ways about it, though, this is the break I've been looking for. It will solve all my immediate problems. And no doubt it's finally my turn to get into the power networks formed at all those country clubs and schools I haven't been able to gain entry to. I couldn't even work there. Instead of watching others get their chance and move beyond the constant money stress, I am now getting a key to being a player in those behind-closed-door deals. This is huge!

After twenty minutes, I slow my adrenaline rush and find a single seat left at a crowded gate bound for Buenos Aires. While babies wail around me and passengers crowd around the velvet ropes reserved for first class, I pulled out my phone to download some notes on the last five minutes of the meeting with Ty.

By that point in the conversation, after he'd revealed the salary, I struggled mightily to stay focused and retain the details accompanying it. He said I'd have to give a presentation to the super PAC board members and explain how I would, in Ty's words, "pull in and deploy the resources." I'd need to quickly become familiar with the rules and regulations around super PACs and stay within those boundaries regarding how I would raise and spend the funds to get Congressman Bryant elected. One public slipup, betraying the fact that I don't know diddly about political campaigns, would be a disaster.

Ty assured me he was as thick as thieves with most of the board members, and we would get the job. I just needed to go through the perfunctory motions of submitting and pitching a proposal in the next few weeks.

As I tap this into my phone, I realize the kink in my plan. The meeting at the IRS is in four days. Securing this job and getting the signing bonus will take a few weeks. The acidic hole in my stomach that momentarily disappeared during the meeting with Ty has started to churn again.

Surely it doesn't matter, I think. In the grand scheme of things, I've put this off for years, but nothing has happened. If they don't hear from me for a couple more weeks, but I show up with a check to pay off the entire balance, everything will be fine.

My intricate, reasoned justification covers the pit yet again.

This is good news! I cheer myself forward.

I do not need to worry about the tax problem. It

will be solved very shortly. I'm about to wipe out the tax debt all at once!

I catch an involuntary giggle just as it slips out.

I text Marie.

6

UP THE JUNCTION

Let's go out tonight. Just you and me. I'll have Julie come watch the boys.

Babe, it's Tuesday, Marie responds immediately. *I have book club.*

Can you skip tonight? I want to take you out.

Her three dots dance.

My thoughts float back to the meeting with Ty. I smile. The dots are still dancing.

At last, *Okay.*

Six hours later, Marie thanks the hostess as she tucks her dress under her legs and slides into the booth. My leg shakes under the table.

"Let's order some champagne!" I grin.

She smiles back. "What has gotten into you? What is going on?"

"Whatever do you mean?" I tease.

"Date night on a Tuesday. Champagne. You tell me."

"Okay." I cut the drama and take a deep breath. "Calvert Struthers called me today."

"Who?"

"Remember? Cal?" Still nothing. "The Ivy League guy from the conferences? He sends me some work every now and then."

Marie shrugs and takes a sip of water.

"Anyway, he called and had me go to the airport to meet with this guy, Ty Banks, today about a gig."

"What kind of gig?"

"That's the thing. I thought he would just be another business guy publishing a book he'd want me to launch. But it wasn't that. It's way bigger."

"What is it?" She's excited now.

"Babe, the pay is a hundred and eighty thousand plus bonuses."

"Wow! That's crazy. For one project?"

"No, not necessarily. It is actually a job offer."

"Job offer?"

I explain the super PAC and running the political campaign for the next two years.

"Who is the candidate?"

"It's such a great opportunity. I would be getting to work with a big budget and actually test out my marketing chops for the first time at scale. I would be able to run tests and multiple campaigns."

Marie waits.

"Congressman Bryant."

"Ricky the Dicky?"

"That's the one."

"Are you serious?"

"Yeah."

"No way...Come on...You're fucking with me."

"I'm not."

"Jesus, Eric!" She's speaking a little too loudly now. "We hate that guy. He is such an asshole. Not to mention just about everything he stands for we loath."

"Not everything."

Marie rolls her eyes and sits back in the booth, folding her arms. "You really want to work for this guy?"

"Technically, I won't be working for him. I will be running the super PAC and working for Ty Banks."

"And this is a full-time job?"

"Yeah."

"What about Andre and Bethany? What are they going to do?"

"I'm not sure yet. I might be able to bring them with me."

"Might? Did you ask?"

"No."

"Would they even want to work for that asshole? That's not what they signed up for."

"Again, they won't be working for—"

"So, if you can't get approval from this Ty Guy, you

will just cut them loose? Bethany quit her primary job to come work with you. What, ten months ago? She has kids she's got to take care of!"

"I know," I say calmly. I have the sense not to tell Marie to calm down in public as it will only piss her off more.

"So let me get this straight. You want to shut down your company, fire the employees that have put their trust in you, and take a job from some guy you don't even know because of another guy I don't even know, helping get Ricky the Dicky elected to the White House? That's what you're telling me?"

Now I start to get heated. "Did you miss the part where my salary is basically doubling, not to mention I'll be able to let go of all the stress of making payroll and bringing in clients and the thousands of other little bullshit things I have to do to keep the company afloat and our family housed, fed, and clothed! All that shit is gone. I could pay off the cars. We could take the boys to Universal Studios and see Hogwarts. This would happen all before any of the big bonuses come through."

Marie burns my argument to ashes. "What happens if he doesn't get nominated? What happens if he does get nominated and elected? Besides the irreparable harm to our country, what will happen to your job? Will you still have one?"

I don't answer. I just sulk.

The truth is, I don't know. The other fact is: I don't

care. In two years, I'll figure something else out. All I know and care about is that in two years, I won't be in the same hole I am in now. I've just got to cover up this mess, and if Cal Struthers hadn't called me, I would never have figured out how to do it.

"You don't know about your employees. You don't know if you will still have a job after the election. So, you haven't actually thought this through. You have already decided to jump before considering how it affects anyone but you, including me and the boys."

Now I kind of lose it. "That is all I'm thinking about!" My teeth clench, and I suspect my temple veins are bulging. I think I might have even pounded the table a little too aggressively because my ice-water glass fell, and now my crotch is soaked.

Marie rolls her eyes again with a look of contempt that any man who has ever loved a powerful and brilliant woman knows and dreads in equal measure.

"Marie—"

"Not to mention, even the idea that you would do anything to support that scumbag is making me sick to my stomach. Is that who you are? Is that who you are wanting to align yourself with? Are you going to update your LinkedIn and Facebook to make sure everyone in the world knows who you are really working for?"

I stare at her, not answering. I've lost the will to engage.

"You know what?" She scoots from the booth and

stands. “Fuck this dinner. And fuck you for making me skip my book club for this.”

“Marie.” I put a hand on her forearm, halfheartedly at best. “Come on. Sit down.”

She snatches her arm away. “You stay. Enjoy your celebratory dinner alone. I will be Ubering home.”

So fucking dramatic. She turns and marches through the dining room toward reception.

I look around the room at the other patrons, who pretend they haven’t been enjoying the free show. I sigh like I’m the victim of a crazy woman, muttering curses as I follow in her wake. Sure enough, Marie is tapping away on her phone when I find her by the host stand.

“I’ll get the car,” I say, knowing perfectly well we don’t have any credit line for the Uber to actually work. I push past her out the door and hand the valet the ticket as I stand there, fuming.

Fucking Marie, I think. She has no idea. No fucking idea of what it takes to keep the house financially afloat. She stays home with the boys, spending the money and driving her car, but has no clue where the money comes from. The stress and anxiety I bear yet still barely squeeze out the necessary dollars.

I feel her presence beside me but don’t turn my eyes. The valet arrives, but I don’t move to open her door. I just plop right into the driver’s seat as a heavy blanket of silence drapes over us on the drive home.

She throws the passenger door open before I put the car into park and marches her way to the house.

I take a tiny bit of joy from watching her realize she'll have to wait for me to unlock the door. Once inside, Julie, the babysitter, questions our early return.

"I'm not feeling great," Marie lies. "We'll still pay you for the full evening, though."

Julie thanks us and heads out to her car. I watch to make sure she makes it and then see her pull out safely, mulling over the argument.

This is bad. My experience tells me I'm in for at least two days of tense silence. If I take the job, who knows how long it will last. I find myself clenching and unclenching my fists as I stare at a three-inch-wide fissure from the street up the driveway's blacktop. Yet another thing that needs care.

I swallow hard, spinning up an appeasing conversation in my head. Bitterly prepping my *baby-I'm-sorries* and *you-were-rights* and all the other ways to acquiesce and end this. What relief I have been feeling since meeting with Ty succumbs to the deluge of anxiety that roars back into my stomach at the thought of that IRS letter. Not to mention the shame of calling Cal and Ty to let them know I won't be taking the job. I'll have to concoct an excuse other than "my wife won't let me."

There's no getting around that I have to turn down this job, which means this will be the last time Cal will ever send me work. You only get one chance to fuck things up with these kinds of guys before they move on to someone else. I sigh and absently shove my fist into my belly before turning away from the gap in the driveway to follow Marie into what will surely be another crevasse in the bedroom.

7

THAT'S THE WAY I'VE ALWAYS HEARD IT SHOULD BE

My multiple apologies and admittance of Marie's unerring judgment thaw the ice enough for a spot in our bed for the night. But the air is still thick with lingering resentment when my internal 4:38 alarm goes off. I stumble out to the kitchen for my morning prework work.

"Um, Eric." Faye stands and begins to gather her things. "I've heard enough complaints about Marie, who seems to be the only one who makes any sense in your story. I just don't see what the point of this is." This is one of the things I love about Faye and Marie. They're honest people who don't hold back their feelings but tell you precisely what is on their minds.

"I get it." I place my hand over her pocketbook to slow down her progress. "If you let me continue, I promise you'll see I'm not here to convince you that I'm a good guy and Marie is some, forgive the expression, 'ball-buster'—far from it..."

She looks at her watch and sits back down.

Marie and I have a long-standing ritual of checking in with one another at 5:30 a.m. for coffee to ensure at least an hour together in the morning before we get David and Matthew up.

No matter what.

I fiddle with the AeroPress while the kettle heats on the stove. Soon after, I deliver Marie's coffee to her on the couch, and a few minutes later, I sit next to her with my own cup.

"I've been thinking," she says. "I want you to see a therapist."

Protests erupt in my mind, but I pinch my lips and hear her out.

"Karen's husband—" *Of course, fucking Karen.* "Peter started going recently, and it's helping him out a lot. They're not fighting as much." *Meaning he kowtows to her even more now than before.* "And he seems calmer."

I would be calmer, too, if I were Peter, a high-powered VP of a bank pulling in north of three hundred grand a year. I quickly cycle through everything I want to say, looking for something that won't reignite the combative fiery shitshow from the previous night. I buy time, opt-out from responding, and remain silent.

"I'm worried about you," Marie continues. "You're stressed all the time. You're short with me and the boys, and now you want to burn down everything in your business, the one you've built from scratch that no one else could have created like you did for this quote-unquote opportunity." Marie is nothing if not caring. "Don't you think talking to someone will help?"

Help with an eighty-thousand-dollar tax bill? I doubt it.

I clear my throat. "I'm not totally against it," I say. I speak slowly as a plan spins up in my mind. Maybe getting a third party's input isn't the worst thing? I am not sure what seeing a therapist will do for me other than cost me money I don't have, but I bet someone tasked with lowering my stress would agree that I should take this job with Ty. I'm pretty sure they have to keep the details confidential, so I could lay out the tax debt without worrying that it would get back to Marie. And then…then I can tell Marie that the therapist told me it would be the best move for me and for the family. Since it's her idea to see the therapist, she'll have to get on board if the therapist agrees with me!

"Really?" Marie's relief is palpable.

I shrug, acting like it's no biggie. "It's true that I'm

stressed all the time. Why not get a professional's opinion on what I can do about it?"

"Oh my god, I didn't think you'd agree. Look." Marie pulls a business card out of thin air. "There's a therapy collective downtown off twelfth. This is where Peter went. Maybe call today and see if she can meet with you?"

Two and a half hours later, I am standing in the coworking kitchenette, sipping coffee and staring at the business card for Dr. Greta Mortenstein LPC, LMFT, MSPC. I'm not so excited about my plan anymore. Everything in me is revolting at the idea of sitting across from some stranger who is getting paid to pretend to give a shit about me and my problems.

According to her website, Dr. Greta is an expert in cognitive behavioral therapy, whatever that is, with decades of experience. I let out a deep sigh. I still have a half hour before their offices open, so I get to stew about it a while longer.

"Whatcha got there?" I look up to find the bespectacled, mustached face of Bob, the Cosmo Kramer of our office space. I have zero memory of his last name. He moved into one of the empty interior offices a couple of weeks before. His Swedish chef Muppet-like lanky six-foot, six-inch frame fills the doorway as he sips from his "Tuesdays! Gone with the Wind" mug. Both his tie and pants are at least three inches too short.

"Just a, uh—" Am I really going to tell this guy, who

is barely an acquaintance, that I am going to see a therapist? I slip the card into my pocket. "It's nothing."

"That was a lot of letters after the name...Doctor? Lawyer?"

I force out a *pfft* and with some inexplicable *What the hell? joie de vivre,* I tell Bob the truth. "Not that dramatic. My wife wants me to see a therapist, so she got a card from a friend of hers."

"You ever been to a therapist before?"

"Not yet. You?"

"Oh yeah. Too many times." He laughs. I feel some relief now. At least Bob doesn't think I'm nuts or something.

"What's it like?"

Bob shrugs. "It depends on the therapist. You gotta find a good one."

I pull the card from my pocket and hand it to him. "You ever heard of her?"

"No," he says, handing it back, "but that doesn't mean anything. There are lots of therapists in Nashville."

I study the card again as if I expect to find some missing information I've failed to discover. Bob continues sipping from his mug.

What even makes a therapist good? Do they give better advice than other therapists and have better empathy? Is that even a thing? What do I even know about this Dr. Greta? That she helped Peter obey his wife better? That's not exactly what I'm looking for.

"Can you recommend anyone?"

Bob studies me for a moment. His lip twitches under his mustache as he dead-eyes me. After concluding that I'm worthy of his intervention, he says, "I can, but just how serious are you about this?"

"What do you mean?"

"If you're just going because your wife told you to or to complain about your problems, my lady's not a good fit for you. She's got all the degrees and everything, but she's what you would call nontraditional in her methods. So, if you want to do the 'tried,' you know what everyone does, you should probably just stick with the lady already on the card. But if you want the 'true,' it's going to be a trial not a bitchfest."

Now I'm intrigued. "If I'm going to spend the money, I'm serious. I don't want to waste my time."

He takes me at my word, sets down his mug, and holds out his hand for the card. I pass it back to him. He pulls one of those old-fashioned ballpoint pens from his shirt pocket and artfully scrawls a phone number on the back of the card.

"Text this number," he says, returning it to me.

His mouth half-cocks into an odd smile. "Her name is Lori. Let me know how it goes." Then he picks up his mug and disappears from the kitchenette.

I text the number. *Hi, Lori, I was given your number by a friend. I wonder if you are taking clients and, if so, when you have openings available.*

I put my phone back in my pocket, but it buzzes immediately with a response.

What's the name of the friend?

I type: "*Bob. I'm embarrassed to say I forgot his last name.*" and send it through.

Can you meet me now?

8

TOKYO STORM WARNING

"Are you trying to tell me to go see a therapist?"

Faye has removed her sunglasses and even sips some of her latte. However, her back is still rigid, and she looks poised to bolt for the door at the first sign of danger.

"No, no, I'm not saying that at all. Trust me." I laugh.

"Because I already am. I have been. David and I have, too."

"I'm not telling you this to get you to do anything. I promise. Just hang in there," I plead. "Especially because the next part gets a little—odd."

"What do you mean?"

"This therapist Bob sent me to…" I clear my throat. "She was a bit, as polite people would say, 'unconventional.' I didn't really know what therapy was, but how she did it was nothing like what I'd heard about from other people."

Despite herself, Faye leans in to hear more. "How so?"

After our text exchange, I walk to the therapist's office, which isn't all that far. Avoiding Nashville's famous hungover but already drinking again bachelorettes, the crowd of selfie-takers in front of the giant "We Believe in Nashville" mural, and the hipsters in too-tight jeans and scarves, I have one of those *Sesame Street* "one of these things is not like the other" moments.

Down the block, a petite woman dressed in a heavy, loose-fitting sweater with a shawl-slash-scarf wrapped around her neck stares up at a giant crane across the street as it slowly pieces together a new skyscraper. As I get closer, I can see that she has a giant muss of mousy brown hair that's barely held together by at least a half-dozen bright yellow pencils sticking in from all directions, her glasses are far too large for her face, and a quick glance at her shoes reminds me of what traveling minstrels wear at Renaissance festivals.

She pings into my awareness, not just because of her insane way of dressing but because she's absentmindedly stepping out into the street directly in the path of the giant purple WeGo public transit bus.

I sprint, swerving out into the street and willing myself to cover the thirty feet faster than the bus. I leap as the bus's horn blares. My shoulder collides with the strange creature's midsection. She grunts from the impact, and I feel a sledgehammer-like blow to my shin before we tumble back onto the sidewalk.

I roll over and onto the pavement, trying to catch my breath. I hear the bachelorettes screaming, and when I open my eyes, several faces are already swimming into my vision.

People yell all around us.

"Call an ambulance."

"Oh my god. Are you okay?"

"Jesus."

"Did you see what happened?"

"Call nine-one-one."

I sit up, ignoring the protests of the onlookers, and search around for the woman. She is also sitting up to my left, staring at me with a crooked smile.

"Are you okay?" I ask.

"Of course."

I remember the sledgehammer to my shin, and my eyes go to my leg. Everything looks in order, so I lean forward and feel around. I hiss when my hands hit the spot right above my ankle. I pull up my jeans to reveal what looks like an egg shoved under the skin.

The crowd choruses again.

"Is it broken?"

"Can you walk?"

"Don't move it."

"Call nine-one-one."

I lift my leg and move my foot around. I definitely feel pain, but nothing feels broken.

The woman is on her feet now and reaches down for my arm. I let her help me up and test the leg by putting weight on it. Again, I feel pain, but nothing like IRS pain.

"I think it's okay," I say.

"You're fine," she agrees.

More people protest around me, but I wave them off, assuring everyone I'm alright. One of the bachelorettes, with mascara streaks from fresh tears, is giving a play-by-play on her phone.

"He's up and walking away," she shrills, seeming almost disappointed.

Soon, everyone scatters, and it's just me and the woman standing still on the sidewalk.

"That was quite a spectacle," she says, adjusting her glasses.

"Are you sure you're okay?"

"Of course," she responds.

"I mean…" I pause, trying to find an inoffensive way to ask this woman if she is mentally stable. "You just seem like you could use some help."

She laughs, "You think *I* need the help?"

"Well, you did just step out in front of a bus."

"And I've already thanked you for that."

"Actually, you haven't."

"So, where are you heading?"

"To a, um." I struggle to reorient back to a time

before I almost died. "I'm going to see a therapist, actually."

"Ha! So you *do* need the help!"

I start to protest but realize the irony.

"You know, I'm a therapist," she says.

"Yeah?"

"I actually have an office a couple of blocks from here."

"What's your name?"

"Lori."

"Oh, weird—" I stare at this insanely dressed woman who almost died moments ago. "My name is Eric. I think I'm your next appointment."

She stares at me, smiling.

"I suppose you are. Come on, we can head to my office."

She turns and starts down the sidewalk, and I fall into step beside her. I keep wanting to ask her questions, but when I try to form them into words, they seem to float away.

We approach the three-story brick walk-up smooshed between two modern office buildings. The whole building can't be more than forty feet wide. I look for a business sign as we approach but can't locate one. She unlocks the peeling front door with a giant brass key before slipping it back into her pocket and holding the door open for me.

She follows me in, throwing the deadbolt behind her.

We head up the dimly lit staircase, the steps creaking and groaning as we ascend and then down an equally dimly lit hallway passing identical wooden doors evenly spaced apart.

We reach her office door.

I look for any indication that I'm at a therapist's office. I saw no "Dr. XX" sign on the door, no diplomas on the entryway walls, and, as far as I can tell, we're the only two people in the building. It's hinky.

At this moment, it strikes me how odd the last five minutes of my life have been. If another person had described this exact situation to me, I would have told them how creeped out they should have felt and been pissed at them for not sprinting out of that place.

Lori swung the inner "sanctum sanctorum" door open, but before I could follow her, she spins around toward me, causing me to stop short. She blocks the door.

"Are you sure you're ready for this?"

I peered over her arm.

A small, clean desk sits in the back corner. In the center of the room, an oversized office chair with a yellow notepad on the cushion and a plush, maroon loveseat fill the space.

Inwardly, I breathe a sigh of relief that it looks like every therapist's office I've ever seen on television.

"I think so…" I respond.

"Things can get pretty intense. And once you start

my process, it's imperative that you finish. No take-backsies."

"I'm good—" My throat catches, and I clear it.

"I am not bullshitting you." She is as serious as cancer.

"I'm ready," I say.

"Then after you," she extends her hand toward the couch.

I feel calm as I cross the threshold and ease across the room.

Lori brushes past me, retrieves the notepad, and sits. She removes one of the pencils from her hair, revealing a perfectly sharpened point.

I turn to face her and begin lowering myself onto the loveseat.

The thing is, I don't stop descending.

I feel my body fold in half as the cushion drops from underneath me. The lights go out, and I fall straight into an inky blackness.

9

CROSSEYED AND PAINLESS

The first thing I notice after my eyes adjust and I begin differentiating degrees of darkness into variants of pitch and gray is my breath. Each of my rapid exhales cast a slight shadow. Then I feel cold or wet, not sure which, maybe both. It's like having cold feet that feel like they're wet. Whatever it is seeps into my jeans at the knees while it simultaneously slithers up my fingers. I think I must be in a dank, cold basement. Lori's floor must have given way, and I've tumbled into the subterranean basement of her office building.

The quiet envelopes me. Dead quiet.

I scramble to my feet, stumbling, I think, to my "right" as the world I've entered remains kilter whirly.

I look around, thinking I'll find an old boiler or cobwebbed garbage can in this basement, but as light begins to shine, I find myself in the middle of a small open field surrounded by a menacing dark forest. The bare branches of the scraggly trees claw their way up to the pale light of a half-moon that hangs low and foreboding in the sky.

A deep memory, a distant recognition, takes root in the pit of my stomach.

I know this place.

The wet cold clings to me, and I shiver as I spin around to make sense of how I've gotten here.

I startle to the shaking in the branches behind me, and I stumble forward away from the sound, certain that if I turn around to confront the noise, I will be attacked. My foot crunches on a bit of rock, which gives way, and the ground slides out from underneath me. As I fall, something stops me short. I'm hanging over a deep black hole as wide as I am tall.

I feel a hand grasping the back of my shirt. It pulls me up from the crevasse. I turn and find Lori standing there smiling with her weird pencil hair, as if this situation was perfectly normal.

"What the hell?" I yell, but my voice doesn't carry. It comes out like a whimper. "Where are we?"

"I have no idea," she says visibly offended. "You brought us here."

Another stomach pit punch runs through my body. "What?"

"Here. This place." She waves her arms around her head, her shawl dancing in the moonlight. "This is your place. You created it. I just followed you down here."

I stare at her for several seconds as she smiles a

lopsided, ridiculous grin. Then I clench my eyes shut and rub the heels of my hands hard into them until colors explode in the darkness behind my lids.

I peek one eye open.

Lori waves at me. "Still here," she says.

I drop my head, staring at the cold, wet grass.

I'm dreaming. This is a dream. I will wake up, like always, scared and disturbed, and then I'll forget the dream and just feel out of place until around dinner when I'll go home to my screaming kids and unsatisfiable, unhappy wife, and that'll push this terror out of me because I'll have to deal with them, and then this place will be gone and—

"How we doing, Eric?"

"Not great, Lori."

"No, not this. I know this is a shock. How're you doing in general? You know, life, marriage, work—that sort of stuff."

"Fine. Great. I'd like to get back to it."

"But you said you needed help."

"No, I said I was going to see a therapist because my wife wants me to."

"So you don't need any help?"

"What do you want me to say? Just—Jesus, can you just take me back or let me wake up or end whatever the hell this is?"

Lori steps close to me, and I see her giant eyes magnified behind her abnormally large glasses. They've shaded from the sharp blue of my recent memory to a deep black. The moon's existence seems to fade away, and the blackness pushes in around us, suffocating out what little light remains. The branches of the trees reach above behind her, disappearing into the inky void that's consumed what was left of the sky.

The remembrance of the dread leaking into my stomach since I arrived wherever this is consumes the remainder of the space and then begins to slide up my esophagus. It's like that weird part in *The Matrix* when Neo dips his finger into the silver fluid that seems like a mirror.

"You said you wanted to do this," Lori says. "You said you were ready. Were you lying? Are you that much of a coward that you're giving up already?"

"I didn't know *this* is what I signed up for. How could I?"

Lori reaches out and tenderly puts the palm of her hand against my chest. The tassels on her shawl wriggle under her forearm, and the pencils in her hair seem to quiver excitedly like Medusa's snakes.

She waits a moment, studying my confused, fearful eyes, and then shoves hard against my chest.

I tip backward, falling heels over head. The rocky edge of the boundary between the solid and the empty rakes against my back.

I claw the air and throw my feet out, trying to catch my balance, but my head topples under my ass, and I slide deeper into the abyss.

I do a complete back flip, wagging my arms and legs in the air, and at last I thud onto the ground, which sucks the air from my lungs and temporarily paralyzes my diaphragm. I lie there flopping like a fish, pulling at my lungs, and trying to suck air back into them.

I flip over to my hands and knees, bow my back, and continue to suck in, like the reverse of a cat spitting up a hairball.

Just as my diaphragm decides to calm down and let a bit of blessed oxygen into my lungs, I hear it.

My head snaps up, and I peer into the darkness.

It is faint at first, but as my eyes adjust, I detect movement, shapeshifting forms in the distance. Monstrous figures prowl at the edges of the sparse remaining light filtering into this place. The whispers grow in volume and number. I can start making out what some of them are saying.

"Lori!" I scream.

I can see her silhouette at the top of the crevasse, outlined from the inky sky.

"Yeah?" she answers as if she has no idea what was going on.

"Get me out of here!" I howl.

"You want out?" she asks, still far too nonchalant. "I have a rope here I could throw down to you."

"Yes! Throw me the rope!"

"But before I do, can you just stop for a second? And *listen*?"

The whispers multiply, growing in volume. They speak over each other, threatening and attacking from the darkness. I catch pieces of what they are saying.

—stupid—

—evil—

—better off without you—

—Shithead—

"No! I want out now!"

"So you don't need any help in your life? You got it all together?"

"Not *this* kind of help!"

"And who are you to say what's the right kind of help? From where I'm sitting, you don't know what you need."

I peer back up into the dark.

"This is your only chance, Eric," Lori calls down. "You said you were ready. If you stop, pull out, it's over. We're done. You'll never see me again. Is that really what you want?"

I open my mouth to beg her to throw the rope, but something stops me. I know what the creatures in the dark are saying. I've heard them all before. I've heard them my whole life.

I hear them when Marie and I fight. I hear them when I yell at the boys. The voices claw at my mind when I read the notices from the IRS. I hear them every night right before I slip off to sleep. They torment me in my dreams, and they are there again when I wake up.

"There you go," Lori says. "Now you're getting it." She pauses for a beat before continuing. "You still want me to throw you this rope, or will you finally face this shit?"

I stare up at her silhouette for, hell, what seems like hours. The entire cave is filled with a cacophony of abuse. Old voices join the newer ones. Some I haven't heard in decades join the party.

The dread pushes up the back of my throat and pours out of my mouth, nose, and eyes. My legs give way under me, and I sink to my knees. I kneel, wait, and surrender. All that is left is for the demons to come and devour me.

"Good man," I hear Lori say, her silhouette disappearing. "I don't have a rope anyway."

10

HELLO IN THERE

"That's our time," Lori says.

I open my eyes to find myself back in her office, sitting on the blood-red loveseat. She stuffs the pencil she was using back into her hair and stands.

"What just happened?" I ask, woozy and discombobulated.

"You did really great work today." She steps toward the door.

"Is that normal in therapy?" I remain seated.

"What did you think would happen?"

"I don't know. I tell you about what's making me anxious, and you give me advice on what to do."

She laughs. "Therapists aren't supposed to give advice."

"That still doesn't answer—"

"Eric, I hate to rush you, but I have someone else I

need to see," she says, opening the door. "So, if you please."

I stand and move toward the door.

"Right, ah, okay." I stop. "But what now? What do I do?"

"Nothing. Don't do anything. Live your life like normal, and then I'll see you again tomorrow at ten."

"Tomorrow? I thought we would meet once a week or something."

"Eric, really, you need to go. You made the commitment. Remember, no take-backsies, or you can go find yourself a therapist who will give you advice." She herds me out the door and forcefully shuts it in my face.

I stand there, collecting myself, trying to wrap my head around what just happened. Nothing about this matches anything I've watched on Netflix or heard from friends about their "healing" from therapy.

I realize she hasn't even charged me for the session.

Back onto the busy Nashville sidewalk, I leave the tiny brick office building door unlocked. I don't see anyone else on my way out. Obviously, Lori hasn't left either. Where is this other person she's supposedly meeting?

I still feel wobbly as I walk the fifteen minutes from the Gulch back to my office parking lot. My shin is still in pain, forcing a slight limp, but that isn't causing the wobble.

Have you seen the original 1980s *Ghostbusters* movie? In the end, when that government prick forced them to power down the Ecto-Containment Unit holding all the ghosts and ghouls, allowing them to escape?

Lori cracked open my Ecto-Containment Unit—that pit in my soul where I cram all the shit flooding into my head that I can't deal with. It now has a fissure in its seal. The ghouls aren't getting out yet, but I can see, feel, and hear them rattling around down there.

I need to settle myself before putting on my "friendly book-marketing guy face," so I take refuge in my parked car and shake my head, trying to clear the fog. Then a tippy tap on the window jolts me back into reality.

Bob's bespectacled face is all but pressed against my window. I now know what it feels like to be a fish in an aquarium.

"Are you okay in there, Enrique?" The only person who ever called me that was my great-grandmother on my mother's side who was born in Mexico, now long deceased.

I crack the door and let him back away as I make room to exit.

"I just had my first meeting with Lori."

"Oh, was it a doozy?"

"Something like that," I mumble. "Look, I'm sorry, but I got to jump on a call."

"Okay, no problem," he says, stepping back so I can pass. "We can talk later."

I avoid Andre and Bethany as I duck into my office instead. I struggle to get myself going on any projects. My handwritten to-do list sits on my desk, mocking me with a long list of pressing client minutia.

Anytime I go to work on something, the IRS letter floats back into my mind along with the voices from the cave, and it all seems so pointless. I can get some work done for a client and send them another invoice for a few thousand bucks, but the money will immediately be eaten up by taxes and payroll.

It wouldn't even dent the debt.

My calendar dings, reminding me of a client call coming up in five minutes. Marilee is a frizzy-haired gardening how-to author with too much time on her hands. She also happens to be my lowest-paying retainer. She loves talking to me, and we constantly discuss ideas that she would never actually implement and, even if she did, wouldn't make either of us much money.

I don't have it in me.

I send her an email apologizing but letting her know something has come up—the more vague you are, the more the other person will assume it's truly awful.

Instead of the call, I decide to start tracking down leads for new work. New work requires deposits, and if I can get enough of those, maybe I can grind my way out.

I sigh and sit back in my chair to do the math.

How much could I actually get? Most of my projects are in the ten thousand to fifteen thousand range. Even if I can get half up front, I'd need to close thirteen or fourteen jobs *and* get paid in the next few days to clear the IRS debt.

No way. I can't even book a dozen initial calls in the next few days, much less complete the proposals, get approvals, and secure payments.

The money isn't going to come from my normal channels.

Brainstorm time. *Come on, Eric, let's come up with some unconventional ideas. How can a man of my lowly status get his hands on eighty large in four short days? There are no bad ideas here.*

I could rob a bank!

Okay, yes, some ideas are bad. I don't see Marie waiting for me to finish up a dime in a federal prison for a botched bank robbery.

My head snaps up at a knock on the door. Strange. Andre and Bethany usually text to ensure I'm not on a call before coming over. Otherwise, no one ever comes by the office.

Wait. That's not true. Someone does come by every once in a while, but only when she's worried about me.

I open the door to find a small gray-haired woman in her sixties clutching a Ziploc bag full of brownies with a huge smile plastered on her face. A man who looks disturbingly like me stands behind her, his expression somewhat pained.

Somehow, my dad still has a full head of hair in its original dark brown shading. I could always get him riled up by accusing him of being a Just for Men hair color spokesmodel.

"Hey, Mom," I say.

"Oh, you're so handsome!" she replies, pulling me forward to peck me on the cheek.

I shake my dad's hand firmly, and he gives me a solid nod.

"I was just thinking of you," my mom says, slipping underneath my arm into my office. "And thought maybe you could use a snack today."

She bustles in and produces a small paper plate. She sits it on the corner of my desk and begins arranging the brownies. My dad takes his usual place in the chair closest to the door.

I sit back in my office chair, put on my "big-shot small-business owner face," and let her talk.

She updates me on Dad's garden club. My frizzy-haired horticulturist's book inspired him, and he started up an allotment in an abandoned field in my hometown using her techniques. And Mom has finally convinced him to sell his two-decade-old Accord—my dad's face scowled at this—she has drama with the ladies at Sunday school, and my niece had a recital.

Then she takes the seat closest to me and rests her hand on my forearm.

"Have you heard from your sister?"

"I haven't," I answer.

My mom knows this. Christy lives in Chicago, and we rarely speak outside of perfunctory holidays or family gatherings.

"I wish you two were closer."

I nod, retrieving a brownie from the plate.

"I talked to Marie this morning," Mom mentions.

There it is.

"Yeah?"

"Yeah, she said you were feeling stressed? That you went to a therapist this morning?"

"Are you asking about the stress or the therapist?"

"Aren't they the same?"

"Mom, don't worry. I didn't talk to the therapist about you. That's not why I'm going."

"Oh, I know," she says, waving me off as if that wasn't the exact thing she was worrying about. "I just..." she pauses for a beat, searching for what she wants to say. "Can we do anything to help?"

"I don't think so."

"Is this about money?"

I force myself to stay still. My mom can pick up on the slightest real or perceived movement and read an entire horror story into it in one-point-three seconds.

"Yeah. Kind of. Money's tight."

"Do you need to borrow any?"

My dad's head snaps to attention at this comment, but he stays silent.

I admit, my soul buoys for a second as I consider it. I know Mom and Dad have some money, but I'm not sure how much. They're both retired by this point. The problem is that my mom would give it to me even if they couldn't afford it.

The hell of being indebted to the IRS burns hot, but there's a special, extra-crispy place for children who take their parents' retirement money.

"Mom, it's fine. We'll be okay."

"We could let you borrow a few thousand. It'd really be fine. You wouldn't have to hurry to pay us back or anything."

My dad clears his throat.

A few thousand? Jesus! If only my money problems were small enough to be solved by a few thousand dollars.

Before I can answer, she ups the offer.

"If it's worse, we could do more. I just don't like you being so stressed out about stuff."

"Mom, I'm fine. Really."

I stand, signaling it's time for them to leave.

She gets the message and comes around to give me a hug.

"You're such a good boy. I know you'll get this figured out."

I pat her on the back and kiss the top of her head. I squeeze her a little longer, risking setting off her radar, but I need it. She filters everything through me being a perfect son. All my childhood woes have long since been whitewashed, and even the adult fuckups are overlooked.

When I finally let her go, I catch the wet glisten in her eye, but she doesn't say anything. She knows—not the specifics, of course—but she knows.

11

MONEY

I slouch back into my office chair. Here I am, a thirty-five-year-old entrepreneur with a wife, two kids, and a mortgage, freaking my parents out to the point that they want to give me a chunk of their retirement funds.

Well, not give me. They said borrow. My mom would never press me on repayment, but it would definitely be a loan in my dad's ledger.

A loan.

No bad ideas!

I fire off two more emails, canceling the last two client meetings of the day, and then run out to my car. Eleven minutes later, I pull into the small branch of Bank of America, where I do all my personal and business banking.

I let Chelsea, the greeter, know why I'm here and take my seat. Nervously bouncing my foot, I stare at nonsense on my phone, trying to distract myself.

Sure, this wasn't the best option, but it would be a stay of execution at the very least. Everybody always said the last person you wanted to owe was the IRS, so maybe I could just owe the bank instead.

"Mr. Bauer?"

I look up to find a Dilberty middle-aged bald man in a dark suit that clings a little too much to his midsection. The pin on his lapel reads: "I'm Guillermo!"

"Yes," I reply, standing and accepting his handshake.

"You want to follow me?"

We cross the lobby and enter a tiny, bland office. The place looks like Guillermo could be cleared out of there in twenty seconds or less. His laptop sits beside a paper pad on an otherwise empty L-shaped desk. He has no picture frames, no clutter, and nothing on the walls—just the desk, laptop, paper, and two chairs.

My father-in-law likes to brag about how he has dealt with the same banker for forty years and about how all business is about connections and relationships and stick-to-itiveness and blah, blah, blah.

It isn't like that anymore. No matter what happens, when I walk out of there, I get the distinct feeling I'll never see Guillermo again, even if I want to.

"I'm a loan officer here at Bank of America, and Chelsea tells me you're looking to open a line of credit. Would this be for your business or personal use?"

"Business."

"Fantastic. Let's take a look."

Guillermo gathers the necessary information and pulls up my business account.

"At this juncture, sir, we won't be able to extend your business a line of credit. Based on your current account status and history, they're not putting through an approval. We could look at a business credit card?"

Oof. Eighty thousand on a card with at least eighteen percent interest makes my skin crawl. Not to mention, no way will they give me a card with that kind of a ceiling on it. "What about a personal line of credit?"

I worry he will ask for some sort of explanation or inquire as to what I need this money for. Business lines of credit are used for business expenses like equipment, office space, and hiring. If I switch to a personal line of credit so quickly, he must wonder what's happening, but Guillermo seems wholly uninterested.

"We can take a look."

Again, he tapped my information into the computer.

"We would need some sort of collateral to do anything. Have you looked at getting a second mortgage? Do you have any equity in your house?"

"Yes, I believe so. We've paid it down a bit, but the market has gone up since we bought the house last year."

"Okay, let's take a look."

After a lot of clickety-clacking and several more questions, he confirms this looks like a possibility.

"What kind of funding are you looking for?"

I gulp. This will be the first time I've said the number out loud.

"Eighty-three thousand?"

He rata-taps some more.

"It looks like we can only approve up to sixty-four thousand."

I sighed. Sixty-four thousand. That would still leave a nineteen-thousand-dollar gap. But maybe it's enough? Maybe I can get some clients to pay earlier for some retainers and go back to my parents and borrow that few thousand dollars?

This might work after all.

"That'll be fine," I reply. "How fast can we get this processed?"

"Once we have all the required paperwork, it usually only takes a couple of days. They're significantly easier to get underwritten than a normal loan or refinance."

"Great. What do you need from me?"

Guillermo and I start going over the requirements. I've been self-employed long enough to know the paperwork will be significant. Twelve months of bank statements for both the business and personal. Proof of mortgage payments for twelve months. Pay stubs. Proof of business income. Picture of my driver's license. And on it goes. At some point in the future, they will ask for a physical and prostate exam before approving a loan for anyone self-employed.

Thankfully, the list is long but doable.

"We can pull a lot of this for you since you do all your banking with us, but you'll need to bring in the other paperwork."

"I can get it all for you," I say.

I'm already spinning up the plan to tell Marie I have to work late so I can come in first thing tomorrow to meet with whatever interchangeable loan officer will be on duty. "Probably by tomorrow morning."

"Great, so we'll look over that, get both of your signatures, and we'll be good to go."

"Both?"

"Yes, you and your wife's. Since she's on the mortgage, she'll need to sign off on the additional loan."

"She's, uh, pretty busy. Could I take it with me to have her sign it and then bring it in?"

"Unfortunately, no. It has to be notarized. We have one here in the office, though. She'll just need to come in for two minutes to sign the paperwork, and then you can take care of the rest without her."

No way could I bring Marie in to sign for this loan without inevitably revealing the tax debt, which would lead to the credit card debt, which would lead to the fact that everything with our finances was a flaming shit ship sinking fast.

"Okay, yeah. That makes sense."

Guillermo turns back to the computer and keeps tapping the keys, and I don't stop him. I can't admit that I'm trying to get this loan without my wife knowing, and it would be obvious if I stopped the process now.

My phone buzzes as I wait.

It's Ty.

Eric! My man! I wanted to check in with you ASAP. Give me a call so we can figure out next steps.

I need to call him, but I still don't have a good reason for turning down the job.

"Okay, Mr. Bauer, I think we're all set!" Guillermo drones on about the next steps and the exact paperwork I need. He slides a checklist across the desk, and I fold it and tuck it in my pocket.

I nod, not listening, as he finishes up. Then he agrees to meet his notary colleague with Marie at 9:00 a.m. the following day.

"We'll be here," I lie.

I shake Guillermo's hand, thank Chelsea as I pass her, get in my car, and spend the next five minutes screaming and cursing at the steering wheel.

12

SORROW

"You're home early!" Marie says as I come in the front door.

I force a tight smile onto my face.

"Yeah, finished up something and decided to come on home."

I grab the clump of mail and slowly sort through it, half expecting another threatening IRS envelope.

"So? You going to tell me about it?"

I look up to find Marie staring at me expectantly. She has her apron on and the first dinner prep items on the counter.

Does she know I went for the loan? Did that asshole Guillermo call her about it or something?

"Tell you about what?" I speak slowly and calmly.

"The therapy appointment. How'd it go?"

Oh hell, I had somehow forgotten about Lori and saving her life and the meeting and—the cave.

"Actually, the craziest thing happened."

I relay the story of tackling Lori and getting clipped by the bus. I show Marie the spot on my shin that has already turned a deep purple.

"She sounds nutty. And this is your therapist?"

I shrug.

"How was the appointment?"

I'm wondering how to relay what happened without sounding insane. My mind still splits from reality when I try to think about it. In the hours since leaving Lori's office, it has felt more and more like a dream. The feelings still linger, but the specifics are getting fuzzy. The only two parts still clear in my memory are entering and exiting the office.

"It was fine. Good, I think."

"Fine? Good? That's it?"

"I don't know, Marie. It's *my* therapy. I don't really feel like talking about it yet. Besides, I have to go back tomorrow."

"Tomorrow? I thought people usually see their therapist once a week or something."

"That's what I thought too."

Marie lets out a little laugh. "You must be pretty fucked up," she says.

I toss the mail on the counter.

"What's that supposed to mean?"

"I'm joking. It's just kinda funny that she wants to see you again tomorrow."

"Well…" I pause for dramatic effect. "That's what

she said." My voice is harsher than it needs to be, but it comes tumbling out before I can stop it. "You wanted me to go, so I'm going and doing what she says to do."

"Okay," Marie says, holding up her hands. "I didn't mean anything by it."

"You know I'm not the only one in this relationship with problems. Maybe you should be going to therapy, too."

"I didn't say you were the only one with problems."

"But I'm the only one in therapy."

"It's for you. You seemed so stressed I thought it would help."

"For me. Right."

Marie's back goes rigid.

"Right," she says. Now she's harsher than she needs to be.

"Not because you see me as the fucked-up shithead in our marriage?"

"I didn't say that."

"You didn't have to."

"I didn't even *mean* that. I just thought—"

"It helped Karen get Peter under control. Maybe it would do the same for me?"

Before she can answer, the sound of a herd of bulls tumbling down the stairs interrupts us.

David and Matthew appear. Matthew is howling and crying, his face fire engine red angry. David follows close behind with a worried look.

Matthew claws at Marie's legs until she picks him up.

"What happened?"

"David hit me!" He points an accusatory finger at his brother.

"No! No, I didn't!"

As Marie gets roped into refereeing yet another sibling squabble, I grab the mail again and finish sorting it while inwardly trying to calm down. I know Marie sees me as the problem. She constantly accuses me of being stressed and short with her and the boys, but she gets that way, too. I mean, hell, I tried to take her out to dinner last night, and she embarrassed me by storming off before we'd even ordered. Was I really the only one with anger issues?

Besides, I wasn't the one who said, "Fuck you." If I said something like that to her, she'd be livid for weeks, but somehow, she's supposed to get an immediate pass on it.

Marie manages to get the boys under control and apparently figures out who is at fault for what. Matthew has stopped crying in Marie's arms, and now David stands between us, looking at Marie expectantly.

"What?" I ask.

"Oh," Marie said. "David has asked me again about getting a dog. He thought maybe you'd be open to it now that he's almost nine."

I start shaking my head before she's finished

making David's case for him. David's shoulders drop, and then his head drops like he's about to cry.

"Please, please, please!" Matthew shouts, now back on his brother's side. It must be nice to have a common enemy.

"Stop. No. That's the last thing we need around here," I say. "It'll just turn into another set of chores for me."

Summoning his courage, David pleads, "No, I'll do everything...take him out, clean up his poop, feed him—"

"I'll help too!" Matthew barks.

"Come on, help me out here, Marie," I say desperately.

She hesitates and then looks back at David and Matthew. "Daddy and I will talk about it," she promises. Somehow, she knows the right way to hold her boys and husband together.

They nod vigorously, happy for the glimmer of hope, and then start up the stairs. Her noncommittal response irks me as if she's not looking out for my interests, pampering those boys.

"Oh yeah, before I forget," Marie changes the subject to something mundane. "We need to get David some new pants for school."

"What happened to his others?" I ask.

"The knee got torn up on them."

I turn to the stairs. Now's my chance to set things right.

"David!" I shout.

He backs down the stairs until he can peek around the corner at me without being completely exposed to my interrogation. "What happened with your pants?"

"I was playing gaga ball at recess and fell and skinned my knee."

"Aren't you supposed to take shorts to change into for recess?" I say like I'm freaking Atticus Finch interrogating a liar and scoundrel.

"Yeah, I forgot today. I'm sorry."

"Sorry? How many times have we had this discussion? You take shorts! If you can't remember to take shorts, you don't get to do recess…Understood!"

David is at a loss. He's just a kid. It's kind of his job to tear up his pants, make mistakes, and not torment himself over things that aren't his responsibility, like money, food, shelter, and security. Now, he has worry smeared across his face. He's confused. He looks to Marie for help.

"Eric, it's thirty bucks. I'll start making sure he takes shorts with him."

I keep my eyes on David as I answer, just to make sure this not-yet nine-year-old boy knows who's boss.

"He's old enough to remember his *own* shorts, and this is the second new pair we've had to buy for him. I think he should pay for this pair."

"With what money?" Marie's had enough. "He's not even nine years old. You want him to get a job?"

I don't take my eyes off David. Instead, I bore into him like he's the cause of our family's suffering. "He gets Christmas and birthday money from his grandparents!"

"Jesus, Eric. Do you want him to spend that on a new pair of school pants? It's just thirty bucks!"

I turn back to Marie and unload on her.

"Just thirty bucks? That thirty bucks has to come from somewhere. *You're* not making any money, so who does it fall to?"

Marie breaks eye contact with me, softens herself, and takes in David. She forces a smile.

"It's fine, honey," she says. "Go on upstairs."

Relieved but ashamed, David hustles up the stairs out of sight. I hear whispering just before Marie hits the counter with her fist and curses.

"What the fuck, Eric? Last night you insisted on taking me out for a dinner that was gonna cost us over a hundred bucks, and today you're bitching about thirty bucks for a pair of school pants for our eight-year-old. What is going on with you?"

The tension behind my eyes threatens to tear my mind in two. I want to spill everything to her—the tax debt, the business troubles, the loan we need, everything.

But I can't. It's too late and too much. Would she leave me? Would she force me to quit my business and get a j-o-b? Sell the cars? The shit keeps coming at me with such velocity that it takes me all I have to push it down below into that pit beneath my surface bullshit.

I let out a deep sigh.

"I'm sorry," I say, running my hand over my face. "I don't know what my deal is."

"I don't know either, but you gotta get yourself together, especially in front of the boys. Do you really want David sitting inside alone during recess so he doesn't mess up his Costco pants?"

"I want him to remember to take his shorts," I say like a complete shithead.

"Eric, he is *eight years old*. Would you have remembered to take extra shorts every day at his age?"

"My dad would have made me pay for my pants."

"And you want to be like your dad?"

Fuck! My dad! She always brings up my dad and how we don't have the best, you know, way of communicating when she wants me to kowtow to my boys and her way of raising them. "Okay, yeah, you're right."

"You need to go apologize to him."

"I will." I surrender before I have a stroke.

"Eric," she waits.

I look up at her.

"Seriously. Is everything okay?"

I hold her eyes for a few seconds, forcing the tension back down, and lie like my life depends on it.

"Yeah," I say. "Everything is fine. I just have a lot going on."

She holds my eyes, too, and then nods at the stairs. I turn and follow David's path.

Before I make it to the first step, she says. "Did you order David's cake?"

13

IS SHE REALLY GOING OUT WITH HIM?

I pull into the Whole Foods parking garage and arrived my usual nine minutes late. The upscale grocer is packed full of East Nashvillians, grown men with top knots and moms in yoga pants fawning over their one-point-five gifted children. Aneel already stands at the breakfast bar chatting with the guy behind the counter making burritos.

We meet up every few weeks. He's the one constant friend in my life, more his doing than mine. I'm the worst at staying in touch with people, but Aneel always reaches out. If I don't return a call or text, he keeps at me until I do.

Honestly, I can't figure out why he cares so much. Since our college days, his life has taken off. Except for a rough patch ten years ago, Aneel's success rolls in steadily and smoothly. Everything about him screams easygoing—from his shaggy dark hair, faded jeans, and screen-printed "Mahalo" T-shirt to his sloped, jaunty way of walking. He seems to know everyone, and everyone loves him.

He's a single serial dater with friends all over the city, including plenty of the big wigs in the music industry and stars I have on my music playlists.

And still, even with the big-time social circles he runs in, he hounds me into a breakfast meeting at the Whole Foods around the corner from his office every couple of weeks.

"Best breakfast burrito in the city," he claims.

He never buys the premade burritos from the hot bar. Somehow, he always works an "in" with the revolving door of cooks who make our burritos to Aneel's specs and deliver them piping hot off the grill for us.

Today's meeting is different, though. I've initiated this one. I join Aneel at the counter, knowing he's already ordered and paid for the both of us. We do an awkward fist bump.

"Eric! Have you met my boy Atticus?" He indicates the twenty-something manning the burritos. Atticus and I nod at each other. I check the weather on my phone while they finish their conversation.

We grab our burritos and head to one of the booths in the front.

"So what's up? How's Marie?"" Aneel asks as we take our seats.

If this friend with everything envies one thing in

my life, it's Marie. It doesn't cross into weird lechy territory, but he thinks Marie is brilliant and hilarious. He comes over for dinner every few months to hang with us and the boys, like he's visiting the zoo or an amusement park.

She's a fan of his, too, always asking when he's going to settle down with a nice girl. His response is always the same: "I haven't found one as cool as you."

"She's good. Nothing new."

"And business? You still raking it in?" he always asks, assuming things are great because things are always great for him.

"Well..." I draw out my response.

I swore years ago I would never ask him for work. I lied to myself, saying I didn't want it to hurt our friendship. The thing is, I've wanted to avoid the embarrassment. More truthfully, I've never thought I was good enough. Aneel's clients are vast and rich. He always seems to have more lucrative jobs he's passed on than ones I've taken.

Years ago, he would offer me gigs, but I turned them down enough that he got the hint. I didn't want him to think he had to take care of me. But now I'm in such a bind that I need to get him to give me work and, assuming it's a possibility, move on to the second, much bigger ask of giving me a sizable advance by Friday.

I clear my throat.

"I'm in a bit of a pickle," I admit.

Aneel nods as he dives into his meal.

"A money one. I'm wondering if you have any jobs you could send me."

Aneel's burrito freezes, hovering halfway between the cardboard plate and his mouth. "You want me to bring you in to work with my clients?"

I nod, gulping.

He slams the burrito down on the plate. Bits of egg and grilled pepper shoot out across the plate and table. "Hot damn!" he says. "I've been waiting years for this! I'd love to work with you, man! I used to offer you stuff all the time. I didn't think you were interested."

"I am now."

"You may very well have perfect timing. I just got a call yesterday to come in and pitch on a huge project. If I get it, I'll definitely need a lot of help." He starts to describe it but then pauses. "Technically, I'm not supposed to talk about it. I actually signed an NDA. Can you pretend you signed an NDA from me? Don't mention any specifics to anyone."

"Of course."

Aneel nods, takes another bite of burrito, and starts talking as he chews.

"A few years ago, I worked for a think tank in DC. I stayed at this cool hotel, walkable to Union Station. It has a great Irish bar as its restaurant." Aneel should have his own travel TV show. "It's awesome because everyone working on Capitol Hill knows about it. I think Howard Hunt used to drink there. Anyway, I met this low-level political staffer over fish and chips, and we ended up shutting the place down. We've stayed in touch, and I always grab a Guinness when I'm in town."

"And..." I say.

"Oh, right. It turns out he's moved up in the world and has been tapped by none other than Congressman Ricky Bryant to potentially run a super PAC for him in the coming election."

A lump of egg catches halfway down my esophagus. I place the last hunk of the burrito back on the plate and slowly wipe my hands and face on the napkin.

"Are you fucking with me?"

Aneel's face goes blank. "What?"

"Seriously. Did Marie put you up to this?"

"Are *you* fucking with *me*?" Aneel pushes back.

I search Aneel's face but only find honesty.

"Dude," I confess. "I just got offered to pitch on this same job two days ago."

"Really? By who?"

"There's a guy named Ty Banks. He's buddies with Bryant's campaign manager. You know, Cal Struthers, the guy I met at the World Domination Summit, connected us."

Aneel lets out a bit of a laugh and shakes his head. "Small fucking world," he says, popping the last of the burrito in his mouth.

"Ty made it sound like he was tight enough with this guy that the job was ours," I say.

Aneel shrugs his shoulders, not a bit put off.

"Then why are you sitting here asking me for work? Do you know how much you'd make helping run something like this? It's nutso money. I don't get it."

"He said it was a full-time gig. I can't swing it with my current client load. Plus, I have employees. How do you have time for it?"

"This is one of those jobs you make time for. Running a super PAC for a brand-name candidate is a game-changer. Have you looked into it? Everybody who runs in this world goes on to high-end jobs and money, money, money…afterward. If there's a golden ticket into the power center of the world, it's running a super PAC."

"And you're okay working for Ricky the Dicky?"

Aneel brushes off the question. "God, that name kills me every time. Why a politician would decide to be professionally known by the name his mom used when he was six years old is beyond me. But it's certainly memorable. But yeah, I'm for it. You know I lean to the other side of the aisle from you and Marie. I'm a boot-strap kind of guy." And then, unexpectedly, understanding sweeps across his face.

"It's Marie. Isn't it? She doesn't want you working for Mr. Dicky. Right?"

I hesitate. "That's part of it."

We sit for the next couple of minutes as I slowly finish my burrito, an uncharacteristically long silence stretching between us.

And, once again, everything goes easily for Aneel, I think.

Here I sit deep in debt with an IRS guillotine perched above my neck with a rapidly fraying rope and a wife encouraging me to keep my head right on the chopping block while my rich friend Aneel coasts in and snaps up the exact same break I'd been working fifteen years to get.

"Look, man," Aneel says, finally breaking the tension. "If you want me to bow out, say the word. It's a life-changing opportunity, but if I had known you were going out for the same job—"

I wave him off.

"Nah, I can't ask you to do that," I say. "Besides, Marie's freaking out at the idea of me working for Bryant, so I think I'll have to pass on pitching anyway."

"Well, Marie's a smart lady. Her being so against it makes me think twice about going for it."

"She just hates the guy's politics. That's all."

I check the time on my phone and start wiping my hands off on the brown, ecologically sustainable napkins.

"Sorry to chow and run, but I've got another meeting."

"Oh. Yeah, no worries."

"Thanks for breakfast," I say, standing.

"Of course. Hey, I'm looking forward to David's party Sunday."

"For sure. See you then."

We bump fists again, and I walk back to the guillotine.

14

THE SOUND OF SILENCE

The nothingness that fills my car takes on a thick and viscous form. The absence of sound so overwhelms me that I somehow lose my sense of space. There must have been movement around me in the Whole Foods parking garage, but I simply didn't register it. When I have the mind to pull myself out of the silent goo, I realize I've been sitting in the car for eighteen minutes after leaving Aneel at the burrito bar.

Friday looms, just the day after next, and I'm out of ideas. The repercussions I've read in the IRS letter loop through my mind in fast, unending succession.

Debt collectors, asset seizure, property foreclosure, prosecution, bank garnishment… I've even heard of them contacting a company's clients and customers.

My mind follows another disturbing tributary of what little reputation I have swiftly burning away as my clients hear from Agent Mason. Every industry is its own small world, and mine is no different. It won't take long for me to be on the blacklist of "scam book marketing" providers.

When that inevitability arises, I'll have to get a job using my double major. Still, the IRS will immediately, with one hundred percent certainty, start garnishing my wages. I already doubt I can find a job paying what we need to live on, but with the IRS taking whatever they want, Marie will have to get a job, too.

When David was born, Marie told me she wanted to stay home with our kids full time. I promised her I would always provide enough so she could work outside the home only if she wanted to.

That's looking like one more promise I'll end up shitting on. Another failure to add to the ever-expanding list.

My phone buzzes to remind me about my appointment with pencil-headed Lori. Even if I leave right now, I'll be late.

That dark cave she dropped me in slipped back into my mind, along with the voices that whispered to me from its shadows.

I don't think I can deal with that at this particular juncture, as Guillermo at Bank of America would say.

I swipe my thumb across the reminder, ignoring it, and my phone immediately buzzes again, this time with a text from Lori.

Please ensure you attend our scheduled appointment. If you are unable to attend, I'll be unable to reschedule.

My unfocused stare goes through the phone as I consider what to do. I still can't see how a therapy appointment will improve my current predicament, especially one that goes like the day before. On the other hand, it would distract me from endlessly picking over the detritus of my fuckups. Plus, when Marie inevitably leaves me over all of this, it will behoove me to have something established with a therapist.

I sigh and pull out of the parking space.

When I arrive, the narrow brick building is unlocked and silent as I climb the stairs. I still don't see any sign that other people occupy the building. At least no one will hear my screams.

Lori opens the door as I reach out to knock.

"Welcome back," she moves out of the way so I can enter.

I step inside and move toward the loveseat but then pause. I put my hands on the cushion and hesitantly push down to ensure it's solid. Then I lift the cushion and run my hands across the fabric underneath, inspecting the solidity of the coiled springs.

"Are you admiring my couch?"

I glance back to find her in her chair, looking at me curiously.

"I'm just—"

What am I doing? Checking to make sure a dark portal to a forgotten realm in my psyche doesn't exist under the blood-red cushions?

"Never mind," I mumble, tentatively lowering myself into place.

It holds fast.

"You came back," Lori says.

"I did. I'm not sure why."

"I'd have to charge you for a no-show if you didn't. How are you feeling after yesterday?"

"Honestly, it's not been great, Lori. I got into this fight last night with my wife and ended up yelling at my eight-year-old about something so stupid, and then this morning… Well, this is actually what's causing me the most stress—"

Lori waves her sharpened pencil in my direction, cutting me off. "That's not what I asked."

"But I'm here to talk about what's stressing me out. Right?"

"No, no. That's not what I do. I don't want to hear about your life, wife, or kids."

"Wait…" I blink, trying to wrap my head around what she just said.

"I asked how you are *feeling*. Not what you're *thinking*."

"Stressed, Lori. Fucking stressed. Because of my life, my wife, and my kids. I thought that's what therapists help with."

She leans forward, the pencil now pointing directly between my eyes.

"I'm not that kind of therapist. And that's not why you're stressed. Now close your eyes."

15

CONEY ISLAND BABY

I hold her gaze for a moment, not wanting to fight and argue with what is now clearly an insane woman before me. I mean, what kind of therapist is she exactly? She doesn't want to hear about my day-to-day problems? What the F?

But for reasons I'll never really understand, I relent and let my eyes fall shut.

"Take a deep breath."

I breathe in slowly.

"Now count slowly backward from five thousand one hundred and eighty-three."

And I do.

When I open my eyes, I stumble and nearly fall. Somehow, I've pulled my mind together—but again, like before, I'm no longer in Lori's office.

Instead, I'm in a long, shadowy hallway that stretches in width and breadth in both directions. It feels like I've entered some weird Escher painting. I'm at the apex with a seemingly infinite expanse spread before me. I can see doors at regular intervals, and each one holds a window at eye level, like in those old movies where weird experiments happen on the other side. Each window has mesh wiring embedded in the glass, forming little diamond-shaped prisms, like chicken wire.

I soon see Lori standing in front of me.

"Ready?" She indicates behind me with her head.

I turn around to find another door identical to the others but directly in my new pathway. The difference between this one and the rest is that light glows from the other side. I approach the chicken-wire window, and I can see the shapes of people inside.

I extend my hand from my forehead, as you do when you focus in the far distance, step close to the glass, and peer inside. I recognize the people in the room and lurch back from the door.

"What is this?"

"It's your birthday," Lori says, standing beside me. She leans toward the window and points, her long black fingernail tapping the glass.

"That's you."

I follow her gaze to a baby swaddled in a white flannel blanket with pink and blue stripes in the center. I vaguely recognize myself from pictures in photo albums—big head, dumb expression—photos I hate looking at. I always avoid looking at any photos of myself preadolescence. Nevertheless, it *is* me.

My mother is holding me in her arms—but not the wrinkled, gray version of my mom I'm used to. This woman is young. Actually, I suddenly remember precisely how old she is.

She is twenty-seven. Dark brunette and stunningly pretty with blue eyes as dazzling as any I've ever seen on a thin, elegant face.

Her eyes aren't on her baby, though. They are looking across the room at my father. There he sits, baby-faced at twenty-five with blond curly hair and a wispy beard.

He stares at the floor with a far-off look into some middle distance only he can appreciate by the banks of his own lagoon.

My parents have been married less than ten months. I am a honeymoon surprise. My mom cried when she found out she was pregnant because she knew my dad didn't want another child—he definitely didn't want one in their first year of marriage.

"Another child?" Lori reads my thoughts.

"Yeah. You see my sister Christy?" I point out the little girl sprawled in the nursing chair situated between my mother, recovering on the bed, and my father in the furthest corner. She's my half-sister from my mom's first marriage. She is ten years old here.

She had never lived with her father, who went out for the proverbial pack of cigarettes and disappeared as soon as my mom told him she was pregnant. My mom raised Christy alone for seven and a half years while holding down two jobs before meeting my father. Plenty of times only my sister got to eat dinner because there wasn't enough money to feed them both. Mom wasn't as thin as she was only by choice.

Christy skulks in the opposite corner, glaring across the room at the baby. Her angry stare shifts to my dad occasionally, but it quickly returns to the bundle in my mom's arms.

A lot had changed for Christy over the previous year. She had to deal with some man she didn't know, and her mom wanted her to call him her dad even though he wasn't. Her new "dad" had zero experience as a parent, and now she had a brother who shared the guy's blood, so he would definitely care more about the baby than her.

"Let's get started," Lori says, placing my hand on the doorknob.

I pull it back.

"What is this, Lori? Where am I?"

"You're in a memory."

"Whose memory?"

"Yours. Who else's?"

"I don't remember the day I was born."

"Maybe not. But it's in there." She taps my head. "Or we wouldn't be here."

I move my eyes back to the baby. "What am I supposed to do?"

"Go in and look around. Whatever you feel needs to happen next will. Just go with it."

I nod but hesitate.

"Go on," Lori says. "You can do this."

Nobody notices the door opening or me entering. I am in the room, but they do not know I'm there. I'm like Ebenezer Scrooge, a ghost.

I walk to the bed and check on my mom.

"Mom?" I say as a test. She can't hear me. I reach out and touch her arm. I can feel the smoothness of her skin, but she doesn't react.

"She looks worried," I say.

"What is she worried about?" Lori asks from the doorway.

I follow my mother's gaze across the room to my father.

"She's worried my dad is going to leave her too. That this is too much for him. She wonders if she can be a single mom again with two kids. It's like…" my voice cracks.

"What?"

"I don't think she's happy the baby's here."

"What about your dad?"

I approach my father across the white tiled floor and crouch before him. I wave my hand in front of his face, but he doesn't notice me either. He's a million miles away, deep in his own thoughts.

"This baby is crushing his plans and dreams," I say.

"What do you mean?"

"He likes skiing on the weekends with his friends, and he's in a softball league. He wants to start building a business. All that's going to change now because of me."

"How's he feeling about you being here?"

I look back at Lori.

"Even worse than my mom does."

"What about her?" Lori nods toward my sister.

I snort out a bitter laugh.

"What's it look like?"

I stand and look around the room some more, my frustration building.

There's a baby here! A brand-new baby! I think.

I then remember the joy Marie and I had when David and Matthew were born. Why aren't these people happy? Why aren't they cooing over the baby, loving on him, and telling him how beautiful he is?

I move over to my mom.

The baby stares up at her longingly. If he could—if he wasn't straight-jacketed in that fucking standard-ass hospital-issued shit-ass bullshit blanket—he'd reach out his arms to her and grab ahold of her attention.

I move her arm out of the way. Then I bend down, gently take the baby in my arms, and step back.

My mom doesn't even notice her baby is gone. Instead, she shifts to her left so she can get a better angle on my dad.

My anxiety spills over into anger, and I stalk to the door, clutching the baby close to my chest. Lori shuffles out of my way as I crash through the door and start speed walking down the long hallway, checking the doors.

I don't know which door I'm looking for, but none are suitable. I pass a few and then dozens more. I pick up my pace. None of them are suitable. I stop and double back.

I see a door with a soft yellow light flickering. I open it and enter.

The room is small and cozy. An end table holds a single candle flickering in a jar. Next to the table is a big, cushy chair.

Marie is sitting in the chair.

"Marie?" I ask, but she can't hear me.

It's like she's just waiting for something, a soft smile on her beautiful face. I look down at the baby, and he, too, has turned his head to face her, so I step close and lean down, offering the baby to her.

As soon as Marie sees the baby, her face lights up, and she reaches out and takes him in her arms.

She immediately starts cooing at him and kissing him on his cheeks, lips, and forehead.

I notice a rocking chair behind me, so I step back, sit, rock slowly, and watch.

"You are *so* handsome," Marie says to the baby. "Look at those long eyelashes! You are so beautiful!"

She continues like this for several minutes, stopping every now and then to kiss the baby or rub noses with him.

After a while, the baby's eyes start long-blinking, and Marie shifts to softly singing a song to him. Soon, the baby is asleep. Marie continues singing for a few minutes but eventually lays her head back in the chair and drifts off.

"Why'd you bring Marie here?" Lori's voice from the doorway.

My eyes stay on Marie and the baby.

"I needed someone to be excited he's here."

"Why Marie?"

"Nobody gets more excited over a baby than Marie."

Lori nods and smiles at this.

My anger has burned off, but it's left behind a heavy, blood-soaked blanket of sadness.

I push myself up from the rocking chair and retrieve the baby from Marie's arms. A soft smile remains on her face as she readjusts her sleep.

Back in the hallway, I begin to walk again, but I feel resistance. I'm stuck. It's like I'm walking but not going anywhere, a treadmill.

Then I start hearing voices. The first is my high school Spanish teacher. The next is one of my pastors when I was a kid. More voices join the chorus. They're all talking about me. It's barely above a whisper. I can't quite make out the specifics, but I know the gist of what they are saying.

Then I see it.

Just at the threshold of thc hallway's darkness, a pair of red eyes appear. They begin moving toward me.

My body starts shaking violently, and I turn to run. I sprint as fast as I can, the baby clutched to my chest. I know whatever is behind those eyes is here for the baby.

A pair of heavy metal double doors appears at the end of the hall, and I quicken the pace.

I reach the doors, turn my shoulder, and slam into the one on the right at a full-throttle run.

It flies open, and I break into a bright green grassy field. The sun is piercing overhead in a crystal-clear sky.

I keep running down the hill toward a distant forest. As I get closer, I can make out a trail cut into the trees and barrel headlong for it. Once safe in the woods, I slow to a walk and catch my breath.

The trail leads down to a slow-moving river about a hundred feet wide. I follow the trail along the river, walking timelessly. I want to put as much distance between me and that sterile hallway, those piercing eyes, and that hospital room as possible.

Eventually, the trail breaks off from the river, following a small stream deeper into the woods. I'm moving downhill now. The trail is getting narrower and more lush, and I must watch my steps so I don't trip.

The pathway and tributary finally end at a still pool of water nestled under a looming cliff of rock. I have nowhere else to go, so I sit cross-legged and rest the baby in my lap. He's awake now, quiet but anticipatory, staring up at me.

I stare back, too. We remain quiet.

We sit like this for a long time.

Eventually, I realize Lori is sitting next to me, her knees drawn up to her chest and her arms wrapped around them.

"What are we doing here, Eric?"

I don't answer. I don't want to answer. I want her and everyone else to leave me alone.

Leave us alone. Let us stay by the water, far from those who don't want us and will hurt us.

"You know what you have to do," she says gently.

"I'm not taking him back."

Lori rests her chin on her knee, her eyes glistening.

"I know," she says.

The baby and I are alone again. She's gone.

I sit longer and then push myself up to my feet. I return to the pathway, take a deep breath, and start walking again.

Within a few seconds, I'm out of the woods, walking through the metal double doors and standing in front of the hospital door. My mom, dad, and sister are right where I left them, still oblivious to me or the missing baby.

I push open the door and step through, shuffling over to my mother.

I hug the baby and bring him close to my face. I kiss him for the first time and then lean into his ear.

“I’m so sorry I have to leave you here alone,” I say. “But I’ll come back for you. Okay?”

I stare into his eyes, hoping for recognition, but he turns and looks back at my mother. I lean down and place him back in her arms. She adjusts and accepts him, pulling him in close.

The room is quiet, the same as I’d found it. But just as I step away, I notice something in the baby. A small light seems to flicker to life inside his abdomen. I reach out and touch the place on his stomach, feeling a warmth spread up my fingers.

“Do you need to do anything else?” Lori asks again, standing in the doorway and leaning against the doorjamb.

“I don’t think so.”

I take one last look around and then join Lori in the hallway, closing the door behind me.

She looks concerned.

“What?” I ask.

“How do you feel about what just happened?”

I shrug. “I don’t know. Sad? I think I knew it was like this, but… to see it…”

“Eric, we’re not time traveling here. I’m not some magical scientist or the Ghost of Christmas Past. This isn’t actually what happened.”

“What is this then?”

“It’s what you feel like happened. We’re in here.” She tapped her sharp fingernail against the front of my head. “Actually, we’re more in here.” And she switched her finger to the back of my head where it connects with my neck.

"Okay, so am I done? Can I go back to my life now?"

"Sure," she says. "I'll see you tomorrow at ten."

"Woah, woah, woah, no. We did whatever the fuck this is. I'm done. Right?"

"How're you feeling?" Lori has a wry smile when she asks this.

"Fine. I'm fine. But I've got shit to do. I can't keep coming here and doing this with you."

"What about the cave?"

"What cave?"

"Your cave. Is it empty yet? Or are the monsters still there?"

I pursed my lips together, not wanting to answer.

16

STEADY AS SHE GOES

"Jesus, you weren't kidding," Faye says. "I've never heard of any therapy like that. More like traumathy."

I shrug. "Now you know what I go through whenever I try to wrap my head around what happened. I always remembered going into her office and then being in her office at the end, but all the middle stuff, the in-between stuff, is fuzzy. I logically know it couldn't have happened, but it feels more real than real."

"I can't believe David hasn't ever told me any of this."

"I've never told David."

Faye's eyes widen.

"I've never told *anyone* about any of this."

"Then why are you telling me?"

"Why don't I keep going? Maybe it'll make more sense as I go on."

When I awaken, I'm alone in Lori's office. I look at my watch and notice two hours have passed. I just sit here, staring into the middle distance, unsure what to do. After a while, it dawns on me that she isn't coming back and I should let myself out.

I make the short drive back to my office in hazy silence. Tears begin to form anytime I think about that memory. I keep having to push myself back down and out of my thoughts. Remembering I have actual problems in the real world I need to deal with does the trick.

My phone buzzes just as I park. I see another text from Ty. He's adamant that we talk.

Which brings my mind back to my breakfast with Aneel.

What are the odds that my best friend would get offered the exact same job as me? Not to mention, he doesn't even need the money or the opportunity. But he's going to get it. I know he will, even if I go out for it, too. Things always work out for Aneel, even when they shouldn't.

Hell. I've already forgotten all about trying to get work from Aneel. The irony doesn't escape me that the only thing he potentially has to offer me is work Marie won't let me take in the first place.

I trudge to my office and slump into my chair, where I sit for several minutes, bathing in self-pity. My options for dealing with the IRS debt are down to zero since my final Hail Mary was trashed by Aneel.

I sigh, wake up my computer, and log in, but I don't click on anything or open any software. Any will to work on open projects has also dwindled to zero.

I open up Google and search for super PACs.

I want to see what kind of opportunity Marie is keeping me from pursuing.

At this point, I know nothing about campaign financing or how a super PAC works. As I search, I see all these campaign finance laws started coming into place in the early 1970s, thanks to, of all people, President Richard Milhous Nixon. Before that, anybody could give any sum of money to any candidate, and the candidate could use that money however they wanted to get elected. The "good old days" weren't as good as I'd initially thought.

So before Nixon, politics was an environment where a single deep-pocketed individual could write a fat-daddy check and fund a candidate's complete run for any political seat. Once that candidate was elected, the fat-daddy check writer would likely come knocking for a return on their investment.

Basically, one person or corporation could buy themselves a state legislator, congressman, senator, or even president.

The Federal Election Campaign Act of 1971 was passed to limit how much a single person or entity could donate to a candidate or campaign to curtail this good-old-boy network, pay-for-play scheme.

But not so fast. A few years later, in 1976, the Supreme Court ruled in Buckley v. Valeo that individual spending on political messaging is protected by the First Amendment's free speech provision and, therefore, cannot be limited. A couple more Supreme Court decisions in 2010 put the nail in the coffin and extended this right to corporations. Wow, that explained a lot about a lot of rot.

As with anything the United States government bureaucracy gets its hands on, this created quite the rat's nest of a system.

Currently, there are still limits to what a single person can give directly to a candidate. Isn't that comforting? When looking at a run for a federal position like congressman, senator, or president, a single person can give thirty-three hundred dollars to a candidate for the primary race and another thirty-three hundred dollars for the general election. So, an individual can give only sixty-six hundred dollars to a candidate.

However, according to those 2010 Supreme Court cases, individuals and corporations can give unlimited funds for political messaging. So, expressing one's message differs from supporting a flesh-and-blood human being. You can buy a Super Bowl ad if you'd like to tell people you want the government to provide free macaroni and cheese on Tuesdays, but you can't donate that money to a candidate who agrees with you.

This is where super PACs come in. They bridge the gap between a person who wishes to buy such an ad and the candidate who wishes to run it.

They're officially called "independent expenditure-only political action committees." Any individual or corporation can give unlimited amounts of money to a super PAC, and those super PACs can spend that "unlimited amount of money" on political messaging in any way they see fit.

Super PACs must just follow two squishy rules.

First, they cannot directly contribute to any campaign. The key word there is "directly." That means all of the super PAC spending cannot be linked in any way to any particular candidate. There can be no record of the super PAC buying a candidate a donut or even a member of the candidate's staff a donut.

Second, the leadership of the super PAC cannot coordinate with a candidate or their campaign on how the money is spent. This, apparently, is the big one that can have serious consequences. Donut buying is generally overlooked as long as the donuts don't turn into vacations in Maui.

But people have gone to jail for directly coordinating with candidates and their representatives.

I look up individual super PACs and the people who ran them. It gets pretty dizzying. Some make half a million a year just running the super PAC, not counting their other consulting and corporate gigs. Many of them become political commentators, lobbyists, and other high-profile jobs.

I lean back in my chair and stare at the computer screen. Being number two at a super PAC doesn't just pay well. It sets your future for being paid well for the rest of your career. Even the less successful super PAC leaders go on to bigger and better jobs. If I do a good job as second in command, the odds of me getting tapped to run my own super PAC go up dramatically.

Even in the number two spot, the high-powered people I'll work with will put me in a whole new stratosphere of connections. I can easily transition out of the political side of things to a role with one of the corporations donating unlimited sums to super PACs. I could be the guy who decides where to direct the money. Everyone wants to be that guy because they have all the power.

Except none of that will happen.

Not for me, anyway.

Even though I have the skills to do the job—and those skills are strong enough to get someone like Ty Banks interested in bringing me on board—none of that matters because my wife doesn't agree with a few political stances of some asshole politician. My chance to not just dig our family out of the gaping void of debt but to actually make something of myself is being blocked by my wife's political views.

And because of this, fucking Aneel, who doesn't

have a wife or kids or anyone pulling him down, will waltz in and get this opportunity to add to the stacks of money and connections he already has.

I stew and seethe. If I were a power plant, I would have been able to light up the entire eastern seaboard.

My eyes slide over to my journal, which is opened to today's to-do list. My stomach churns at the thought of fixing a typo on a client's website or sending out an email campaign for their book about Amish intrigue that will sell a few hundred copies.

I'm about to turn down a job managing millions in spending on marketing campaigns that matter worldwide. This makes the already mundane tasks I spend my days doing seem unbearably trite.

I jolt at a knock on the door.

For fuck's sake! Is my mommy back for another visit? More brownies for her loser-ass, panty-waist son?

I open the door to find a tall, scrawny kid in his mid-twenties wearing a white, short-sleeved button-up and dark slacks. He looks like a white Steve Urkel from the old TV Show *Family Matters*. His mud-brown hair is already thinning, and he has a manilla folder tucked under one arm.

"Mr. Bauer?"

"Who are you?"

"My name is Ashley Whittaker. I'm from the Downtown Nashville Internal Revenue Service Taxpayer Assistance Center. May I come in?"

"I, uh—" I notice Bob stepping out of the kitchen into the hallway.

He stops, coffee in hand in a mug that had "Hump Day!" written on it and then starts in our direction.

My vocal cords refuse to produce more sound, so I step back and motion for Urkel to enter before quickly closing the door behind him.

Urkel takes a seat, his eyes momentarily dropping to the brownies still sitting on my desk.

No way are you getting one of those, motherfucker, I think.

He opens his official folder and scans whatever the fuck is on those pages.

"Agent Mason sent me down to check in with you to ensure you received our latest correspondence and are planning to make your 10:00 a.m. meeting this Friday."

He then stares at me like some cold, uncaring, malicious machine, waiting while letting the silence hang between us. After the longest thirty seconds of my life have passed, he speaks again.

"Did you receive the correspondence?"

I nod. Urkel makes a note in his folder.

"Good. And you plan to meet with Agent Mason at the appointed time and day?"

"What, um—" I clear my throat, pick up the brownies, and extend the plate to him, "What's the meeting about?"

Like a lizard, he snaps a big fat one off the plate,

takes a big bite, and mumbles, "Did you read the correspondence?"

"Yes. I mean, most of it."

"Are you aware of the amount and penalty of back taxes you owe?"

Again, I nod.

Again, he stares, letting the silence stretch and doing that weird thing with his tongue that people do when they savor sugary sweets.

"Agent Mason would like to discuss that with you," he says.

"What if I don't have the money to pay the taxes?"

"I'm only here to confirm you received the correspondence, are aware of the time and place of the meeting, and are planning to arrive for the meeting."

"What happens if I'm not able to make it?"

Urkel retrieves his phone from his shirt pocket.

"I have access to Agent Mason's calendar and am happy to book another time with you this week."

"Can we push the meeting back?"

"Unfortunately, to do that, you would need to visit the Nashville office in person to inquire about changing the appointment to a later date. I'm only authorized to move it closer. In fact, Agent Mason wants me to tell you that if you could come in this afternoon, you could get the process started," he says with a degree of sympathy I hadn't expected.

"No. No, I can't today."

He nods and replaces the phone in his shirt pocket

as he asks, "So you plan to meet Agent Mason at 10:00 a.m. this Friday, February second?"

"Yes."

"And you understand the repercussions spelled out in the correspondence if you do not attend the meeting."

I nod.

"Unfortunately, Mr. Bauer," says Ashley, "my job requires me to get verbal confirmation of an answer to that last question."

"Yes, I understand."

"Thank you," a relieved Ashley says, checking off the final item on his list and closing his folder. "Do you have any other questions I can help you with right now?"

I shake my head.

He stands.

"Thank you, Mr. Bauer."

He begins to leave, but just as he opens the door and enters the hallway, he turns back to me.

"That's the best brownie I've ever had."

17

ACROSS THE BORDERLINE

After Ashley-Urkel leaves, I pop out of my chair and I not so subtly poke my head out the door in time to see him turn the corner. I hurry down the hall and watch as he exits the glass front door of the building, entering the sunlight.

I creep to the entrance and peer out, watching the young man climb into his white Toyota Corolla, adjust the mirror, and back out of the space. I pull out my phone as he drives out of view and dial Ty's number.

"What the fuck, Eric?"

"Sorry, Ty, I—"

"This isn't going to work if I can't get ahold of you. Shit's changing fast, and I need to know I can get my number two on the phone."

"Yeah, that's what I wanted to talk to you about." I pause for dramatic effect. "The thing is, I'm in. I want the job."

Ty doesn't answer. I check the phone to make sure we're still connected.

"Ty—" I break first.

"Of course, you're fucking in! This isn't something you turn down, Eric. Don't be a shithead. Now, are you ready to get to work and make some fucking money, or do you want to contemplate your situation some more?

"I'm ready."

"Great! Now, John Smith called me last night."

Did a blander American name ever exist?

"John Smith?"

"The congressman's campaign manager. He's the guy bringing us in to run this super PAC? Two big things have shifted. First, the pitch is on Saturday. We must be in DC to pitch the super PAC's board members. John will be there too, unofficially."

"And second," Ty continues. "Looks like we have some competition. Another one of Ricky's staffers, probably some prick after John's job, has his own guy he wants to run the super PAC instead of us. This fuck's going to be there to pitch too. Some asshole named Aneel Bana—Benna—Banar—I don't know, some Indian name."

"Banerjee," I said. "Aneel Banerjee"

"Yeah! How'd you know?"

"He's actually a friend of mine. I had breakfast with him this morning," I stammer.

"No shit? Small world. Well, he's now your sworn

enemy. Either we're running the super PAC, or he is. What do you know about him?"

I give him a quick rundown on Aneel and his business.

"So he's for real? Fuck! And they'll probably give it to him, too, so it'll look good for the Dickie to have some colored guy running it."

"Ty—"

"Yeah, yeah. I know. Alright. Got any dirt?"

I hesitate.

"Spill it, Eric."

I clear my throat. "Nothing of note."

"Sure, sure," Ty says. "John's still confident he can sway the board in our direction, but we still have to do the dog and pony to get the gig. I'll need you in DC on Friday night to prep for the presentation to the board on Saturday morning."

"*This* Friday?"

"Yeah, it got moved up."

Dread and relief swirl into a funky cocktail deep in my bowels.

I'm relieved that the pitch has been moved up, which means I'm that much closer to paying off the IRS debt. However, I dread how I will tell Marie about the trip and the job. Leaving town is a lot harder to hide, especially having to go that close to—oh *shit*.

"I'll be able to fly right back to Nashville Saturday evening. Right?"

"Why?"

"My older son has his birthday party on Sunday." As I tell Ty how important David is to me, I remember yet again that I still haven't ordered his cake.

"We get this job, and you can buy your kid a new birthday."

I laugh nervously. "Ty, I can't miss it."

"Yeah, yeah," Ty says. "Book your return ticket for Saturday night, and we'll have you back in plenty of time for your kid's party."

"So it'll be official by this weekend?" I ask.

"Looks that way."

"Documents signed, check in the mail?"

It's Ty's turn to laugh. "You seem anxious to get this moving. The official campaign won't start for another six weeks, you know."

"Look, I should probably tell you something."

"Aw fuck, what now?"

"No, no. It's not a huge deal. I just—I've got a pretty big tax bill hanging over my head. The signing bonus would let me wipe that out and stop the interest and penalties from accruing."

"Oh, I gotcha. Yeah, we'll get you that bonus, Eric. You show up Saturday with a bangin' presentation, John will use that to lock down the board, and we'll be rolling along by next week."

I let out a deep breath and nod into the phone.

"Alright, Eric, I gotta roll. I'll call you tonight at seven, and we can start prepping."

He hangs up as I'm saying goodbye.

18

TAKE TEN

Ten minutes after 7:00, Ty still hasn't called. A couple of hours ago, I texted Marie to let her know I'd be working late. She promised to leave a cold plate in the refrigerator for me like Stella in *A Streetcar Named Desire*.

The truth is that I could have gone home for dinner with the boys and helped clean up the kitchen before taking the call with Ty, but I didn't want to face Marie. No option exists in our universe that includes me going to DC without pissing her off royally.

The trip alone will be enough to set her off, but tack on David's party on Sunday, and the stressors will snap her something fierce. I don't get why it kicks her anxiety up to a ten. Only friends and family make up the guest list.

The thing is that anytime we have people over, she goes into cleaning hyperdrive. And you better believe

I'm the elbow grease she uses to make the house sparkle. Now, I'll be away the day before the party, so she'll have to juggle the kids and prep for the party and guests without me to order around.

She just doesn't understand why this party is so important. She originally wanted to keep it small—have over a handful of David's friends for a sleepover. But we haven't had a big shindig since moving into the new house. Most of our friends have never even seen it. Neither has her father since he lives a couple of hours away. He raised Marie by himself after her mom left when she was two. He did it all while growing a successful chain of small hardware stores, which he sold three years ago for somewhere well north of seven figures—a real Horatio Alger, or so he pretends.

He's never thought much of me and still likes to take sideways verbal shots any chance he gets. I want him to see the house I bought for his daughter. Our new place is twice as big as his house, with a half-acre, fenced-in backyard and one of those big, fort-style swing sets. I even spent a month building a treehouse for the boys, which I am confident will put an end to his jokes about my handiness with tools.

A birthday party for his grandson is enough of a guilt trip to force him to make the drive and behold the power of his son-in-law.

I picture myself walking him through the house, pointing out the various features, and then letting the awkward silence hang long enough for him to fill it with a compliment.

Now, all I have to do is avoid the IRS foreclosing on my Shangri-La.

My phone buzzes. At last, Ty's name pops on the screen. Like a teenage boy waiting for his girlfriend to call, I pick up immediately.

"Eric! My man!" Ty is shouting over a din of voices in the background. "I got someone here I want you to meet. Hang on."

I hear the shuffling of Ty's phone being handed off.

"Hey, Eric, John Smith. Nice to meet you."

John Smith. The congressman's campaign manager!

"Uh, hi, John. Nice to meet you, too."

"I have heard good things about you." John's flat, monotone voice comes at me fast. "You will be a good addition to the team for this super PAC." *Geez, how many did this guy oversee?*

My mind scrambles to keep up. If this is Ricky's campaign manager, why is Ty hanging out with him, and why am I currently on the phone with him? Doesn't this break the main rule of super PACs—no coordinating with the candidate?

"Thanks. I'm excited to be a part of it."

"This Saturday should be straightforward, but you need to show up with a comprehensive presentation. I have good relationships with three of the four board members—Reggie especially—but I must insist you cover a few main points. Do you have a pen?"

John talks in hyperdrive. I swear he gets five words out in the time I can say one. It feels like a battering ram to my frontal cerebral cortex.

According to my app, it's a twenty-seven-minute-thirty-one-second masterclass monologue covering the ins and outs of the super PAC's goals, what they expect to accomplish, and the media onslaught they will run during the primary and general races to ensure they do.

I write furiously but only get down half of what he's throwing at me.

My anxiety rises at an exponential pace as the onslaught continues. Ty had made it sound like this pitch was a perfunctory exercise, but getting everything John is assaulting me with will require hundreds of slides and a very long presentation.

A presentation I have to give in three days.

I fight to focus on John's words while also looking ahead to the rest of my week. How can I possibly have time to put the deck together, rehearse, and prepare appropriately for the meeting? I don't have a chance without working crazy long days and barely sleeping.

And why am I even talking to this guy? Doesn't John's explicit directions for the pitch count as coordinating? I assume, especially with my number two status, that I'm not supposed to meet the congressman or any of his staff until after the election.

Finally, John's stream of consciousness ends, and he hands Ty the phone back.

"You get all that, Eric?"

"Actually, I—"

"That's my man. I'm sure you've already got the presentation mostly prepped, but just work in John's details, and we should be good to go. Do you have any questions?"

I hesitate, unsure where to start. I have so many questions I'm struggling to organize them in my head.

Before I can answer, he cuts back in.

"That's great. Oh, one more thing. I overnighted a package to your office for delivery tomorrow. Text me when you get it. We're counting on you, Eric. Gotta run. Our table just got called."

I hear a click, and the line goes dead. I pulled the phone back, staring at it like a crystal ball, hoping it will reveal answers to questions I hadn't even formulated yet.

I walk back through what just happened in my mind. Ty said he would call tonight to start prepping the presentation. We had talked for about ten seconds, and part of that was him assuming I had the presentation "mostly prepped." I haven't even started building the slide deck yet. I've never done a pitch like this before.

Not taped and on YouTube, but live? In front of a bunch of rich political suits? Not desperate-for-validation writers?

I open PowerPoint and stare at the suggested templates.

What colors should I use? Red, white, and blue? The unknown unknowns are killing me. I know nothing about this process and, even worse, have no idea what I don't know but desperately need to know.

Back to Google.

I don't come up for air until, wouldn't you know it, 4:38 a.m. By this point, I've read every article on the internet about super PAC fundraising and spending as well as listened to my conversation with John a half-dozen times. I've even bought and read a book titled *The Political Campaign Desk Reference: A Guide for Campaign Managers, Professionals, and Candidates Running for Office*. I also skimmed through *The Victory Lab: The Secret Science of Winning Campaigns* and *The Campaign Manager: Running and Winning Local Elections*.

Those books have been a godsend. I've credited huge portions for my deck to demonstrate I'm not a shithead but someone who actually keeps up with the tools of the trade. I don't miss anything significant and even manage to sprinkle in the extra nuances from John as I go.

One hundred and eighty-two slides later, I'm feeling much more confident about my situation. I estimate the whole thing is about seventy percent done.

I close out everything on my computer before packing my notes and lists into my dive bag. On the way out to the car, my mind keeps pulling back to my conversation with John. His advice about the presentation was helpful but also extremely specific. And it all related to how we would run the campaigns financed by this super PAC.

How does that not count as coordinating with the candidate's campaign?

I yawn as I lock the front door of the building and unlock my car. It's too late to worry about all this. I'm overthinking it. Ty and John obviously know what they're doing. I'll give Ty a call in the morning to get some clarity.

For now, it's time to get home and get a half hour of sleep before Marie and the boys are up and a new day starts.

19

GOTTA GET UP

Marie's alarm sounds at 5:30 a.m. I groggily bench-press my face off the pillow and start sliding my body off the bed.

"No, no." Marie's lips are close, whispering in my ear. "You sleep. I'll get the boys up and going."

I mumble something resembling a thank you. She kisses me on the cheek, and I'm back asleep before her feet hit the floor. A few seconds later, I feel her hand on my arm, shaking. *I thought she was going to let me sleep in.* I open an eye and look up at her. The room seems awfully bright for this early. Why would she turn on the lights?

"Eric, it's almost eight," she's crouched down by the bed. "I'm taking the boys to school. When do you want to get up?"

A weird moan escapes my throat. I needed to get moving. I still have to finish the presentation and… the

IRS meeting slams into my consciousness, and my eyes pop open.

"You okay?" Marie asks.

I clear my throat and struggle up to a sitting position.

"Yeah," I croak. "Just need to get going."

"You got everything done last night?"

"Mostly. I need to finish it up this morning."

"What project is all this for?"

I scratch my head and cleared my throat again, pretending to wake up still but mostly buying time until I can form an innocuous lie in my sleep-deprived mind.

Heavy steps come bounding down the hallway, and Matthew appeared, shirtless, in the doorway. He looks very proud of himself.

"Where's your shirt?" Marie asks.

"I got milk on it, so I put it in the sink."

Marie stands.

"The sink?"

"Yeah, Mommy. You always soak stuff to get the stains out. Right?"

"So your school uniform shirt is soaking in water in the sink?"

Matthew nods, still very proud of himself.

"Oh, for god's sake." Marie laughs and hurries out of the bedroom, shooing our youngest down the hall in front of her.

I stand, rubbing my face and shaking my head,

trying to force consciousness on my body. I'm brushing my teeth when David and Matthew come in to kiss me goodbye. Matthew has a non-uniform shirt on inside out.

I pat them on the head and mumble a goodbye through the toothbrush. They run out as I spit in the sink. Marie comes in next, flustered but smiling.

"We gotta go," she says.

"Thanks for taking them this morning."

"Did I have a choice?" she quips.

"I would have gotten up," I shoot back.

"Sure, sure." She pecks me and hurries out.

I was *getting up.* She *told me to go back to sleep. Why is she bringing it up like I wouldn't have done it?*

Frustration pools in my mind as I struggle to understand it. Far too many things are going on today. I don't have time to deal with Marie's passive aggressiveness.

I need to finish the presentation. Getting to seventy percent took me eight hours, but getting it completely ready to go will take at least another eight—probably more. I'm sure I'll still be proofreading on the plane.

Shit. The plane. I still need to buy a plane ticket and break the news to Marie that I will be leaving the next night. I'm not sure how I'm going to do either of those. I spent the last of my credit buffer on the plane ticket and visit to the airport lounge on Monday to meet Ty.

I check our bank account to find only a couple

hundred dollars left. That's enough to cover food essentials and the final stuff for the party, but that's it.

I go into the closet to select the T-shirt for the day, and my eyes go to the small, black safe tucked in the back corner under a couple of boxes. Several seconds pass as I stare at it before I dig it out.

Inside—among the passports, birth certificates, insurance papers, and final house closing documents—sits a sealed freezer bag containing a thousand dollars in twenties.

The emergency cash!

Marie made me swear to only use it in the case of total societal anarchy or zombie apocalypse—both of which would probably render the cash useless.

She also never checks on it.

I stuff the freezer bag in my pocket, dress, and head to the car. Just as the back tires of my Tesla escaped the driveway, I remember my dive bag inside. It holds my notebook with the notes I scrawled when talking to John.

I throw the car into park and run back to the front door. I can hear the house phone ringing. I try to ignore it as I enter, but the caller ID reads "Ashley Whittaker." Fucking Urkel!

"Hello, Mr. Bauer. This is Ashley Whittaker from Agent Mason's office."

I freeze, gripping the landline.

"I'm calling to confirm your meeting downtown at the IRS Taxpayer Assistance Center at 10:00 a.m.

tomorrow, Friday, February second. Be sure to bring the documentation outlined in the correspondence you've received. Agent Mason wants me to pass along the importance of your attending this meeting on time. Do you have any questions?"

My bag drops to the floor with a crash.

"Are you there, Mr. Bauer? Do you understand?"

"Yes, I understand. Thank you," I say and then hang up the phone.

My stilted legs barely carried me across the living room. If Marie had been home, if Ashley had called earlier, if I had gotten up in time to take the kids to school—any of those, and Marie would have been the one to get that message.

Fucking Ashley. Apparently, embarrassing me at my office wasn't enough for him. He had to come for me in my home.

I have to get out of this meeting.

I retrieve my laptop and Ashley's business card and compose a new message to Mr. Whittaker's email address.

Hi Ashley, thanks for the call this morning. Unfortunately, I will not be able to attend the meeting tomorrow. I have an appointment with—

I tapped my finger on the laptop's metal casing and stare out the window at two cardinals fighting for dominance over our bird feeder.

What is severe enough to warrant missing the meeting and also something that can't be questioned?

Anything business would be something I could postpone. Personal errands are out. Something with the kids? I've gotten out of meetings before claiming family stuff. I don't know. Being vague here won't work. I could fake being sick? Call tomorrow morning with a stomach flu? They would probably want a doctor's note—

Then the flash of insight!

—an oncologist that I am unable to reschedule. They were able to get me in only because of a cancelation. I'm happy to set a time late next week for me to meet with Agent Mason. Let me know some days and times that work, and we'll get it set. Thanks so much! —Eric

There we go. Extremely important, solid reason I can't reschedule, and no way will he question anything having to do with cancer.

I fire off the email and close my laptop.

That will buy me a week and a chance to get this job.

My phone buzzes.

I had a cancelation this morning. If you'd like to come in early for our session, please do —Lori.

Perfect. I can get therapy over with and make it to the office before noon.

Twenty minutes later, I sit on the blood-red loveseat across from her.

"Ready?" she asks.

"Not really."

"Close your eyes."

20

THE RUN AND GO

The roof is yellow, and the exterior is brown with light gray mortar running the bond between each brick in that one-over-two half-pattern. This sort of color combination—pee over poop with interlocking phlegm—could only have emerged from the nineteen seventies.

Lori stands next to me at the end of the ranch house driveway.

"I don't want to go in there. Can't we hit pause and do this one tomorrow?"

Lori shakes her head. "Once we start, we have to finish. That's the rule."

"How long is this going to take?"

"That's up to you and how long you want to stand here and argue."

I sigh, stalk up the driveway, and open the front door without knocking.

There he is. The baby sits alone on the green shag carpet in the living room. His rosy cheeks and a swirl of sandy blond hair adorn a worried face. His eyes dart around and then back to the front door, where he looks through me, fervently searching.

I hear a creaky car door slam shut behind me, and I turn to look. The woman in the driver's seat checks over her shoulder and reverses the idling gray Cutlass. Briefly, the woman turns back to look at the house, and my breath catches.

It's my mother, just a few months after the last time I saw her in my mind hospital. She sniffs hard with red-rimmed eyes and then turns to look behind her again as she backs down and out of the driveway, turns around in the cul-de-sac, and drives away.

The baby cries, and I turn back, shutting the door gently behind me. I kneel next to him, searching his face. I want to ask him why he is afraid, but obviously, he's a baby and can't answer. Also, more obviously, I already know why.

I look between the baby and the empty hallways and kitchen, waiting for someone to come rescue this wailing child. Pick him up. Dance with him. Sing with him. Tell him his fears are unfounded.

When nobody comes, I kneel down again and reach for the baby.

Just as I feel the touch of his skin, the floor opens up underneath me, and I start sliding into the depths that lay beneath the green of the shag.

The baby seems not to notice. His wailing continues, and his eyes remain fixed as if he's looking at a private landscape that escapes me. As the world fades to black and the abyss consumes us, I see the red eyes from the hospital hovering just behind the baby, ready to devour him.

With my free hand, I claw at the carpet, but the void seems to suck at me, creating a vacuum at my feet and pulling me down into and through the darkness.

At least, I assume I'm falling. There is no wind. No sound. No light. Nothing passes me by. I scream but can't hear myself. That same vacuum sucking my torso is also pulling the breath from my lungs, leaving my cries unacknowledged, unheard even by myself in the vastness.

Panic washes over me.

Somehow, the baby is still with me but also not with me as I transport back in time.

I've returned to my fourteen-year-old self. I'm back in Grand Cayman, scuba diving with my father. While he is thrilled to take me on a special hundred-foot-deep night dive, I'm terrified the second we tip over the side and into the water. I suck at the bottled air on my back faster than any of the other divers around me. I can tell because of the bubbles. I'm making a lot more than the others. Soon, realizing I don't have enough air to return to the surface, I yank on my dad's dive vest and frantically point at my air gauge.

He checks it, nods, and points up to the surface. We

start the ascent—no more than thirty feet per minute—just like he'd told me a million times before. Any faster, and the nitrogen from the compressed air will get stuck in my joints and fizz like a shaken soda, causing bends and permanent deformity if not death.

My dad hands me his spare breathing valve, and I grip the valve in my left hand and the air gauge in my right. I watch as my air ticks down with every breath.

I remember imagining during the safety training that the air would slowly get cut off. I envisioned it becoming harder and harder to breathe until nothing was left to pull into my lungs.

That's not how it works.

The air snaps off mid-breath.

I am breathing in slowly, and then there is nothing. For an eternity, I forget my dad is there with his extra air and spare valve and suck harder and harder at mine, desperately trying to extract some spare oxygen from the metal walls of the air chamber.

He was there then, but he's not here now.

This is the feeling I'm reliving as I fall deeper into that suspended darkness beneath the green shag carpet, sucking hard at the nothingness, desperately begging the world around me to allow a bit of oxygen to flow into my airways.

And then I realize I'm not falling down. I'm falling up.

So, I kick hard with my legs against the emptiness around me, and my head bursts above the water's surface. I can suck a half breath of air in before rapids engulf me and spin me through a trio of somersaults within the turbulence.

My back rakes against a rocky shore, which burns across my shoulder blades. I spin around again, and my head cracks against another rock in the vortex. My vision explodes with static as I tumble around again.

Kicking as hard as I've ever kicked, I find my way back to the surface and pull with my arms against the current to keep my head above the water, gasping to fill my lungs.

The rapids I find myself in are racing downward in an undulating spiral through a rough-hewn half-moon of rock. Water splashes over the jagged boundaries, and I follow the entryway with my eyes to see a seemingly endless dark cavern beyond. Enormous black stalactites emerge from the black above, pointing down into the nothingness I am approaching.

I continue to spin and fight the current from dragging me under. Twice, it threatens to shoot me into the fissure. The spiraling downward continues for what seems like hours as I fight to keep my head above the churning, racing water.

The bottom of the half-moon rips at my feet as the water recedes and gets shallower, racing the current faster.

Suddenly, everything drops, and I am weightless again. I swing my arms and legs wildly against the waterfall, which spits me into the emptiness. I flip another three times and then hit hard against the water's surface.

Once again, I'm plunged into blackness, and as I beat at the water frantically, I realize I don't know which way is up. I stop thrashing, trusting the air in my lungs to pull me back to the surface.

I burst through and look around to find myself in a large stone silo a hundred feet wide. The water is still now. Flat. Placid. The only sounds are from my slaps at the surface, looking around, trying to find where to go. High above me windows have been cut into the stone and are lit from behind by torchlight. In each window is a silhouette of a person sitting, silently watching me.

They don't answer my cries for help. They don't move. They only watch.

I swim over to the border of the stone walls and start feeling around counterclockwise, looking for an opening or a crack or something to find a foothold or a way out. But the stones are smoothed from millennia of holding water, and I can find no gaps.

Fatigue sets in. I call out more as I beat my legs and arms against the water to stay afloat. I keep swimming around the edges, looking for an opening I know isn't there.

I call out to the silhouettes and then switch to cursing them, those silent, watching bodies as they sit in warm light and comfort, waiting for me to drown.

I try to lie back on the water, using the air in my lungs to hold me afloat and keep some energy in my body, but each time I exhale, my head slips below the surface. Water runs into my nose, threatening to fill me up and pull me down. I gag and vomit.

I begin to cry. I'm lost, and I now realize I've lost the baby. The red eyes have him. There is no way out, no way back to him and no way back to myself. I will die here, and my body will sink down to the bottom of this well to join the countless other lost souls.

I close my eyes, take a deep breath, flip myself below the surface, and swim downward. As I descend, something whispers past my ears, but I miss what it says.

I kick hard against the water, using my last strength to drive downward. The voice comes again, louder this time, from the deep.

"Here. Here. Here."

I struggle against the water, stretching my arms as far as they can go, and pull my cupped hands back, pushing my body down.

"Hurry. Here. Here."

As I push my way down, a blemish in the stone emerges—a break in the wall. I hurry toward it as the burning in my lungs works its way up my throat and tongue.

I grab the edges of the break and pull myself into the opening, a long chute leading back upward. I now claw above me at the wall and push off the sides with my feet, but the black at the edges of my vision begins closing its way in.

The internal blackness takes over just as my head breaks the surface. I fall backward, cracking my skull against the stone wall. The pain brings me back from the engulfing unconsciousness.

I wedge my back against the wall with my feet out in front, holding myself in place as I suck in air and let the oxygen drive the numbness out of my extremities.

Nothing lies in the darkness above me but a vague bit of potential light.

I allow myself a brief period of rest before I begin the arduous climb toward the possibility, shimmying my way up through the opening. I move inches at a time, stopping to rest as needed, constantly checking to measure the vague but increasing brightness of light above me.

Time passes—months perhaps, maybe even years. I rest, shimmy, check the light, and do it over and over again.

Eventually, the light clarifies into an orange flickering glow. I speed up, resting less. Soon, my fingers reach a ledge. I find purchase, push against the walls, and flop my body onto, at last, a blessed horizontal surface.

I crawl across the floor, following the fiery light, and find myself in a large enclave at the edge of a virtually unending cavern. Torches along the cragged wall light up the area, and my eyes scan the liminal space that disappears into the darkness.

I stand and snatch one of the torches embedded in

the wall before unsteadily creeping to the edge and looking down. The yawning abyss disappears into infinitude. I squint and look off into the cavern, seeing what could be the rapids I had descended, but I have no way to be sure. This topsy-turvy world morphs and complexifies faster than my mind can comprehend.

As I move along the edge, looking for an escape pathway, I sense movement behind me. I spin around, and the light from my torch flickers off the black scales of a giant serpent, slowly raising its head, like a cobra, to full height. The wet, undulating tongue of the slick, slithering beast darts out of its mouth, and the burning red eyes stare down at me as it raises itself two, six, and finally eight sizes above me.

I stumble back and sit down hard. The torch skitters away.

Somehow, I know this snake. This is the 4:38 snake that has followed me and chased me in my dreams. No matter where I hide or how hard I run, I've always found myself in the devouring embrace of this monster for as long as I can remember.

This snake has no name, but I know his role in this turbulent underworld. He is the snake that eats the unwanted babies.

I make my way back to my feet, my knees shaking beneath me. As soon as I am vertical, the snake darts down at me, snapping its fangs inches from my face, and I fall back again, cowering under its gaze.

"Tell me," the familiar voice is slick and thick as oil

flowing over me. I hide my head between my knees and under my arms. "Why are you here?"

I peek between my fingers and somehow choose to get back on my feet to stand up like a man instead of a child before answering.

"I've come for the baby."

"The baby's gone."

"Where is he?"

"I ate him."

Confusion and then a spark of anger lights inside my abdomen.

"You are the eater of unwanted babies," I accuse.

"I am."

"But if I am here for that baby, he is wanted. He doesn't belong to you. He belongs to me." I'm shouting now.

"It's too late. I have eaten him, and he is gone."

Now, my insides are inflamed. I stand taller, stiffen my spine, and clench my fists.

"Give him back."

The snake's head lolls back and forth before me, taunting me, and a shrug runs through it.

"I am bored now. And tired. Leave me so I can sleep."

I step forward and push out my chest.

"I want him back. Give him to me."

The snake ignores me and begins slithering back into the darkness, its thick body coiling up on itself.

I break into a run, leap on top of its looping body,

and grab the first scale I can wrap my hands around. It is the size of a dinner plate, and I can see my face reflected in its inky translucence.

I pull hard, my back straining and my shoulders bowing. It sticks fast at first, but then, with a sickening wet sucking sound, the scale peels loose. I fall back off the snake, tumbling onto the stone floor.

A sound between a hiss and a roar emits from the snake, and its great diamond head shoots into my vision. It snaps at me again, its fangs inches from my face, but I hold still. It snaps again and hisses.

I stand, tossing the scale to the side, and rush toward the bleeding hole.

"No! Stop!" the snake hisses.

"I will tear you apart until you give me back that baby!"

"The baby's gone! I ate him! He's mine!"

I rush back up his scales and dig my hands into the flesh beneath the wound. I place my foot against the snake's body and yank as hard as I can. With another wet sucking sound, another scale skitters across the stone floor.

The snake screams and hisses. He curses and threatens me, but I can't hear what he's saying exactly.

This time, I dig my fingers into the bleeding meat the missing scales expose. I claw and grab handfuls, throwing the wet mess behind me. His dark purple blood runs down my arms. My feet become slick. I can feel the tissue spattering against my face and matting in my hair, but I don't relent. I become crazed, digging and clawing, ignoring the curses and threats that have now transformed into pleas for mercy.

"Stop! Please stop! Here, here, here! I will give you the baby."

Hearing this, I relent, my hands buried to the elbows in the serpent's flesh, and look up at the head hovering above me.

The snake begins to convulse and gag. I yank my hands out of the dark flesh and slide off its body, backing away. The snake drools big milky yellow ropes as it hacks and spits.

Its great jaws unhinge and bulge open as the baby tumbles out of its maw to the floor in front of me. As soon as the baby emerges, the snake falls back, defeated, and slides off the cliff's edge, disappearing into the abyss.

I turn to the baby, who is now sitting upright, and my jaw falls open. He's the same, but he is now three stories tall. I walk up to him and gaze up at his magnificence. I can still feel the blood of the snake dripping off the ends of my fingers and pooling next to my feet.

The baby, seemingly nonplussed, looks around and then down at me. When he smiles, a light emanates from within his belly, lighting up the entire enclave—but not just the enclave. I'm sure the entire unending underworld is bathed in his light, illuminating and revealing everything once hidden from me.

I smile and look up at him. "What am I supposed to do with you?" I laugh.

The baby smiles back, and something shifts. I look down, and the snake's blood is gone. I am clean again with a fresh shirt, clean pants, and familiar shoes.

I look back up at the baby, but he is gone as well. I hear the slamming of a car door behind me and turn to see through the living room window of the 1970s ranch house.

My mother has returned.

I spin around again to find the baby, normal-sized, sitting on that ugly shag carpet, smiling and bouncing in place, beyond excited.

I hear my mother's Sunday service high heels click and clack across the concrete walkway, see her slam through the door, and watch her scoop up the baby. She holds him tightly, twirling and dancing in place. The baby coos and laughs as she dips, spins, and sings him a song.

Embarrassed, I take a step back and give them the space to move around the living room without regard for me. I try to catch the baby's eye and wave goodbye, but he only has eyes for his mother.

I skirt around them to the front door and back myself out, gently closing it and catching the latch behind me.

As I make my way down the driveway, I run my hand over the old Cutlass, the car my father bought for my mom a week after she'd given birth to me.

Lori meets me at the mailbox.

"That was some good work you did in there," she says.

"I have no idea what happened. What was all that?"

"It's hard to say. We're not down to the bottom yet."

"How much further?"

"You never know until you're there."

21

FAST AS YOU CAN

"I don't know what to say. That's really hard to process." Faye looks confused and unsure about what I want her reaction to be.

"You don't have to say anything. I'm just telling you what happened."

"And you lied about having cancer to get out of an IRS appointment?"

I shrug.

"Why didn't you just tell them you were having a mental breakdown?"

"I'm not convinced it was a breakdown... I'm not proud of the cancer lie, but it was the only thing I could think to do at the time."

"That's some bad karma you put out there. Did it work?"

I laugh and pick up where I left off.

I sit down on an empty bench in front of Lori's office. The sun burns brightly and hot for a winter day in Nashville. This kind of solar intensity is usually reserved for the late spring and early summer months.

My eyes squeeze shut against the glare, and images of snakes, rapids, and giant babies flicker through my mind. Surely, I'm losing it. This can't be normal. I know it must all be in my head, that Lori was hypnotizing me somehow, but it felt so *real.* I rub my hands together, remembering the sucking, slick flesh of the snake. I wipe tears out of my eyes as the picture of my mother dancing with the baby replays in my mind.

The phone buzzes in my pocket. Ty.

Did you get the package? I'm showing it as delivered.

I haven't been in yet. Heading over now.

Call me when you get it.

As I walk slowly down the sidewalk to the parking lot, I keep telling myself to pick up the speed, go faster. I've got a lot of shit to do. But I can't break out of the slow-motion daze.

Once in the car, it takes me five minutes to pull out of the parking lot.

At the office, I nod to Bob, who sips idly from his steaming "Keep calm. It's almost Friday!" mug.

"You doing okay there, Eric?"

"All good, Bob," I respond, slipping by him.

I turn the corner and see the FedEx package leaning

against my office door. As I bend down to grab it, the package starts vibrating. I jump back, staring at the white envelope as it shakes and shimmies to the prone position.

Once it stops, I pick it up and rip open the perforated cardboard.

Inside is a small Android smartphone. I extract the device and click the button on the side. The screen lights up, revealing three missed calls from a blocked number.

I enter my office and drop into my chair, staring at the phone, unsure what to do with it. I bring up the home screen again and tap around, but the only app on the phone is for making actual telephone calls. No email. No web browser. No maps. I can't even find a texting app.

My main phone buzzed. Ty again.

Get it yet?

I think. A phone?

Ten seconds later, the new phone rings again from a blocked number.

I answer.

"Hello?" I ask.

"Eric?"

"Who is this?"

"It's John Smith."

I don't answer. I have no idea what to say. Why wouldn't John just call me on my main phone? We talked two days ago.

"Eric? Are you there?"

"Uh, hey, John. What's up?"

"I'm making sure you received the phone we sent you."

"Yep. Got it right here. Talking on it now."

"It is an unlocked phone with a new SIM card and one thousand hours prepaid, which should last us a while. It only has one number in the contacts, which is the phone I'm talking to you on right now. Only call that number. Nothing else from this phone. Never call anyone else. Do not install any other apps or use any other functions. Only phone calls. Also, set up a lock screen passcode. Do you know how to do that on an Android phone?"

"I can figure it out."

"Don't use the face passcode. Only a number passcode—a unique one."

"I'm sorry, John. I'm confused. Did you just send me a burner phone?"

John doesn't answer for a beat, letting the silence answer for him.

"How is the presentation coming together?"

"Fine. Good. I should finish it up today."

"Do you want me to look over any of it?"

I pause again, still trying to wrap my head around what's happening. I can't think of a single good, legal reason why I need such an untraceable form of communication.

"Send it to me when you are done," John says.

I nod but don't say anything.

"Go ahead and set up the passcode and then keep this phone on you at all times. We will talk soon."

"Sure. Thanks, John," I hear myself say.

John hangs up, and I'm left staring at the new phone.

A thousand hours? No texting, only calls, and only to a blocked number?

I pull out my primary phone and dial up Ty.

No answer.

I go to text him but then think better of it. Why would John insist on no texts? Should I be careful what I'm texting Ty as well? My last text to him was, "I think. A phone?" and he didn't respond. Maybe I shouldn't have put in writing that he'd sent me another phone. But why?

Again, I can't think of a single good, legal reason.

A fist of anxiety pounds in my stomach as I lay both phones on my desk and stare at them. I'll have to keep the second one hidden. If Marie finds it, she'll probably think I'm cheating on her.

What now?

The only thing I can think to do is continue working on the presentation. I will double-check with Ty before sending John what I have, but either way, I need to get this thing done, and the clock is ticking.

I wake up the computer, and my inbox reveals anxious inquiries from several open client projects. I hope mightily that these projects will be irrelevant in a few short days and ignore them as I reopen the PowerPoint and dive back in. For the next several hours, I make good progress, filling in the gaps and tightening everything down.

Honestly, as far as I can tell, I have a solid plan for running the super PAC for Congressman Bryant's primary campaign. The books I've read, combined with my experience running online product launches, put me in a really solid place.

Also, if I'm honest, John's input has been a huge help, giving me several insights into how my history uniquely connects to Bryant's. I am a "self-starter" without much pedigree. That was precisely how Bryant positioned himself for his run—an outsider ready to go to Washington and "get the foxes out of the henhouse."

The connection he made between me and Bryant causes me to Google John, which is uniquely challenging given his name. It takes a while to track him down, but once I do, it becomes clear he's at the top of his field. Bryant is just one of many politicians of all stripes he's run campaigns for, and he has deep alliances with people like James Carville and Karl Rove.

An old magazine article in the *Washingtonian* reported that he'd gotten his start as a pimple-faced teenager who finagled a job getting coffee for the legendary Lee Atwater at Black, Manafort, Stone, and Kelly. He has a reputation of being unflappable and relentless, and his nickname "Prestone," as in the antifreeze, was earned. Eighty-three percent of his clients won their races, and the seventeen percent who didn't either died before voting day or dropped out to "spend more time with their families and pursue private sector work."

The lion's share of credit for Bryant's successful run for Congress was attributed to him. Simply finding a way to sell "Ricky the Dicky" was miraculous in and of itself. Now, I'm working with him—more accurately, for him. Again, it washes over me how crazy it is that I'm suddenly running in these kinds of circles. All I have to do was what this guy tells me to do, and I'll never have to worry about money again.

I check the clock. It's almost 2:00 p.m. It's been more than three hours since I called Ty, and I've had no return call. I check my phone but see no messages. I check my email.

No messages from Ty, but I do have one from Ashley.

22

CREEP

Hello, Mr. Bauer, thank you for the update.

Agent Mason is very sorry to hear that you will be unable to attend tomorrow's meeting.

Please provide the name and phone number of the oncologist's office so we can confirm your appointment. You'll also need to call them and give them permission to confirm your appointment so as not to break HIPAA laws.

As you can imagine, people often fake these sorts of things to get out of their meetings. Once you send that over and we confirm your appointment, I'll be happy to reschedule for early next week.

Sincerely,

—Ashley Whittaker, Executive Assistant to Alex Mason, Internal Revenue Service

---

I read the email a second and then the third time.

Fuck.

Now, I need an appointment with an oncologist. How hard are those to get?

Turns out pretty hard.

I call every oncologist's office within a twenty-five-mile radius. I wait on hold for fifteen minutes only to be told the earliest appointment is a month away, six weeks away, or, for one office, four months.

What if I really had cancer? I'd be screwed.

By the sixth call, my desperation has pushed me to begging. Still, it becomes apparent that most people calling an oncologist aren't in a position to take their time. As a result, the staff at these offices have become numb to desperation. They all have the same calm, pseudo-sympathetic demeanor.

"I'm sorry you're having difficulty finding medical attention; we recommend you call your employer's health care representative to aid you in your search... blah, blah, blah."

Phone calls aren't working.

Then I remember when I once called the dermatologist to get a weird infection on my scalp looked at, and they were booked for the next two weeks. After another day, the infection had gotten worse. So, I drove to their office at 7:30 a.m. when they opened the door and told the receptionist I needed to see a doctor that day. I'd brought my laptop to get some work done and was happy to camp out in the waiting room all day in case of a cancelation.

Twenty-five minutes later, I was sitting on that waxy paper on an examining table, and a dermatologist had a flashlight shining on my head. Ten minutes later, I was out the front door, prescription in hand.

I punch the closest oncologist into the GPS and start the twelve-minute drive. I confidently push through the front glass doors but am turned away a few minutes later. No appointments are available, and waiting in the lobby won't change that.

For the next two hours, I drive to every oncologist's office, slowly circling outside the city, all but pleading with them to put me on the schedule. Several times, I even try implying something dire is going on, but I can't talk them into putting me on the schedule.

I pull into the parking lot of my last chance oncologist in Columbia, about forty-five minutes south of the city, at 4:53 p.m.

I almost lose my nerve when my eyes land on the receptionist. I imagine the first line of the want ad this man must have responded to: *Are you an ancient individual who regularly gets mistaken for a corpse?*

"Hi there, young man," he croaks. His genuine smile only deepens the terrifying crevices embedded in his face. "How can I help you?"

The reason for my visit has somehow vanished as the crypt keeper waits patiently behind the large receptionist desk in the surprisingly warm waiting area. Dark brown, overstuffed chairs line the walls, and fresh flowers poke out of ceramic vases on every end table. The lights emit a soft yellow, and jazz Muzak gently floats down from the ceiling.

"I, um," I pause again, refocusing. "I need to make an appointment."

He dons the glasses hanging from his ropey neck by a dull gold chain and leans close to the boxy monitor.

"Let's see. Are you a current patient?"

"Actually," I say.

His eyes squint above his frames as he looks up at me.

"I need an appointment for tomorrow at 10:00 a.m."

He collapsed back from the monitor.

"Unfortunately, all of our appointments are booked for tomorrow. The earliest appointment is a month out."

Irritation invades my voice.

"What if this was an emergency? Wouldn't you be able to get me in?"

"Are you a current patient?"

I shake my head.

"*Is* it an emergency?"

"I'm not saying it *is* an emergency. I'm just asking, what would you do if it was? Don't you leave some room in the schedule to fit in extra people if they need to get in?"

"If it *is* an emergency, I would tell you to go to the hospital's emergency room. We could fit you in if you were an existing patient dealing with a complication, but considering you are neither a patient nor in an emergency, I'm not sure what you are asking me to do."

"Sir," I lay the politeness on as thick as possible. "I know this may sound crazy, but I just need to have an appointment on the books for me at 10:00 a.m. tomorrow. I'm even happy to pay my copay up front right now."

The ancient man stares at me, the gears moving slowly behind his eyes.

He folds his hands on the desk.

"I think you need to leave...sir."

"No, you don't understand. I know this sounds crazy—"

"Yes, it does sound crazy because it *is* crazy. You want to pay to book an appointment for tomorrow at an exact time, for god knows why. I've never heard of this before, and I can't imagine it would abide by our policies."

As he says this, a much younger woman, closer to my age, shuffles into the receptionist area behind him, several patient files tucked under her arm.

The old man glares at me, but I look at the new arrival, pleading with my body language.

She meets my eyes and then looks down at the receptionist.

"Hey, Grady, anything I can help with?"

"This man." He points a crooked finger in my direction. "Is trying to make an appointment for tomorrow, but he's not a patient, and I don't even think he's sick."

"Grady, you can't say that!"

Grady ignored her and kept glaring at me instead.

"I *am* sorry." The woman turns to me. "But if you're not a current patient, there's nothing we can do. I would suggest calling around to other offices and maybe having your insurance try to book you an appointment. Sometimes, they can push something through."

I sigh and nod. The woman turns away, and Grady stares menacingly at me until I back away and head to the parking lot.

Out in my car, I sit motionless as my mind's eye stares into an empty abyss of ideas. *How can it be this hard to get a doctor's appointment?* It's the end of the day, which means all the offices are closing, and I have no options left. I can email Ashley back, letting him know my appointment was canceled, but how would that help? I'll still have to go to the meeting, but he'll know I lied without the appointment he can confirm. I suppose I could send him the information for one of the oncologists, and when they don't confirm the appointment, I'll tell him it must have been a mix-up. But then I'm sure he'll ask for some kind of receipt or confirmation.

Again, though, what will they do if I just don't show up? Sure, the letter contains threats, but would they really go through with any of them? I can just call on

Monday, let them know I have the money coming, and *then* go to the meeting and clear it all up.

Have the money coming.

This job is getting more and more complicated. I'd started to worry a bit when Ty first put me on the phone with John. Still, technically, from the understanding I picked up via Google since I'm not currently working for the super PAC, I guess it isn't directly illegal to coordinate with the Bryant campaign.

However, after receiving the burner phone—did those ever show up in real life for *legal* or morally uncompromising purposes?—with a blocked number and a thousand hours prepaid, that could only mean they had many future expectations for me to talk directly to John.

This is feeling sticky.

Surely, John and Ty wouldn't risk their reputation and potential legal troubles playing so fast and loose with the regulations. Right? After all, the burner phone can be burned, and with no other records of us speaking other than each of our collusion in the operation, plausible deniability is pretty much locked.

But Ty still hasn't called me back.

I recheck my watch to see that it just clicked past 5:00 p.m. Still nothing. When I look back up, I see a door on the side of the oncologist's office swing open, and little old Grady stumbles out. He reaches into his Mr. Rogers-esque cardigan sweater pocket and produces a pack of cigarettes. He deftly removes a single and sticks it between his craggy lips. His previously shaky hands hold fast as he strikes one of those old-fashioned self-lighting matches on the building stucco, expertly brings the flame to the tip, and inhales deeply.

What a shithead, I think. *Fuck it.*

I throw the car door open and hurry across the parking lot toward Grady, slowing as he turns toward me.

Holding up my hands in surrender, I put on my kindest, most innocent, Southern aw-shucks smile as I continue my approach from about twenty feet away.

His eyebrows narrow when he recognizes me.

"Look," I say, "I really am sorry. I know it sounds crazy, but can you just hear me out? Twenty seconds?"

He stares without answering, and something shifts in his demeanor, so I take it as a yes.

"Again, I know it sounds nuts, but all I need is an appointment on the books with any of your doctors or registered nurses at 10:00 a.m. That's it. Like I said, I'm happy to pay the copay up front."

I continue approaching slowly as I speak, now ten feet from him. He holds his ground, cigarette dangling from his lips. I reach for my wallet, and my hand brushes the bulge in my pocket, which gives me an even better idea.

"In fact," I produce the freezer bag of twenties. "I'm happy to pay you for the trouble. How's a hundred bucks?"

Grady turns back toward the door.

I shoot my hand out, trying to gently put it on his shoulder to stop him from going back inside, but he spins around with surprising speed and sticks a Taser directly into my palm.

At first, I think he's screaming, but by the time my knees hit the sidewalk, I realize the high-pitched sound is coming from me. I look up, trying to force my vocal cords back into working order, but before I can speak, he steps close to me and hits me again with the Taser right below my collarbone. My back goes rigid, and I tumble over onto my side, hitting my head on the curb.

I roll over onto my back and watch helplessly as Grady replaces the Taser into the other pocket of his cardigan. Smirking down at me, he calmly drops the cigarette, rubs it out with his toe, and goes back inside the office without a word.

Will he call the police? Send one of the doctors out to deal with me?

I need to leave there before Grady's minions get to me.

My muscles start regaining their function, and a few seconds later, I make it back to my feet. I sway as the horizon seems to rock back and forth in front of me. I stumble back across the parking lot and fold myself into my car.

Thankfully, the parking lot is empty, so I can pull through unimpeded. I slowly turn onto the road and begin the forty-five-minute drive home.

23

TAKE THE LONG WAY HOME

Ten minutes into the drive, I stop at an old Exxon gas station. My head still feels woozy from my confrontation with Grady, so I decide to avoid the high speeds of the highway and work my way home on the back roads. Still, I need to take a break, grab a snack, and drink some Gatorade to see if I can get my head on straight enough to contend with what awaits me at home.

I park the Tesla in front of the dilapidated building and sway a bit as I walk into the convenience store and pay for the snacks with cash.

Back outside, I lean against the bumper. I take a couple of sips of the red-flavored sports drink and let out a sigh.

My head aches where it hit the curb. The bleeding has stopped, but it left behind a nasty bump. It looks like someone has shoved half a lemon under my skin.

How exactly am I going to explain this to Marie?

The phone starts buzzing. Ty. I hurry to answer.

"Hey, Ty, thanks for calling me back."

"You got the phone? Have you talked to John yet?"

"Yeah, he called me. Actually—"

"Great. Make sure you keep that phone on you at all times. It's the only way John will be able to get ahold of you starting next week."

"Yeah, that's what I wanted to ask—"

"I've got some good news for you. I spent the afternoon wining, dining, and sixty-nineing those assholes on the board. Eighteen holes of golf and unlimited drinks usually do the trick. I'm pretty sure one's still holding out on me, but the other three are solidly in our corner. We're about to head out to dinner, but I saw you called. How's the presentation coming together?"

"It's good. Great actually. I've got a solid plan for the primary and have outlined the whole thing."

Ty yells something incomprehensible to someone, apparently really far away. Then he's back on the phone.

"Good man. You get John's input in there?"

"Yeah, it was really helpful. He's a smart guy."

"For sure. You have no idea. Look, really quick, let's just switch to talking on the phone from here on out. No need to text me. Just call if you need me. I'll always call you back first chance I get."

"Okay. This is actually what I wanted to talk to you about."

"Can it wait, Eric? The car just arrived. They're waiting on me to roll out to dinner."

"Um, yeah, well, it's important."

"Okay, shoot. You have two minutes. *Two minutes!*" he shouted, apparently to the car full of drunk super PAC board members.

I cleared my throat. "So this phone."

"Yeah?"

"What exactly is it for?"

"It's so John can get ahold of you when he needs you."

"It's got a thousand prepaid minutes on it."

"Yeah, Eric, I know. I'm the one who sent it to you."

"You sent me the phone? Not John?"

"Right."

So Ty sent me a burner phone preprogrammed with John's number and a thousand hours of prepaid talk time.

"Ty, what are the expectations here? Maybe I missed something, but from what I can tell, once we're running the super PAC, we're not allowed to coordinate in any way with Bryant's campaign."

Ty lets the silence hang. He must have been tutored by John.

I fill it.

"I mean, I'm not saying we're doing anything illegal, but I just, I don't know, it seems weird."

"What seems weird?"

"Why do you need me to talk to John for a thousand hours?"

"Eric, we're running a *presidential* campaign here. This isn't your shitty little online gardening book promotions. This is a big deal."

"I get that, but—"

"This is going to take a lot of work. Long hours. We're not fucking around here. We need Bryant to lock the nomination and then make it all the way to the White House. You're going to play an integral part in that."

He continues before I can respond, "Do you have any idea what this is going to do for your career? What an opportunity this is? Fuck the money and your little snafu with the IRS. By the time we finish this campaign, you'll have a hundred powerful connections and your pick of jobs."

"I know. It's just—"

"You're worried about the rules?"

"Right. I want to make sure—"

"We're not breaking the rules. Right?"

"Yeah."

"You a rule follower?"

"Well, when it comes to laws and fines and jail time."

"Which is why you've filed and paid all your taxes on time?"

"This is different."

"You're fucking right it's different. Do you think the other side is following all of the rules? Do you think *anybody* who isn't eating shit in this world follows the rules? Look, you have an untraceable phone that can't be tapped, and you'll get calls on an as-needed basis. That's it. You've got to live with certain discomforts, Eric, and in the grand scheme of things, this one is a fucking breeze."

I stare up at the sky. It's a beautiful pink as the sun lowers behind the sagging Exxon station.

"So I *will* be expected to coordinate with John."

Ty lets out a long sigh and mutters a few curses.

"Eric, I thought you were tired of being a shithead, fuckup, panty-waist, small-business nobody. I really did. I come along and offer you not only a chance at doing something that actually matters in the world, but it'll pull you out of this money pit you've dug for yourself. I thought this was what you wanted. But if not, just say so."

It's my turn to let the silence hang.

"Do you have any idea how replaceable you are? There are a thousand of you out there who would jump at this opportunity and not think twice about the sacrifices required. So make a fucking decision. Are you in, or are you out?"

24

LIKE A HURRICANE

I stay at the Exxon for another thirty minutes, sipping my red Gatorade and watching the sky turn black.

Even though my head has cleared, I keep to the back roads, stretching out the drive home as long as possible. I leave the radio off and let the conversation with Ty loop in my mind.

My head throbs where it had bounced off the sidewalk. My body still twitches every minute or so due to the electric jolts old Grady gave me.

Total darkness has set by the time I pull into the driveway and make my way through the front door. I can hear Jamie Hyneman's dull, dry voice explaining something sciency upstairs, which means the boys are watching their pre-bed episode of *MythBusters*. A plastic-wrapped plate of food lies solitary on the otherwise clean countertop in the darkened kitchen.

I drop my keys off on the side table and absently

touch the tender spot on my temple as I make my way back to the bedroom.

"Hey, hon." I steel myself as I call out an artificially cheerful but familiar announcement of my arrival.

No answer.

I check the bedroom and bathroom but no Marie. Then I go through the laundry room and out the back door to find her head in a book, reading on the porch.

She looks up as I open the door.

Standing in shadows to mask my injuries I say, "Hey, hon, I'm just letting you know I'm home."

"Okay," she says and then looks back at her book.

I study her for a bit.

"Everything okay?"

"Yeah," she says, not looking up. "Just tired."

I wait a bit longer to see if she'll respond in some other way before backing into the house and closing the door. I decide a shower will come before the lukewarm dinner.

Once I'm shirtless in front of the mirror, I can see the full extent of the damage Grady did to me. Two welts sit right below my collarbone, and though the initial swelling has gone down on my temple, it still stands out bright red.

I can hide the mess on my chest but not on my head.

My phone starts buzzing as I finish undressing. The automatic caller ID flashes for the IRS. I silence the phone and push the meeting out of my head. I will email Ashley tomorrow morning apologizing for missing the meeting but assuring him I'll be there first thing Monday. By Monday, I should have confirmation of the job, and the meeting will go entirely differently. I'll be in charge, not the IRS.

I hear the back door open as I step into the steamy shower. I stand under the hot water, letting it sting my skin while I suck the humid air deep into my lungs.

I've just finished soaping up my hair when Marie appears in the bathroom doorway. I can't see her well through the fogged-up glass, but her body language looks menacing as she slings open the glass shower door. I back away into the corner to get as far from her as possible.

"What the fuck?" she screams at me.

I have no idea how to respond. The list of things she could be referring to has grown too long. If I guess, the probabilities are I'll admit to something she doesn't even know about.

I opt for noncommittal silence.

"Some guy named Ashley from the fucking IRS just called about a meeting tomorrow morning? Apparently, we owe eighty-three thousand dollars in back taxes?" She's screaming now. "Oh my god, Eric! What are we going to do?"

I stand in shocked silence, wet and naked with suds running down into my eyes as the spray of water lands at my feet.

"Say something, Eric!"

"I..." I clear my throat and shuffle closer to her. "I'm taking care of it."

"You're taking care of it? What the fuck does that mean?"

I hold out my hand, trying to touch her, to calm her, but she smacks my hand away.

That seems to spark something in her.

She smacks my arm. Then again. Then smacks my chest, harder than Lori had. Then she swings for my head, but I instinctively lift my shoulder and arm, blocking the blow, so she shoves me.

I slip on the tile and reach for something to grab, but I can't stop the fall. I smack into the tiled wall and tumble into the bottom of the shower. I lie there as the water sprays down onto me, shocked and assessing the damage before I try to get up.

"I can't even look at you right now."

She turns and walks out of the bathroom, leaving me naked on the floor of the shower. I turn off the water and slowly work my way back to my feet. My mind races as I towel off, trying to wrap my head around what just happened. How can I mitigate this and assure Marie I have everything under control? I rub the soap out of my hair the best I can and then pull on some joggers and a T-shirt before shuffling out of the bedroom.

I find her sitting rigid on the couch, her face in her hands. I sit on the ottoman, facing her, and place my hand on her knee. She smacks it away, looking up at me.

"Don't touch me," she barks.

I hold her gaze.

"How long has this been going on?" she asks.

"What do you mean?"

"What the fuck do you think I mean? How long has it been since you've paid our taxes."

"I didn't *not* pay taxes. I just didn't always have the money to pay all of them."

"How long, Eric?"

"I don't really know. It's been off and on for a while."

"When did it start?"

I don't answer.

"Tell me when you missed the first payment."

"I don't really remember."

"Then give me your best guess."

"Four, maybe five years ago."

"Five years?" she's yelling again. "You haven't been paying our taxes for *five years*? Oh my god. Oh my *god.* You *shithead!*"

"No, I told you. I paid them off and on. It's not like I just *didn't* pay any taxes."

"Why? *Why* didn't you pay all of them?"

"I couldn't all the time. I had to make payroll and pay myself and David's school—"

"But you kept spending money like we had it. You bought me the Navigator almost four years ago."

"I got the Navigator for *you*. You needed something safe to drive the boys around in."

"I didn't even want that car. I was happy with the minivan, but you insisted on getting me the upgrade. You said we could afford it."

"I thought we could at the time. The payment seemed doable."

"That car is less than four years old. You were already missing tax payments when you bought it for me. And then what, a year ago, your Tesla shows up? Did you pay taxes that month?"

"Jesus, Marie, I needed something to drive too."

"I asked you—both times—I said, 'Can we afford this?' and you assured me we could."

"We *could*. At the time, I was doing well and paying everything, and I wanted us to have nice—"

Marie shoots to her feet and starts pacing. She shakes her head in frustrated disbelief.

"And this house! This *fucking* house! I never even wanted this house. It's too big and needs too much maintenance, but you and that fucking realtor you hired talked me into it. Again, you assured me we could afford it."

"I was trying—"

She holds up her hand to cut me off and keeps pacing, muttering to herself. I want to assure her that everything will be okay and I'll figure it out, but I'm worried I will only add fuel to her white-hot anger.

After a couple of minutes of pacing, she stops.

"We have to sell it," she says barely above a whisper.

"Sell what?"

"All of it. The house, the cars, all that fucking workout equipment you bought for the basement. *All of it.* It has to go. It won't be enough to pay off the debt, but it'll make a dent in it. Then we have to—"

"No, no, we can't do that," I creep to my feet. "We're not selling the house and cars."

She looks at me as if I'm a dimwitted child.

"We can't afford it, Eric!" Her yelling has escalated to screaming. "How can you not see that?"

"I can fix this. I'm going to—"

"No, I'm not trusting you to do anything. I'm taking all of this over. *I'm* going to handle selling the house and cars. *I'm* going to tell David he can't go to his school anymore. *I'm* going to get a job and put the boys in aftercare."

"Marie, no, I already have a plan to get us out of this."

"You have a *plan*?" Her voice shakes with anger. Tears roll down her cheeks, but she ignores them. Her wide, angry eyes bore a hole through my skull.

"Like I would trust the shithead that has fucked all of this up," she spits out.

You're not even a man. You're a loser. A small-time little boy who's acting like a man. All you'll do is fuck it up more. She's right, you are a shithead!

My body freezes in place, and my brain seems to phase shift out of the present moment. The voices from the torchlit silhouettes in the cave, the ones watching me flush into the vortex, have crowded into my mind as Marie yelled. Her voice just punctuates the chorus of criticisms and insults already resounding in my head.

"No, *no*!" I yell, putting my hands over my ears.

This cuts Marie off, but her face stays twisted in anger.

"I can fix this. I can do it. The job. The job with the super PAC," I say, talking at hyperspeed and staring at the floor. "I'm going to pitch for that job. If I get that job, I'll be able to pay off all the IRS debt—all of it. We won't have to sell the house or the cars or take David out of school."

I look up and see Marie. I'd forgotten she was there for a moment.

"The job? With Ricky the Dicky? I thought you turned that down."

"I—uh—I did. But I can call Ty and see if I can still pitch for the job. If I get that, the signing bonus alone will pay off the debt. It's one hundred thousand."

"Do whatever the fuck you want, Eric. That's what you were going to do anyway." She turns and storms off down the hallway, slamming the bedroom door behind her.

25

ALL APOLOGIES

I stumble out the front door in my slippers and run like a madman desperately trying to break out of the looney bin. The darkened houses that line our neighborhood mock me as I sprint by them. Homes with up-to-date mortgages whose garages protect wholly owned high-end vehicles and house dual income partners and their beautiful children enrolled at Nashville's best college prep private schools.

I only know one thing. I *have* to get the job.

Marie has taken anger into a realm that has no words. I know she's serious. She'll sell the house, the cars, and anything not nailed down. I bet she's looking at job postings right now, trying to find some way to make extra money.

There will be no stopping her. All I can do is fix it and pay off the debt, and then she will calm down and see that I can handle it. None of our friends will need to know. I won't have to deal with her dad.

At the end of the block, I bend over, hands on knees, sucking in air and trying to pull myself together. When my hands stop shaking, I retrieve my phone and text Ty.

Sorry again about earlier. Just reiterating I'm excited about the job and looking forward to seeing you in DC. I'm going to knock this presentation out of the park for you.

My anxiety climbs as I stare at my phone, willing a response.

Good man. No worries. We're both under a lot of stress. I know you'll do great. See you soon.

Then one more.

No more texting.

I take a deep breath, let it out slowly, and then look back toward my house. As much as I want to sequester myself to the living room and not face Marie for the rest of the night, unfortunately, that's not an option.

My feet seem to move through thickened air as I return. I enter through the front door, still lost in thought when I startle at the sound of steps on the stairs.

I look up to find Marie descending.

Oh. Right. It's already pretty late. She must have been putting the kids to bed.

She ignores me as she sweeps past, heading back toward the bedroom.

"Marie..."

She freezes in place but doesn't turn around.

"I just got off the phone with Ty."

She slowly turns around to face me. I search for any sign of what is happening beneath the surface of the only person I've ever shared ineffable true joy and sorrow with, but I can only register ambiguity.

I clear my throat.

"I have to fly to DC tomorrow. Ty is going to the pitch meeting on Saturday, and he still wants me to be a part of it. So I have to fly out tomorrow."

Marie must stare at me for a dozen seconds, but it seems to stretch for at least three hours.

"The meeting is on Saturday?" she asks. "David's party is Sunday at noon." Her speech is steady with low intonation.

"I'll be back. I can take a return flight on Saturday evening. I'll make it back in plenty of time for the party." I can't seem to slow my speech to a normal cadence. "I already told Ty that was a nonnegotiable. I already told him. I know I won't be here to help get everything ready, but I'll do what I can Sunday morning, and I'll take care of all the cleanup."

"You're actually going to work for that man?"

"For Ty?"

"You know what I mean."

"What choice do I have?" Now, my voice takes on an unfortunate, shrill tone. "This is the only way I can pay off the tax debt!"

"Keep your voice down. The boys can hear you," she

growls. "You're still playing the victim. Acting like you don't have a choice in this."

Rage inflames me.

Through gritted teeth, I quietly respond, "I'm not playing the victim. I'm taking care of things. Do you think I *want* to take this job? I don't. But I have to. I know I've made some mistakes, but I'll do whatever it takes to fix them."

She shakes her head and folds her arms.

"When does your flight leave?"

"I haven't booked it yet."

"But in the afternoon? Because you have the meeting at the IRS at ten."

Fuck. The meeting—the one I was planning on skipping, except now Marie knows about it.

"Of course."

"You're going to that. Right?"

"Yes, absolutely."

Marie waits a few more seconds and then turns on her heels and heads back down the hallway.

"Marie, wait—" but my voice is drowned out by the bedroom door slamming again.

26

REELIN' IN THE YEARS

All night, whenever it comes to mind, I tell myself I will go to the IRS meeting. I plan to slink in, hat in hand, apologize profusely, and beg the supreme power behind Ashley, Agent Alex Mason, for a week extension.

I keep myself awake until almost 2:00 a.m., pecking at the keyboard and continuing to make progress on the presentation. Then I strip to my boxers and curl up on the couch, resting my head on the frilly decorative pillows and pulling Marie's grandmother's throw blanket over me for warmth. It isn't long enough to cover my entire frame, so I'm forced to choose between warm feet or shoulders.

The nightmares don't wait for me. They come as soon as I drift off to sleep.

I'm a little boy, about six years old, trapped somewhere dark, cold, and damp. Long, low-ceilinged cobblestone corridors stretch before me, twisting and turning as I run. I keep taking random turns at intersections, hoping to find a hiding place. Every time I pause to catch my breath, I hear the scraping and scratching of the serpent as he keeps pace with me. I can feel him moaning and cursing my name as he pursued. My only choice is to wear him out and keep moving to stay alive.

A smack on my feet rescues me. Marie looms over me.

"Go back to the bedroom so I can get the kids going."

"No," I say, throwing off the blanket and burying the grogginess. "I can help. I'm fine."

"Okay, I'm going back to bed then."

I watch her walk away from me once more.

Is she really going to make me do all the chores with the boys this morning, knowing I'm going out of town and have the biggest presentation of my life to give?

Once again, when she gets angry, she takes the liberty to act however she wants. If I did that, there'd be hell to pay and no money to settle the bill.

If that's what she wants to do, it's fine with me. I'll show her I'm not a loser idiot shithead. I know for a fact how much her friends envy how much I help with the kids. Most husbands are checked out at work during the week, getting home way after dinner, and on the weekends, they played six-hour rounds of golf, foisting all the responsibility for childcare and house maintenance onto their wives.

Not me. Sure, I've made some mistakes with our finances, but I could make more money if I worked the hours most men did instead of taking the boys to school, being at all their school functions, and making sure I'm home for dinner almost every night.

I stand, stretch, tidy the couch, and redress from the night before. Within a few minutes, I have David and Matthew up and moving and eggs spattering in the frying pan. My laptop sits open and plugged in on the counter, recharging as I look over the presentation between flipping eggs and buttering toast.

The boys tumble down the stairs a few minutes later and take their positions on the stools at the kitchen island. I lay out two fried eggs each, runny yolks for Matthew, hard for David, and two pieces of toast cut into perfect triangles.

"Can I have some orange juice?" David asks nonchalantly as if his mother always lets him have a liquid sugar bomb first thing in the morning. We always seem to have orange juice in the refrigerator, but the boys are never allowed to have it.

Well, fuck her, she went back to bed.

"Sure, go for it."

David's head snaps up in surprise, belying the nonchalantness he portrayed just a moment ago.

"Me too, me too!" Matthew yells excitedly, bouncing on the stool.

I laugh.

"Sure! David, set your brother up too!"

The next two-point-five seconds all happen in horrifyingly slow motion.

David hops off the stool to sprint the six feet between him and the cabinet that holds the mugs and plastic cups. His left hand catches the power cord, yanking my laptop off the counter. I watch helplessly, spatula in hand, as the computer shoots off the counter, hits David's arm, and then somersaults down to the floor, hitting perfectly on the top corner of the screen.

I scream something as it falls, but I have no memory of what I said or whether it only came out as a gurgled shrill.

I dive to the ground and grab it, but it's already clear it's unsalvageable. The top half hangs limply by exposed wires, and cracks run through the screen at odd angles.

"What the *fuck*!" I spin on David. "Jesus, David, can't you control yourself at all? What is *wrong* with you?"

"I'm-sorry-I'm-sorry-I'm-sorry," he says, backing up against the cabinets.

"What am I going to do now, huh? What? Are you going to buy me a new laptop?"

I hear the bedroom open and footsteps pounding down the hallway.

"What's going on?" Marie shoots as she enters.

"David just knocked my laptop off the counter. It's destroyed. Unusable."

"So you had your laptop on the counter while cooking and feeding the boys, and it's *their* fault it got broken?"

"*Fuck!*" I yell, standing with the devastated laptop piled in my hands. "What am I going to do? I have to finish the presentation and then *give* the presentation. On what? This?" I hold out the mess to Marie.

"You know what that sounds like?" Marie demands, stepping between me and the boys.

"What?" I shoot back.

"Not our problem."

"But he—" I start.

"Not another word, Eric."

I lock eyes with her, almost blackout furious. I'm enraged over the laptop, David's careless ineptitude, and Marie's undermining me in front of the boys, painting me as the bad guy yet again.

Her eyes are molten steel, implacable and unyielding.

"You've got your busy day," she says. "And your big trip is obviously more important than anything or anyone around here, so why don't you go get ready for it."

I seethe and churn internally. In a dozen years of marriage, I've never once thought about laying a hand on Marie in anger, but as I stand here in front of her, the urge wells up inside of me.

This woman stands in front of me as if she were a guardian over our children, as if she needs to protect them from *me,* the one actually earning all of the money to take care of them. And she mocks and belittles what I'm doing over the next forty-eight hours to provide for them while she stays home and—what—plans a party?

I retreat to the bedroom, afraid of what I will do if I stay in the kitchen and take any more of her verbal blows. I toss the wreckage of the laptop on the rumpled bed and lock myself in the bathroom. I want to scream and curse while I tear the chrome-plated towel holder off the wall and use it to bash in the mirrors, puncture the drywall, and shatter the shower.

I don't do any of that.

So what am I going to do? I built the presentation with online software so I didn't lose it, but I must have a laptop to present it. Plus, I need to finish the presentation and practice giving it before the meeting tomorrow in DC. Still, I need more money from the freezer bag, which isn't nearly enough to pay for a new laptop. Plus, I still need that money to pay for the flight to and back from DC.

27

INVISIBLE SUN

The IRS Taxpayer Assistance Center—how's that for a name?—is nestled inside the Estes Kefauver Federal Building in the heart of downtown Nashville. It's surrounded by three aged stone churches with towering spires. If you walk five minutes further north, you will hit the honky-tonk bars where tourists gather every weekend to buy cheap boots and pretend to drink like cowboys.

While I would have loved to step into one of those taverns, I'm here to enter the flat concrete rectangular building that could easily pass as a prison.

I've always wondered about the people government buildings are named for, so I Wikipedia them. Carey Estes Kefauver was a Tennessee Democrat who served in Congress and the Senate. Famous for leading congressional hearings investigating organized crime, he ran for president a bunch of times and was the democratic running mate for Adlai Stevenson's campaign. He died pretty young, at the age of sixty, of an aneurysm. I'm half hoping I have one myself.

Do you think he dreamed of having his name on a building where bureaucrats self-loathed the days away and ordinary citizens dreaded being summoned to?

Fuck, I don't want to be here, especially after losing my shit and practically blowing my life up this morning.

By the time I'd taken a shower and dressed, Marie had already left with the boys, making sure I didn't get to say goodbye to them before leaving town for the night.

That's fine. I told myself I would call them from DC and be back the next day. No big fucking deal.

My previous two and a half hours were spent running the necessary errands to replace my laptop. Most of that time was spent at my parents' house. I couldn't just take the money and run. I ended up having a cup of coffee while my mom made her breakfast vegetable smoothie, and my dad sat at the kitchen table stoically hand-tying fly-fishing lures he sold online to other crazy control freaks who spent hours catching fish, just to release them.

I fended off personal questions about work and Marie with vague half-truths and redirects. Patience was the key in these situations. Lots of nods and "is that so?"

Eventually, my mom slid the folded check into my

hand, hugged me, and kissed me on the cheek. She expressed her undying belief in my perfection, and I hurried to the car.

I was waiting at the bank when it opened at 9:00 a.m. so I could cash my parents' check, then walked into the downtown Apple Store a few minutes later. I deliberated over the various models but ended up with their high-end MacBook Pro. I wondered if I should get one of the cheaper personal models—they were plenty powerful enough to run a slideshow—but decided I should get the upgrade as I would need it for the new job. I didn't want to come across as some hillbilly who didn't have enough money to upgrade.

At 9:55 a.m., I found street parking across from the Estes Kefauver Federal Building.

A reminder popped up on my phone for the meeting with Lori.

When she set the appointment at 10:00 a.m., I had already emailed Ashley, so I assumed I'd be free to meet with her.

I start to text Lori a cancelation but then stop. My eyes slide up to the concrete structure looming in front of me.

Marie will lose her shit if I skip this meeting, but does that really matter at this point? She's already pissed at me. I'm thirty-six hours away from fixing this problem anyway. Would I rather spend the next hour or so getting mind-fucked by Lori or for-real-fucked by the IRS?

I put the car into drive.

A few minutes later, I'm back on the blood-red loveseat.

"You know, I'm not getting any better," I say.

"What do you mean?"

"Isn't that why we're doing all this? To make me feel better? To make me happier? To make me less likely to break down?"

Lori starts laughing. "No," she says. "Now come on, you've got work to do."

"I don't know, Lori. I'm having nightmares and screaming at the children. I've got this huge meeting in DC tomorrow. I think I need to put a pause on this."

"That's not an option. I told you, once we start, you have to keep going, or you'll get stuck."

"Stuck how?"

Before I can hear her answer, the room begins to melt away and reconfigure around me.

"I know it was him! I know it!" a voice shouts from the hallway. I sit on the L-shaped sectional in the basement of my parents' upgraded 1980s split-level house. The carpet is an orange shag this time, and I know the hallway off the living room runs to my sister's bedroom. I follow it to find her, now several years older than when I last saw her at the hospital, standing nose to nose with my mother. Her bedroom is a wreck. The bed is in tangles, and clothes are strewn on the floor. A floor lamp leans against the wall in the corner.

"Why would he steal your money? What does a five-year-old need with forty dollars?"

"I'm telling you, Mom, I left it right there." She points at the nightstand near her bed. "Now it's gone. He's the only one that could have taken it."

"Right. I can't imagine a teenage girl misplacing something in this pigsty."

"I worked for three full Saturdays to earn that money! There's no way—"

Mom waves her off and turns to leave the room. My sister, arms crossed, remains fuming. She stomps out of the room into the bathroom, slamming the door behind her.

Time shifts. Nothing seems to change around me, but I can feel a fast-forwarding of a few days.

"Enrique Miquel Bauer! Get up here right now!"

I snap to alert.

I hear rustling from the downstairs den. I look down the hallway and catch a glimpse before feet hit the stairs. I follow the sound up the stairs and then into my boyhood bedroom.

It is the boy again but no longer a baby. He is six years old, standing with his shoulders slumped. My mom kneels by his bookcase with purple rubber gloves on. A dirty rag is draped over the caramel bottle of Pledge at her feet. She holds an open copy of a hardcover King James Bible in her left hand and two crisp twenty-dollar bills in her right.

"Where did this come from?"

The boy stares at the floor, not answering.

"This is Christy's. Isn't it?"

The boy nods.

"What is wrong with you? Why would you steal this money? What do you need it for?"

My sister walks through me and stands next to my mother.

Crossing her arms, she says, "You're an awful little brother. All you do is make my life harder. I wish you were never born."

Now, my dad enters. He stands with the two of them and verifies their sentiments.

"You're an evil, sinful little boy. This is what you do if we don't watch you constantly. You steal, lie, and cheat. You hurt the people who love you the most."

As they speak over the boy, darkness fills the room's edges. It pushes all the light to the center, and I can no longer make out the walls around us. It's as if the five of us are standing in a big empty space and the only light source I can detect emanates from the boy's solar plexus.

More voices start calling from the darkness. My third-grade teacher. My old pastor. My Sunday school teacher. Vaguer, ever more monstrous voices join the chorus.

"You are such a little shithead," a high-pitched voice wails at the boy from behind my parents like that sing-songy *nah-nah-nah-nah-nah* way kids taunt one another. "Shit, shit, shit, shithead. That's what you are. That's all you'll ever be. Shit, shit, shit, shithead."

A new voice emerges. This one is silky, feminine, and sounds on the edge of tears.

"Why do you keep hurting everyone? All of these people love you, and all you ever do is fuck up their lives and make everything worse. You know what you are? The epitome of Suffering. *Suffering*. That's what people should call you because that's all you bring to them."

The little boy drops to his knees. Long, dark, oily, tendril-like worms slither from the floor below and climb to envelop him.

"No!" I say, snatching at them, but my hand moves through them like vapor. I throw my body between them and the boy, but it doesn't matter.

The longest of them darts straight through me and pierces into the back of the little boy.

He lets out a scream as he falls to his hands, crying.

Two more tendrils dart out and attach to him. I can see them moving into and snaking through his body.

They are looking for the light.

"Stop!" I scream. "Please stop! Let him go!"

I run over to the boy and grab him under the arms. He is limp and heavy, but I start dragging him back away from my parents and my sister and those voices.

But the tendrils hold fast, pulling him back away from me.

I resist them and cling to his arms. His poor body

hangs in the balance, suspended between me and the dragging darkness.

Two more viscous worms, this time thicker and stronger, latch on to his legs. They shake him violently and yank him back.

"No, no, no, no! Please don't take him! He'll never—"

My grip slips off the boy's arms, and I fall backward, losing my bearings in the topsy-turvy nothingness until I collapse and discover that I'm now sitting hard on a cold cobblestone floor.

Everything around me has transformed.

My childhood bedroom and my parents, my sister, and the boy are gone.

I am alone in a low-ceilinged room that looks like it has been carved straight out of the rocky earth. A flickering torch hangs on a distant wall, providing the only paltry light source. Openings in each of the walls lead down four dark passages.

Aural exclamations of pain circulate around me. Screams of suffering and torment push into the room from each quadrant's byway.

I stand, turn around slowly, and try to get my bearings.

"Lori?" I rasp out in a loud whisper. I don't know if it is safe to call out here, wherever here is.

No answer.

A piercing scream stands out from the rest of the indistinguishable moans, and I whip around, beginning to follow the source of the voice down one of the four pathways. I keep my hand on the wall as I move, inching my way via touch.

Soon, my hand scrapes across what feels like wood, and I investigate. It's a door. I find the handle and attempt to open it, but it holds fast. No light escapes.

The scream comes again, calling me deeper into the labyrinth.

I move on, continuing to feel my way along the wall. I repeatedly trip over loose stones on the ground and then discover another locked door. I hear moaning from behind the door twice, but I can't get in. I reluctantly continue.

Every so often, the piercing scream returns from an incalculable distance, and I quicken my pace. I trip several more times and hit my head twice, but I keep going. The scream. I have to find the screamer of that scream.

At last, I turn a corner and find a third door. Like the others, it is fastened shut, but light escapes from the threshold edges. I skulk up to the door and put my ear to it. As I do, I hear a thick thwack of a body being struck, and then the scream pierces through and hits me right in my guts.

I grab the door handle and, with unfamiliar resolve, yank it open with enough ferocity to break the locks.

Inside is an enormous, twisted, monstrous soldier, a head taller and a quarter wider than I am. He's shed his overcoat and uniform shirt and now stands barebacked. His vast shoulders are slicked with sweat, and his muscles are swollen and red. His shoulders, torso, and skin are covered with scales, like armor, resembling snake skin. He has a short sword dangling from his waist, and his long black hair is slicked back and wet.

A braided leather whip dangles from his wrist. The handle is about a foot long with nine individual leather strands splayed off from the end.

He towers over a small boy who is face down in the fetal position. What little I can make out of his small, delicate back hangs in long, bloody ribbons. Blood pours out of his wounds, and I can see the meat and bone underneath. I begin to gag but am somehow able to suppress it. I don't want the boy to know how truly awful his situation is.

The torturer, hearing my entrance, begins to twist around to discover who's broken through the door. As he does, the boy starts to turn too and looks up, but before I see his face, something grabs me from behind and forcibly yanks me out of the room.

I fall to the ground as I hear the door slam shut.

"You can't be here!"

I look up to find Lori standing over me. Her breath is coming in short gasps, and worry clouds her face.

I scramble to my feet. "What is that?" I scream at her, pointing at the door.

"It's not time for that yet. We have to go."

She grabs my shoulder and pulls me back down the passageway, away from the door. I shrug her loose.

“Not time for that? That boy! He’s being beaten! I have to do something.”

I turn back toward the door to find Lori standing between me and it.

“You can’t go into a new memory without finishing the one you’re in. It’s too dangerous.”

“But—the boy! I have to save him.”

Lori softens. She walks toward me, grabs my arms at my biceps as orderlies do to restrain madmen, and laser-focuses her eyes into mine.

“It’s not time yet. Another little boy needs saving right now. The darkness has him and is dragging him away. Remember? The one back at the house?”

I look over her shoulder at the door.

“What the fuck! How many boys getting the shit kicked out of them are there!”

How can I leave this one behind? But then I think of the other five-year-old boy being torn from my grasp by the worms at the split-level.

“Okay,” I say, calming down a bit. “We’ll come back for him, though. Right?”

“Of course. Let’s go.” She grabs my shoulder again, and this time I follow. We run down the pathway I came from and flow back into blackness.

Before I know it, I am back in my five-year-old bedroom. The boy is on his hands and knees, breathing hard and sobbing. My parents and sister stand over him, their voices continuing to curse him. The other offstage voices have grown louder and more numerous, too. The darkness crushes in as the voices move closer with ever more sharpness.

A dozen black, oily tendrils have attached to the boy. Two wrap around his neck, four run down his arms and legs, and another six intertwine at various points along his back. They seem to be undulating, secreting, and pumping some necrotic essence that will eat the light within him.

I step in between the boy and the voices. The incantations seem to be the source of the tendrils' sorcery, and I scream at them to stop. They ignore me. I turn back to the boy and grasp uselessly at the black worms. I cannot get a grip on them.

I look up to Lori, who stands at the edge, watching.

"What do I do?"

"What do you want to do?"

"I want to rip these things out of him and tell all of these fuckers to shut up and leave him alone."

"You can't, though. Can you?"

I shake my head.

"What can you do?"

I look at the boy. His small back heaves under the constriction of the worms. It's all he can do to pull in enough air to stay alive. I kneel down in front of him. He looks up at me, his eyes leaking tears and debilitating sorrow at finding himself so powerless.

"It's not true," I say. "None of it. None of it's true."

He shakes his hanging head—not listening, not answering—and brushing me off. Tears flow like torrents from his eyes, reminding me of those weeping Virgin Mary statues people pilgrimage to see.

"Sit up," I say, taking his hands and helping him to his knees. I come close to him. For the moment, the voices subside and dial down to a whisper.

"I have to show you something," I say.

I straighten up and dig my fingers into my abdomen. I feel thick, oily ropes jolt at my intrusion. My insides burn and convulse, but I keep digging with my fingers until I find a hold. I strain as I pull my hands apart, like Superman pulling off his street clothes, and a tiny sliver of light blooms out of me to light up the boy's face.

He blinks against the bright light, but then, his river of tears relents, and the darkness retreats, if only momentarily, from his eyes.

"You see it?" I ask, grimacing. The effort to hold back my own tendrils is exhausting.

He nods excitedly.

I let go, collapsing before him. I feel the ropes reformulate and recoil around my light, blinking it out. Sweat pours down my face.

I point at his abdomen.

"You have the light, too, and these assholes hate it. It makes them see their own darkness, which they can't handle. All of these things they're saying to you are enchantments. They're calling the darkness to take more of your light. But it's *your* light. It's already there. Can you see it? I can see it!"

As I speak, the tendrils attached to the boy's back start to wither, and the ones around his neck snap off. The boy regains strength and pushes himself to his feet. Four more give way as he stands.

I stand, too, and push back my shoulders, standing tall.

He mimics me. The rest snap off his back and retreat to wherever they come from.

His light fills the room, and I hear shrieks behind me.

"Hurry, cover it!" I say to the boy. "Cover it with your hands!"

I grab at his hands and put them over his abdomen. The light diminishes but still glows behind his fingers.

I keep my hands over his and kneel in front of him again.

"Now, you listen to me. This is *your* light. As you get older, you can let it shine. You won't have to cover it up. But your parents, your sister, and your Sunday school teachers—they're going to be too scared of it. So, for now, just keep it to yourself. But when they try to tell you lies, you remember your perfect little light. Okay?"

The boy nods, his face serious, resolute.

"Good boy," I say, standing. "You going to be okay?"

He nods again fiercely.

I step out of the way and turn toward my family

and the monsters, but the light, even covered by the boy's hands, is bright enough to scare off the voices from the dark. I can barely even hear what my parents and sister are saying.

The boy smiles at me and turns to run out of the room and back down the stairs to watch television.

I turn back to Lori, but she is gone.

Now, I am back in her office on the blood-red loveseat.

Alone.

28

CAROUSEL

After getting my bearings, I sit in Lori's office and absolutely lose it with gut-wrenching sobs and tears bigger than I can ever remember releasing.

I sit here a long time.

If you ask me why I'm crying, I couldn't put it into words. I feel swallowed up by an unnamed sadness.

Flashes of all the memories I've explored with Lori keep floating through my mind, and I continually return to that dungeon she yanked me from. Is that little boy still in there? Does he need me to rescue him? Lori promised we would return for him, but I have no idea where he is, let alone how to get back there.

After some time, I check my watch. I need to pull myself together. I have to get to the airport, buy a last-minute ticket, and finish setting up my laptop before the plane takes off at 2:40 p.m.

I heave myself up off the loveseat, and forty minutes

later, I'm being herded onto the transfer bus at Economy Lot B at the Nashville International Airport. The woman at the ticket counter is surprised when I pull out a freezer bag full of twenties to pay for the ticket. The laptop cost more than my parents lent me, so I have to dip into the emergency cash. Still, I have plenty left over to pay for the round trip four-hundred-and-thirty-eight-dollar ticket for the second to last seat on the plane.

Twenty minutes later, I am through security, camped at the gate for a good hour and a half before boarding. I find a place to plug in my laptop, connect to the free wi-fi, and start downloading, installing, and configuring everything so I can work on the plane.

The presentation is about ninety-four percent done, but I still have to create six or seven new slides and do a couple of run-throughs to prep for the next day. I needed to make the most of the time at the gate and the hour above ten thousand feet.

The waiting area slowly fills with travelers as I click and tap, hunched over the laptop.

"Eric?"

I looked up to find Aneel standing over me with a huge smile and a coffee in hand.

"What are you doing here?" I shoot back, appalled that he has entered my sacred public privacy of the airport.

He slides into the seat beside me, dropping his JanSport backpack down at our feet.

"Same as you, I'm assuming. Heading to DC to pitch the super PAC bigwigs. So you decided to go for it after all?"

Oh, right. Somehow, I hadn't put together that he was pitching on this job at the same time I was, so we could very well be on the same flight. I suddenly feel awkward but don't know why.

"I wish I'd known we were on the same flight," Aneel says. "We could have probably gotten our seats next to each other."

This is the last thing I need, Aneel distracting me from nailing my presentation prep, which is obviously his goal.

"I actually just got my ticket this morning. Everything was up in the air until last night."

"How're you feeling about it?" Aneel asks as he slouches back in his chair, popping the top of his coffee and blowing at the steam.

"Okay," I say. "Good. I'm actually finishing it up on the plane."

I shut the laptop but left it out.

"Dude, it's *all* I've done the last few days."

"Oh yeah?"

"Yeah, man, I got connected to a few politicos who have run super PACs before, including one guy who lost. I paid them all for an hour of consultation and picked their brains clean for as much information as I could get."

He rattles on for the next fifteen minutes about

everything he's learned. It isn't just the guys from the super PACs, either. He asked former candidates and a sitting congressman for their feedback and ideas about optimizing advertising and outreach to key "undecideds." He also drew from his broad experience in online and offline marketing to figure out the practicalities of separating the wheat, the ones who hadn't decided who to vote for yet, and the chaff, who were locked into Democrat or Republican identities.

While my experience is deep and laser-focused on the direct messaging appeals that convert interest into action, it's also narrow. With the eclectic nature of his career, he's gotten a look at lots of different avenues at a macro level that I have yet to consider or address in my deck.

I let him talk, ask leading questions at pauses, and furiously take mental notes.

First, he'd gathered a vast breadth of information and research that I didn't have. I was deep, concentrated, and all-in in just one sliver, the messaging, of his broad spectrum of finding the people to send the messages. Apparently, when you don't have the IRS and an ungrateful wife breathing down your neck, you can get a helluva lot more done.

Second, I can't figure out his angle. Has Aneel forgotten that I'm pitching on the same job as him? Why would he tell his competitor the material he'd paid a premium to attain? Information is power. Isn't it? Did he just hand me a bunch of powerful stuff out of some kind of generosity? I mean what is he telling me this for? What is in it for him?

The gate agent's voice cracks on the intercom as she lists all platinums, medallions, and upper-class statuses now allowed to board.

"That's me!" Aneel says, popping to his feet and throwing his bag over his shoulder.

Of course, he's in first class.

"See you on the other side!" he says.

I bump his outstretched fist with mine.

"You want to grab dinner tonight?" he asks.

"No, I shouldn't. I need to run through my presentation a couple more times."

"Sure, okay."

Aneel takes a step away. I start to pop open my laptop, but he turns back, snapping his fingers.

"Oh! When is your flight back tomorrow? Are you on the 6:55 p.m.?"

I close the laptop again.

"Yeah, gotta get back for David's party on Sunday."

"Right, right. Me, too. Why don't we meet at the ticket counter at 5:30? I'll use my points to see if we can bump you up to first class so we can fly back together. How does that sound?"

"Perfect!" I say, forcing a grateful smile onto my face. "Thanks."

"Cool, man, that'll be fun!"

"Totally!"

As if.

29

SYMPHONY NO. 7 IN A, 2ND MOVEMENT

It's Saturday, my professional D-Day, and I'm up, showered, and dressed by 4:00 a.m. I've only slept four hours, but I'm too wired after overhauling my entire presentation to go back to sleep. Besides, every time I drifted off, nightmares flooded into my unconsciousness. On the plane, I used an old wi-fi voucher I had in the pocket of my dive bag to check all of the information Aneel spilled at the airport, and it panned out. Turns out he wasn't bullshitting me.

It took me a couple of hours just to incorporate all of the juicy bits Aneel had given me preflight. I skipped dinner to save time and cash and spent the next few hours pacing the room, going through the entire presentation out loud. Each time, I found new areas to tweak and improve.

Somewhere in there, I stopped to call the boys. Marie let David answer the phone, and when I was done talking to Matthew, he handed the phone to her. She hung up without speaking.

I texted her after, but she didn't respond. My frustration started boiling up again, but I shoved it back down. I had far more important things to worry about.

Ty has booked a private room for 10:00 a.m. at a greasy spoon a few blocks from the hotel. I spend the six hours catching up on some emails. I assure my annoyed clients, Andre, and Bethany, that everything is fine, and I'll catch up with them in the coming week. Then I dive back into my presentation.

When it's finally time to meet Ty, I emerge from the Phoenix Park Hotel bundled up against the dreary, bone-deep cold day. A mist blows in my face as I walk, and I arrive with damp hair and a shiver.

As soon as I step into the waiting area, over the din of the other ham and eggers, I can hear Ty's loud, barking laugh in the back of the restaurant. The place is a rundown, old-fashioned diner with black tiled floors and brightly colored booths. The framed grade of B from the health department is displayed a little too proudly out front.

I nod to the gray-skinned man behind the counter, who could have been thirty or sixty. He's happy to ignore me as I pass.

I tentatively pull aside the curtain separating the dining area from Ty's booming voice and stick my head through.

"Eric! You son of a bitch!" he hollers with a wide smile. "Come on in!"

I survey the small room filled with a neon green booth with overstuffed plastic cushions.

Ty looks just as disheveled as when I'd met him at the airport. He gestures to a stolid figure on the opposite side of the booth.

"This is John Smith, who you've already talked to."

John is mostly bald with a long, narrow face that hasn't been shaved in a few days. He has the haggard look of a man who rarely gets enough sleep.

"Of course." I shake his firm hand as he stands to properly greet me.

"And this is Haley Parker, John's—we're calling her your assistant. Right?"

Ty barks out another laugh while John squints and smiles tightly. Haley, a strikingly beautiful pale, blonde girl in her mid-twenties, reaches out her hand as her neck and face rapidly blush.

We exchange pleasantries before I take my seat next to Ty. We talk briefly, and then John asks to see my presentation. I slide my laptop over to him, and he starts clicking through my slides while Ty continues talking loudly with a mouth full of steak and eggs, and Haley keeps her eyes on her plate.

I nervously shift my coffee mug back and forth, glancing up at John while waiting for the verdict.

Ten minutes later, John hands the open laptop back to me.

"It's good," he says dryly. "Impressive. You have some stuff in there I had not considered."

I'm about to relay my airport conversation with Aneel but think better of it. I'd rather keep an air of mystery around how I acquired my knowledge, especially around these guys.

"But look at slides twelve, eighty-one, and one hundred twenty-two. You have typos on each of those, so clean that up." I start navigating through the presentation as he speaks. "When discussing interacting with fundraisers, add a bit to show your understanding that Congressman Bryant cannot be in the room when funds are pledged. Also, on slides fifty-one and sixty, take out references to me. There is no need to add that complication."

I dart around my slides as he quickly monotones another dozen changes to my presentation. Each time, he fires off the exact slide that needs something added, changed, or deleted.

Ty checks his Rolex and claps his hands.

"Time to go!"

He throws a bunch of cash on the table and then elbows me in the ribs. I toss my laptop back in my dive bag and scoot out.

"Jesus, kid, who the fuck are you, Jacques Cousteau! We need to get you a proper fucking bag." Ty laughs.

The nerves hit hard as we walk the four blocks to the meeting space back at the Phoenix. I'm glad I haven't eaten anything because I would have definitely had to stop and puke it up along the way.

Ty and John are as calm as can be. Clearly, they both feel confident it's in the bag for us. It would be bad form to come off as the doubting Thomas, so I do what I can to stiffen my resolve.

My phone buzzes—an unknown Nashville number. I send it to voicemail and pocket the phone. Three seconds later, it buzzes again. My thoughts shoot to Marie and the kids, so I pull back from the group and put the phone to my ear.

"Hello?"

"Eric, hi, this is Bob."

"Bob?"

"From the office. Sorry to call you. I know you're out of town, but, er, there's a sheriff's deputy here looking for you."

My feet cement to the sidewalk, and white noise fills my head. My body threatens to disintegrate right here on the spot.

"Eric?"

I clear my throat.

"Did you hear me?" he asks.

"Yeah."

"What do you want me to tell him? What can I do to help?"

How the fuck should I know?

"Can you put him on the phone?"

"I don't think so. I told him you were out of town

and offered to give him your number, but he said he had to deliver the subpoena to you in person. Is everything okay?"

"Obviously not, Bob! Fuck. Just—I don't know. Tell him I'll be back in the office on Monday by 8:00 a.m. I can talk to him then."

I hang up before he can answer.

My feet stay rooted in place while I sway around, wobbling like a Weeble. Cold mist spits in my face as sweat runs down my back.

"Eric!" Ty yells from half a block ahead.

He holds his arms up like, *What the fuck?*

I can't move. My system is shutting down, and I can't do anything about it. It's too much. An actual member of law enforcement is driving around Nashville looking for me, a uniformed officer with a badge trying to track me down.

Am I going to jail? Bob said "subpoena," so maybe not. The sum total of my knowledge of subpoenas comes from *Law & Order* and *The Closer*, which always had someone showing up saying, "You've been served." It rarely came with handcuffs.

"Eric!"

Suddenly, as if teleported from fifty yards away, Ty stands before me. Oh, a lot of time must have passed. I stand here thinking about subpoenas, handcuffs, sheriff's deputies, and Kyra Sedgwick instead of the meeting I'm currently heading to with Ty and John and what was her name? The blonde assistant-slash-mistress. I mean, it's apparent they're sleeping together. Right? Or did Ty just insinuate that because he's constantly fucking with people?

My body started shaking, and I look up.

Oh, right. Ty is in front of me. His hands grasp my shoulders, shaking me as if trying to wake me from a standing nap. He snaps his fingers in front of my face a couple of times.

This slams me back to the moment. I blink—twice—forcing my vision to focus on Ty's bulbous and craggy face.

"You freaking out on me, Eric?" Ty spoke at a low, even volume. He had something like concern on his face. It was unsettling.

I shake my head to clear it.

"No. Yeah. I—" What do I say? At this point, should I just be straight with him? He's my partner in this, after all.

I take in a deep breath and let it out slowly. "That was a guy from my office complex. A deputy showed up to serve me a subpoena."

Ty takes this in slowly.

"The tax thing?"

I nod.

Ty turns back to John and the blonde assistant-slash-mistress.

"You guys go on ahead. We'll meet you there."

John turns without a response and continues, almost as if he's been around my kind of behavior before. The assistant-slash-mistress follows closely behind.

Ty comes in closer and puts his large hands back on my shoulders. He gets at eye level with me and speaks clearly and plainly.

"Eric, it's going to be okay. I promise you. They do this shit to scare people, and it works. Normal, law-abiding citizens with mortgages and Hondas and two-point-five kids never interact with cops outside of the occasional speeding ticket. They've never even met someone from the IRS."

He pauses for effect.

"But I'll tell you this. You're not normal anymore. You're going for much, much bigger things. We are one meeting away from you making plenty of money to pay off your IRS bill and get these fucking maggot bloodsuckers out of your life. But they'll be back. You know why? Fuck the money. That's not what matters here. They hate when normal citizens like you and me have power. These fuckers get these shit government jobs so they can feel powerful. They feel small, so they want to lord over other people. But that's not real power. What you're about to get is *real* power. You're going to meet the men who run this fucking country. Not politicians and judges and fucking cops. You will meet these powerful men and women and sway their opinions in the direction *you* want them to go. That's real power."

Now he closes.

"And fuck the people who want to stand in your way. I'm sure your friends and family don't get what you're trying to do here. They want you to stay the same. Living a small, insignificant life. Like them. That's not what you want. You're ready to level up!"

He steps over beside me now, puts his arm around my shoulder, and points down the sidewalk in the direction John kept walking.

"And right that way is where we're going to do that. You and me. Are you ready? Are you with me?"

My system floods with relief and gratitude. Finally, I feel like someone has crawled down into the trenches with me. I haven't realized until this moment how alone I've felt with all of this—how alone I always feel—with everything.

I turn to him, fighting back tears, and stare at him for a moment, trying to figure out how to express what I'm feeling. Then I grab him in a tight hug right there on the sidewalk.

30

LET'S GO CRAZY

The meeting room is far less impressive than I imagined. Honestly, I don't think I had imagined anything. Still, if you had asked, I definitely wouldn't have said the room where it happens is the Powers Court Living Room on the mezzanine level of the Phoenix Park Hotel. It was literally the waiting area of a bigger conference room with some of those cheap shoji screens you can buy at Ikea closing off the space from wayward hotel guests.

On the cocktail-stained carpeting sit six rickety plastic fold-out tables draped in cheap white linens, around which squat a dozen threadbare cushioned chairs. In the far corner of the windowless space stands a little roll cart with a coffee carafe, powdered creamer, and a sweating pitcher of ice water.

Ty and I have walked the rest of the way to the meeting in silence, but as soon as we step foot into the room, he turns on the loud boisterousness and starts glad-handing everyone in the room. He introduces me to the four board members who do not get up when I shake their hands.

Reginald is the first and the oldest. He's short, bald, and almost as wide as tall. Priscilla, the only woman, is dressed in a Hillary Clinton pantsuit and gives me the firmest shake of my life. The last two, Spencer and Montgomery, could have been brothers. Both look to be in their mid-fifties with brown hair and wear high-end suits. Unfortunately, Spencer has one of the worst cases of halitosis I've come across. Thus, I'll never forget the difference between the two, remembering them as "stinky Spencer," and "mild Montgomery."

The handful of other people in the room are various worker bees with clipboards and stilted half-smiles. Ty and the others ignore them, so I do, too.

I take my seat across from the board members and pull out my laptop so my shaking hands will have something to do. Haley—I heard John introduce her to the suits—takes up the role of waitress and begins serving everyone coffee and water.

The overhead projector fits the room's institutional stereotype, and I started trying to connect the adapters and cords to get the connection working.

Before long I realize nothing will fit.

My brand-new Mac laptop doesn't have the correct ports because, of course it didn't. I had been in such a hurry buying it that I turned down the forty-year-old beanie-wearing hipster sales guy's advice to buy a couple of adapters to have on hand for a time just like this.

I check the map on my phone, and we were six blocks from the closest Apple Store. Even if I cab it, that would be at least a twenty-minute venture across town, but what choice do I have? I pull Ty aside and tell him the situation. He laughs and shrugs it off.

"I have to give my own little presentation before you start anyway. Go get the gear you need, and I'll keep things going until you're back."

Again, I apologize and thank him profusely, feeling the relief of someone having my back. He waves it off and tells me to get going with a wink.

Out the door, I hustle through the lobby and, thankfully, grab a cab being slowly vacated by an older couple who takes for-fucking-ever to call the footman to get their luggage out of the trunk. Four minutes later, I enter the packed Apple Store and force my way into the awareness of one of the salespeople. He seems offended and repulsed when I pay with my freezer bag of cash, but he accepts it. I sprint back to the waiting cab, which delivers me to the hotel less than fifteen minutes after leaving.

I give the cab driver some extra cash and several thank-yous before heading back to Powers Court Living Room on the mezzanine level.

John stands outside the meeting room smoking a

cigarette, his tie loosened, and staring off into some middle distance.

I slow to a walk when I see him. As I wonder, *Surely you're not allowed to smoke in here,* he mistakes my expression for inquiry about the status of the proceedings.

"Ty just got started." He smirks. "You have at least twenty minutes until your turn."

"Thanks," I say. "Why are you hanging out here in the hall?"

He shrugs.

"Keeping up appearances."

He stares at me, his jaw moving slightly. I desperately want to get back inside and hook up my laptop, but I sense he has something more to tell me, so I stay in place.

"Are you good with all of this?" He gestures to the meeting room with his cigarette.

"Yes sir, of course. I've gone over the presentation several times. I have your fixes worked in. I'm ready."

"Yeah, yeah. You're gonna kill it in there. I have no doubt."

He pulls a tissue out of his pocket, spits in it, and carefully dabs the half-smoked cigarette out. Then he wraps the cigarette and tucks it into his front pocket.

"I mean all of this. The super PAC. The campaign. It is a lot." Then he gets that faraway look back in his eyes: "There is a good chance I will drop dead by fifty from the stress and excessive amounts of steak dinners.

Plus, a lot goes into these things, that is..." He pauses, studying me.

I wait.

"I will just say, more than a nice kid like you should want to be involved in."

I don't know how to respond. Something about what he said grips my gut. I have a sudden urge to turn and run away, shitcan the second phone in my pocket, catch my flight home, hug the boys, and apologize to Marie.

I clear my throat, my thoughts racing and crashing through my head.

But then what? I still have the IRS and the subpoena. The credit card debt. The car payments. The school bills. The mortgage. None of that would simply go away because I suddenly grew a conscience around what was being asked of me for the super PAC.

I only have one way out, and that's moving forward, not running away.

John doesn't know any of this, or he would understand.

"I have to," I say simply.

This seems to satisfy him. He nods and then indicates the entryway, so I slip in as Ty loudly proclaims the brilliance his experience and connections have brought to the super PAC.

Back in my chair, I unpack the first of the adapters, which thankfully click into place.

I double-check everything, settle into my seat, and

wait for Ty to turn the meeting over to me. At this moment, a calm falls over me. I don't know if it's John's confidence I would kill it or the realization that I'm in this all the way and have Ty's full backing did the trick, but all the nerves leak out of me, leaving a quiet assurance.

Within a few minutes, Ty launches into an introduction of me full of adulation, exultation, and the most incredible exaggeration and half-truths ever uttered about me. According to him, the online business world would collapse without me, and the entire internet marketing economy was basically my idea.

I thank him as he finishes, turned on the projector, and begin my presentation. I slip into that blessed flow state and, for the next hour and forty-five minutes, give a perfect presentation. I drop in jokes where appropriate, extract laughs from the board members, and deftly maneuver through the complicated content. The additions from John and Aneel have superbly shored up what I'd already compiled.

My eyes scan the room as I speak, and every time they land on Ty, he nods with a smile.

In short—as John said I would—I kill it.

At the end of the presentation, the suits pepper me with questions, most of which I easily answer. I note the handful I can't and assure them I'll follow up with well-researched answers.

Once their questions died down, Ty joins me at the

front and concludes the meeting. After that, every single one of the suits approach me, thanking me for my presentation with big smiles and firm handshakes. Ty works the room as well, glad-handing everyone. He stops to speak quietly with each board member as I make my way out.

Outside the meeting room, John stands alone, his arms folded, staring off toward yet another distant shore.

Nearby, Aneel stands in quiet conversation with a tall blond man about my age dressed in a tan suit with perfectly combed hair. When Aneel sees me, he smiles and motions for me to join them.

"This is my friend, Eric Bauer," he says as I approached. "Eric, this is Fred Harrington. He's Congressman Byrant's staffer who brought me in on this project."

I nod at the man and hold out my hand. He eyes me for a split second, a bit reticent, but eventually accepts.

Ty bursts out of the meeting room laughing loudly, Haley following in his wake as he saunters over to John.

"Some interesting company you keep there, Eric," Fred says, his eyes following Ty.

I cock my head and shoot a questioning gaze at Aneel.

He laughs, trying to cover a nervous tremble in his voice.

"Forgive Fred," he says, clasping his companion on

the shoulder. "He's got some strong opinions about John and Ty, but I assured him you are the real deal. How'd it go in there?" He seems eager to change the subject.

"I think pretty good. Hard to know."

"I'm sure you killed it."

I shrug and cut my eyes to Ty, who motions for me to follow.

"I gotta run," I said.

"Okay, man, I'll see you in a few hours. Right? At the ticket counter?"

"Sure thing."

I hurry off to catch up with Ty, John and Haley as they navigate through the hallways and lobby.

Outside, the misty rain has burned off, and the sun shines brightly and warmly. I smile at Ty, and he slaps me on the back, continuing to laugh at some unspoken joke.

"Let's get a drink," I say. "It's time to celebrate!"

The three of them agree, and we headed off toward the sun.

31

FISHERMAN'S BLUES

Ty obviously picked the presentation location for one main reason. The Phoenix Park Hotel's in-house restaurant is The Dubliner Irish Pub and Restaurant, where Guinness on tap flows day and night.

The interior is straight out of a setting for a Eugene O'Neill play with dark wood, green padded chairs, and little seating nooks carved out around the exterior. When we enter, a hunched, authentically severe Irishman stands behind the bar with his arms folded, barking at a patron to put out his cigarette or take it outside.

Ty's phone buzzes, and he excuses himself, taking the call outside. John and I grab a small booth enclave that could handle the four of us while Haley fetches four pints of Guinness.

John extracts the cigarette from his shirt pocket,

relights it, inhales deeply, and leans back in the booth, shooting his exhale at the ceiling.

I cut my eyes back to the bartender, who pretends not to notice. I'm uncomfortable with the silence, but John seems uninterested in engaging in any conversation, intent on getting the most out of every drag remaining in his cigarette.

Haley arrives, expertly embracing and balancing the four pints without a tray, and arranges them on the table with cork coasters before sitting next to John. I take a long pull off the top of the glass, letting it slink its way down into my empty stomach.

We remain in silence with me gulping, Haley sipping, and John ignoring until Ty slams down four full shot glasses on the tabletop, ripping us all out of our personal thoughts. Whiskey splashes, but our eyes all focus on Ty, playing the charismatic titular role of Hickey in our own contemporary version of *The Iceman Cometh*.

"Hot damn, we did it! Double J for everyone!"

Ty slides into the booth next to me, all smiles and energy.

"Reggie called me and said the gig was ours!"

"Are you serious?" I ask, straightening up. "But Aneel hasn't presented yet."

Ty waves this off.

"Fuck him. Reggie said they were over the moon with our presentations. After they let the other team give their spiel, they'll do a due process deliberation.

Still, we'll get the confirmation by first thing Monday morning."

My elation from the meeting shoots even higher, and I look around at my booth mates. Haley is all smiles, feeding off Ty's energy. Still, John looks unfazed, edging toward boredom. Same shit, different day.

Ty spreads out the shot glasses and holds his up. We all join him, tapping the glasses together, and then I take mine down in one big gulp.

I shake my head against the burn and pull out my phone. I still haven't told Marie any news.

Meeting's over. My presentation went great! Looks like we got the job!

Ty is off and running, bitching about which board members will pose what obstacles and talking through what will happen once we get started. John finishes his cigarette and drops it into the empty shot glass. Haley has switched from sipping the Guinness to sipping the whiskey.

I keep checking my phone, waiting for a response. I know the boys play flag football on Saturday afternoons, which means Marie is sitting in a lawn chair on her phone like all the other parents.

Ty pulls my attention back to the bar when he slides four more shots onto the table and picks his up. We cheers again. John and Ty knock theirs back, Haley takes a sip off the third full glass in front of her, but I hesitate.

I have two hours until I'm supposed to meet Aneel at the airport, and I'm already one pint and a shot deep on an empty stomach.

"Eric?" Ty asks, eyeing me.

"Sorry, Ty," I reply, setting down the glass. "I gotta be sober enough to get through the airport in a couple of hours."

"You're still going back tonight?" Ty is loud, even for him. "I thought you'd push your flight to tomorrow. It's time to celebrate! Your future's blindingly bright!"

I shake my head.

"No, I can't. I would, but David's birthday party is tomorrow."

"Ah, fuck that. He won't even know you're there."

I pretend to laugh.

"Even so, Marie would kill me."

I recheck my phone. She's responded. I eagerly unlock my phone to find a simple, *K.*

K? That's it? I responded.

I stay glued to the phone as the three dots blink.

What do you want me to say?

I don't know. Good job? Congratulations?

Sure, Eric. Congratulations on fucking up our finances, lying to me, being an asshole to the boys, and then working so hard to get a bullshit job being a bitch for a grade-a fuckface politician.

The blinking dots again.

Is that what you were looking for?

I stare at the phone. The anxiety and fear I've had

under control, quietly simmering beneath my surface as it turned into anger, boils over. I felt my head get hot.

All she can do is point out all of the mistakes I've made. That's all she ever sees with me. How I'm a complete fuckup shithead. While here in the capital city of the Western world, I sit accepted among successful, powerful men. I came from nowhere and impressed these guys so much they're going to rain money on me.

They see my value.

They don't think I am a fuckup or shithead. I'm the guy who delivered.

They understand what I'm trying to do.

Fuck Marie. Fuck her, I think.

I slam my phone down on the table, grab the shot, and down it. Then I reach across the table with both hands, nab the still mostly full shots sitting in front of Haley, and down them both—one and two.

"That's my man!" Ty shouts, slapping me on the back. "Let's get this going!"

Everything immediately begins to blur. More drinking is soon followed by greasy baskets of various fried foods, followed by more drinking. At this point, my memory starts cutting in and out. I remember lots of laughing and yelling. I think I slurred my way through singing "Molly Malone" with the bartender.

In Dublin's Fair City

Where the girls are so pretty

I first set my eyes on sweet Molly Malone

The bar fills, and everyone seems to be ringing in the Saturday revelry.

John leaves at some point. Ty finds himself in a loud, mostly friendly argument about American football versus everywhere else's football and, for some reason, professional table tennis.

I've lost track of my phone, so I'm back in the tiny booth, supposedly looking for it but mostly trying to stay upright. Haley appears next to me, offering help. We laugh as we flop around the booth, both too inebriated to be useful. Something urgent pinged at the edge of my consciousness.

I really do need my phone.

Instead, I find myself nose to nose with the gorgeous young blonde. I blink and laugh. She kisses me. I let her for just a moment.

Then I fall back away from her, startled and scared.

This isn't what I want. It certainly isn't what I need.

She smiles at me.

"Where's John?" I ask.

She shrugs. "He's not here."

I try to lock on to the blurred vision of her perfect, pale face as it sways before me. It's been a long time since I've seen that look on a woman's face. What is it? Desire? Lust?

Does it matter?

"Oy! Eric! You looking for this?"

Ty tosses my phone onto the table.

I cut my eyes away from Haley as I fumble with my phone.

The first thing I see is the time.

6:48 p.m.

A long litany of curses blow through my mind.

My flight is taking off in less than ten minutes.

The phone buzzes and adds another notification to the long list of unanswered calls and texts.

I unlock my phone and read through Marie's texts in reverse order.

WHERE THE FUCK ARE YOU?!?

The plane's about to take off.

Aneel said he's at the gate, and you aren't there.

I'm getting worried, Eric. Please call me.

Aneel just called. He's waiting for you at the ticket counter. He said you were supposed to meet him but you're not there and not answering your phone.

Please let me know when you get to the airport.

Eric?

Did you get that?

Hey babe, I'm so sorry. That was a dick move texting you like that. I know you've worked hard for this. I'm exhausted. And worried. Just get home, and we can talk about everything tonight. I love you.

That first text had come in two minutes after her text blasting me.

I have more texts from Aneel wondering about me.

I hit the button to call Marie but then immediately end the call. What would I say? How could I explain what happened? She would hear the chaos of the pub behind me for sure. I could go outside to make the call, but I still have the issue of being drunk off my ass and slurring my speech.

I have to do *something*. She's obviously freaking out. Probably worried I'm dead in a gutter somewhere.

This is where I should have called her. Tell her I'd gotten pissed at her texts, started drinking, and missed my flight. I should simply own up to what I've done. But I'm not ready to do that yet.

I'm so sorry, Marie. I got pulled into another meeting and lost track of time. I'm fine. Everything is fine. I'm about to head to the airport and get on the next flight home.

What the fuck, Eric? Why didn't you call or text me?

I'm so sorry. I left my phone in my bag, and these guys were super intense. I didn't feel like I could pull away.

That doesn't make any sense. You said the meeting was over, and you got the job. What else did they need?

I start typing out a response, making up bullshit about what we were doing in the meeting, when my phone rings. It's Marie.

My thumb hovers over the answer button. I shake my head, trying to clear the alcohol and figure out if I can handle having an actual conversation.

I send the call to voicemail.

Sorry, babe, I have to get back to the meeting. We're almost done. I'll call you when I get to the airport.

32

WHO ARE YOU

"Nothing? Not to Chattanooga either?"

"I'm sorry, sir. We only have one flight to Nashville in an hour, and it's fully booked. Would you like me to add you to the standby list?"

"What number will I be?"

"Eight."

"I'm not making that flight. Am I?"

"No, sir, I doubt it."

I sigh.

"Sure, that's fine."

The ticket agent clickety-clacks into her computer while I wait, sullen and sagging against the counter. I've already been to the other airlines, but no one has any flights to get me home by the morning. I'm now back at my airline, converting the flight I'd missed into a standby ticket.

What about renting a car? Well, I'm still too drunk

to even think about doing that, and even if I sober up, I don't have any credit line or cash to make it happen.

Another flight in the morning will land at eleven, an hour before David's party starts, but it's full, too. The only flight that looks promising puts me home after 6:00 p.m.

I still haven't called Marie.

She hasn't responded to my last text an hour ago, and I was hoping to call her with news that I'd still be home tonight or first thing in the morning, but that hope has faded.

I need to come to terms with the fact that I'm not going to make it back for my son's birthday party. My parents. My father-in-law. Our friends. Even fucking Aneel. They'll all be there.

Not me.

After the ticket counter lady finished my reservation, I slink to a back corner and make the call.

It goes about as you might expect. Marie is so furious that she sounds like a zombie. This is a coping mechanism when stress crosses a threshold into the "unbearable" zone. The emotional input of so many bombs falling at once—finding out about the tax debt I'd hidden from her, finding out about my agreeing to work for someone she thinks is (and probably really is) irredeemable, and me disappearing for hours when she was expecting me to be on a plane—is too much for any sane person to handle, so she stopped handling me and had given up.

She definitely isn't buying the bullshit excuse I'd made about the meeting, but she won't come right out and call me a liar. I apologize profusely, but none of it matters. She's out.

Eventually, we have nothing left to say, so we hang up without goodbyes or I-love-yous. It's almost eight o'clock now. I don't have enough freezer bag money to pay for a hotel, so I'll be sleeping on the airport floor somewhere.

An hour later, the gate agent for the last Nashville flight lets me know I won't be making it on standby. I nod and wander off through the thinning airport crowd. I find a nook behind a row of chairs and a large pillar to wedge myself in, mostly out of eyesight. I looped the strap of my dive bag through my suitcase's handle and hooked it around my leg before slumping back and trying to force myself to pass out.

Somewhere deep into the night, thanks to the booze and extreme exhaustion, I'm pulled down into something like a deep sleep, though I feel trapped more than refreshed by it. Just another drop into yet another abyss. I fight against it, knowing that isolation and pain lie at the bottom. I kick against the current only to discover those dark, oily tendrils from my sessions with Lori climbing up from below and wrapping themselves around my legs. I thrash to free myself as I scream out and jolt awake.

The row of chairs I've hidden behind is now full of people, several staring back at me with fear and surprise on their faces. My mouth tastes sour and feels like a ragged wool sweater. I feel as if my brain twists around in my skull as I struggle up from my prone position. I untangle myself from my bags and stumble out of the gate area into the main hall. I can hear sighs of relief from the other passengers when I absent their periphery.

I check the departure boards.

I have an hour before I need to be at the gate for my next standby attempt. Ten minutes in the airport bathroom, adjusting my clothes, reapplying deodorant, and brushing my teeth put me in a better spot.

My thoughts spin toward doing another round through the other airlines, attempting to find a flight that will at least put me home *during* the party so I don't miss the whole thing.

However, the abstraction my whiskey-addled brain didn't realize while I was canvassing all possible solutions the night before was that I have no way to actually pay for the ticket, even if one is available.

Not yet, though, I muse.

This week, I'll pay the tax debt, getting the IRS and sheriff off my back. Then I'll begin a salary that will allow me to pay down the credit cards and start getting my feet back under me financially.

Granted, the last week has been awful, and Marie has sunk into the fifth level of hellish anger, but it will pass.

And it will definitely be worth it.

For the first time since I doubled down on Ty's John Jameson shots and ever-flowing Guinness drafts, I encourage my mind to wander into the future. I imagine my life with no debt and no stress on me to get clients, pay taxes, and keep the bills current. Then after we win the primary bid, I'll get a bonus and probably a bump in salary, too. And that's just for winning the primary, which Little Dicky is projected to win by a landslide.

Plus, the contacts I'll make along the way will be like none other I'd ever made. Knowing an honest landscaper and a skilled burrito griller was one thing, but knowing the money behind congressmen, senators, governors, and even presidents is another realm of knowledge. If the super PAC gets to be too much, I'll have my pick of jobs at Fortune 100 companies or can restart my agency and rack up consulting fees.

But I'd be working with clients with actual budgets instead of the two-bit horticulturalists and genre fiction writers I constantly find myself with now.

I check in at the gate, and the empathetic older gate agent confirms what I already know. I won't be making the 11:00 a.m. flight either.

He checks the 5:40 p.m. departure and assures me I'll make it. The hour-and-a-half flight would land a few minutes after 6:10 p.m. with the shift in time zone. Then it will take another twenty minutes to ride the economy long-term parking bus to my car, another twenty to drive home, and sure enough, I'll arrive a couple of hours after the party ended.

I have four and a half hours to kill before my flight boards. A quick check of the freezer bag reveals I have less than fifty bucks left before I'm destitute. Somehow, I paid for most of the drinks the night before, which just about wiped me out.

I need to eat, so I pick a sit-down restaurant and spend seventeen bucks on a sandwich and some chips, mainly to get the unlimited water. I drink it heavily, trying to put down my hangover.

After my pittance of a meal, I wander through the airport shops, looking for a present for David. I'll miss his party, but at least I won't show up empty-handed. And like Ty said, he probably won't even notice I'm not there.

An hour later, I settle on a soccer ball with a large American flag emblazoned across it.

$26.98.

I head to my flight's gate and settled in for the wait. I kill the time watching a couple of sitcoms on my laptop and flinging birds at pigs on my phone. The gate slowly fills as we approached departure, and the agent starts making initial announcements. She tells the first group of passengers to line up to board. I check in with her, and she confirms what the previous agent had told me. I'll make this flight. She hands me a boarding pass.

Relieved, I return to my seat just as my phone starts buzzing.

Ty.

"We have a problem," he says. "Are you still at the airport?"

"I am. What's the problem?"

"What gate?"

I tell him, and he hangs up.

Ninety seconds later, I see him barreling down the corridor like Chris Farley in *Tommy Boy*, all but shoving people out of the way. When he gets to me, sweat is running down his flushed forehead.

He dabs at it with his sleeve as he starts talking.

"That curry-eating son of a bitch has fucked us right up the ass!"

I look around, embarrassed, wondering how many people his booming voice just carried to.

"What's going on?" I ask, lowering my voice and hoping he will match me.

"I don't know what he did or said or threatened or —*fuck*. Reggie just called me and said the board is leaning toward hiring your buddy to run the super PAC."

"Why? I thought we had this locked."

"That's what that asshole told me yesterday, but now I guess that's out the window. He listed off a bunch of impressive stuff in his presentation. Stuff I guess you decided *not* to include in yours."

Shit. This was what was gnawing at me after talking to Aneel at the airport. He's more qualified than me, and the stuff he told me was so apparent to him that sharing it with me didn't matter. Obviously, he hadn't told me anything close to everything he knew about running super PACs. He held some back for himself and his meeting. Hell, for all I know, he gave me bullshit info knowing I'd lap it up and copy-paste it into my own presentation so he could debunk it after I'd left. He knew I was presenting first, so he basically told me what to say.

"What stuff? Did Reggie give you specifics?"

Ty shakes his head and shrugs simultaneously, like some animatronic robot at Disneyworld. He's flustered and frustrated, and his ordinary, chaotic boisterousness transforms into an uncontrolled whirlwind. He's targeted me to settle his turbulence.

"You need to do something about this, Eric," he says. "*Your* friend is fucking us. What are you going to do?"

"Jesus, Ty, I didn't recruit him to pitch against us. It was a coincidence."

But Ty isn't in a state to hear me. He keeps going, ranting about Aneel and Reggie. It quickly expands to the whole politically correct system, where white guys get fucked over just for being successful.

I let him roll on as I keep cutting my eyes to the dwindling line of passengers waiting to board.

I jumped in when I finally get a break in Ty's tirade.

"Look, give me Reggie's number. I'll call him as soon as I get to my seat, figure out what I missed, and put together a short presentation I can send to the board. If they were already so excited to hire us, I'm sure I can get them back."

"Get to your seat! No, no, no. You gotta stay and help me figure this out!" He looks like his head is about to explode.

"Ty, I can't. I already missed my son's birthday, and my wife is freaking out. I'll work on it on the plane and take care of it."

Ty opens his mouth to argue, but something clicks, and he relents.

"Fine, okay, but if this doesn't work, I need to know you'll do whatever it takes to make this go our way."

"I will, Ty. I'll do everything I can."

Ty grabs my shoulder and pulls me close. His voice drops low, and his tone has a newfound menace.

"You've got some dirt on your little brown buddy. I know you do."

He locks eyes with me.

"Like I said, I need to know you'll do whatever it takes."

33

THE PASSENGER

I squish my way into my middle seat between two large individuals spilling over the armrests, compose myself, and then call Reggie.

"It's hard to say. Honestly, after your presentation, we were all sold. You did a fantastic job. And it's not that Aneel did *better*. He just seems like a better fit. He already has deep contacts with people in this world, and he was able to spout off the winning tactics of other super PACs from memory. We peppered him with a few specific questions, and he was able to give clear, precise answers to every single one. Again, it's not that you did anything wrong. You brought up several tactics and ideas Aneel didn't mention, and you have a lot of experience putting those tactics into action, but on a smaller scale. But when we step back and look at the enormity of this project, Aneel has more experience with bigger undertakings."

"Is there anything I can do here, sir? I'm happy to put together an addendum or send over another presentation. Can I answer any questions? This is a significant project to me."

"Look, Eric, you did a great job. And nothing is final yet. I called Ty to let you two know it wasn't as locked as I thought it was after you guys presented. I didn't want to spoil relationships and everything. No one likes to be blindsided."

"Can I talk to the other board members? I'm happy to give them a call."

"No, I wouldn't do that. It definitely won't help."

I nod to myself and let the silence speak for me.

"Look, son. It sounds like you're on a plane. Get home to your family. Enjoy the last of your weekend. The board is meeting Monday afternoon, and we'll give Ty a call with a final decision after we meet."

The flight attendant is giving me the stink eye to get off the phone.

"I can do this," I say just above a whisper.

"We'll call you tomorrow. Have a good night, Eric."

He hangs up.

Nineteen minutes later, we break through ten thousand feet. The two men in full ooze into my seat as they snore, and I seethe, helplessly staring at the back of the reclined seat in front of me.

I spend the hour and a half in the air silently ruminating on the pitch, my preparation for the pitch, Ty's final injunction, Haley and me in the booth, practicing my presentation, Aneel's info dump at the airport, my first meeting with Ty, my fights with Marie, back to the pitch, and over all of it again, and again. My mind pokes at every part of the last few days, desperately trying to find a hole somewhere, something it can exploit to get what it wants. Once it's unsuccessfully rotated through all the possibilities, it loops back to the beginning and starts again.

Each time I consider using what I know against Aneel to secure my future, I force my mind to keep moving on, to find something else to do instead.

The wheels slam into the Nashville tarmac and jolt me out of my mind trance.

With bags in hand and David's soccer ball tucked under my arm, I stagger through the airport, ride down the escalator, and bus to the self-parking wasteland.

I sit quietly and remain still in my car, putting off the drive home and facing Marie. I could handle the confrontation when I knew I had the job and could write it off as a blip on the radar on the way to much better times, but now… I put my head on the steering wheel. The tears start to come, but I push them back down. They will do no good here. It's time to man up. *Suck it up, buttercup.*

I face the truth. Once again, I've fucked up a great opportunity and let the people down who care about me the most. I think of Ty and how he trusted me with this project and stood by me.

What am I going to do?

I finally begin the twenty-minute ride home. The driving side of my brain goes into autopilot as I return to the realm of rumination.

As I approach the house, I notice Marie sitting on the front stoop. It's dark except for the dim single porch light, which casts her in a dusky silhouette. The street light across from the house is on and adds its orange tint to the gloomy, surreal scene. It's like an Edward Hopper painting, stunningly beautiful in the honest portrayal of an indescribable sadness.

Something is definitely wrong.

Of course, I knew I wouldn't be arriving at a happy homecoming welcome, but as I pull into the driveway, something more profound collapses within me.

Marie stands as I pull in beside her Navigator. I grab the soccer ball for David from the passenger seat, plaster an insurance salesperson's smile on my face, and climb out of the car.

I can tell she's exhausted and drained, her movements stiff as if she's steeling herself, as little kids do, to do the honorable thing even when it would be far easier to run away from a problem than solve it.

She stands silent, staring, as I approach.

"Marie, I am so sorry. I—"

She holds up her hand, silencing me.

"Eric, I need you to listen to me. Don't talk. Don't argue. Just listen. Can you do that?"

I nod, swallowing against the knot that has formed at the back of my throat, trying not to throw up.

"I'm leaving," she says. "I've already sent the kids with my dad. I'm going to stay with him for a while."

I open my mouth to protest, but she puts her hand up again.

"Not done," she says, her voice reaching above her calm.

She takes a deep breath and continues.

"I know you've been struggling for a while, but you don't tell me anything other than to reassure me that everything is fine. Then you come home with this *opportunity* that involves you abandoning all your clients and employees to work for this horrible, *horrible* man just for the money. Then I find out about this enormous tax bill you've put us under. Then you run off to chase this job and miss David's party. All the while, you're freaking out on the boys and lying to me. I know you're not telling me the whole truth about things. You're hiding and manipulating, and I just..." Her voice cracks as emotion fights its way through, but she pauses and forces it back down.

"I don't know who you are anymore. I know you to be a good man. The best man. But you don't know that, and it's become dangerous for the boys and me to stay with you."

"Dangerous?" I punch back incredulously. "What do you think I'm going to do?"

"I don't know!" she yells. "That's the problem! You've come completely unhinged. I have no idea what you're going to do next. You lie. You steal. You—"

"Steal? What did I steal?"

"I tried to use our credit card, but it was rejected. Then I checked our bank account and found it was overdrawn. I need money for things like, *I don't know*, gas and food, so I went to get the emergency cash out of the safe and discovered you'd taken that too. I had to borrow money from my dad just so I would feel safe driving around!"

"Marie, look—"

"Then, *then*! After you assured me you would go to the meeting with the IRS before you left town, you skipped it."

I stare at her, my eyes wide.

"I'll tell you how I know." She returns to the stoop, retrieves a yellow, legal-sized envelope, and throws it at my feet. "While I was hosting your son's birthday party all by myself. With your parents and my dad and our friends here and Aneel, who apparently was able to magically make it back from DC for our son's party, a deputy showed up at our house looking for you. He has a *subpoena* for you, Eric. A cop is trying to find you so he can deliver a fucking court summons! I just..."

She takes a deep breath and, again, forces herself to calm down.

"I can't do this anymore. So I'm leaving. I'll be at my dad's with the boys. I don't want you coming over, calling, or doing anything right now. Do you understand?"

"No, please. Don't do this. I can fix this."

"You don't even know what that means, Eric. You can't fix a problem you don't understand. You'll only make it worse."

"I do. I do understand. I've lied and hidden the money stuff. I've not been great to be around. But I'll work on it. All of it. Whatever you want me to be, I can do it."

Marie shakes her head sadly and turns to get in the car.

And then I get desperate. "Marie! No, you can't. You can't just leave. I've just tried to do what I'm supposed to do. I just don't know..." I trail off.

At that moment, I realize those four words are probably the only entirely true things I've said to Marie in a long time.

"Please," I say, holding out the soccer ball. "At least take this to David. I got it for him."

Marie looks at me, her face sinking into an even more profound sadness.

"David doesn't even like soccer."

34

YOU ARE NOT ALONE

The rest of the night is a foggy blur. The inside of the house is a wreck with the ragged remnants of David's party. Half-eaten food lies piled across the counter. The sink is full of dishes. The trash overflows. Everything—from the kids' toys strewn across the floor to the decorative pillows in disarray on the couch —shows the aftermath of a stampede of children and adults having gone through the house.

I begin to clean the mess, assuming Marie had left it behind purposely for me to deal with, but I quickly give up. I miss the boys terribly and almost get in the car several times to drive the two hours to Marie's dad's house and demand to see them.

Each time, I give up on the idea, partly because Marie decreed that I don't and partly because I'm in no state to drive that far safely.

So I spend most of the evening either wandering

through the house or sitting somewhere random in a hazy daze, unsure of what to do. My mind races and chases itself in loop after loop from Marie, Ty, and the board to the boys, the overdrawn bank account, and on and on.

Somewhere around ten, I retrieve the giant, cheap bottle of rum from the top of our closet. I take the time to pour the first few drinks into a glass before I down them but quickly switch to drinking straight from the bottle as fast as I can stomach.

Soon, I lie sprawled on the kitchen floor, moaning. Then I'm sobbing. Then I pass out.

A pounding on the front door jolts me awake much too early Monday morning. Still on the kitchen floor, I peek around the corner and see a deputy in his tan uniform. He squints, looking through the door window, and I duck back out of sight. He pounds the door again, I wait several seconds before poking my head out again.

The deputy shakes his head and turns, walking off our stoop. I crawl over to one of the windows and watch as he returns to his cruiser and drives off.

The relief melts away as the headache pounding my temples slams into my consciousness. I crawl back to the kitchen and manage to get some water into the rum glass from the night before. I suck it down. Two more full glasses, and I have to sprint to the bathroom. I don't make it all the way to the toilet before the vomit starts exiting.

I kneel in my bile and heave into the bowl. My stomach keeps clenching and retching long after it's empty.

Crying again, lying there with my face against the cool tile floor, I force my sluggish mind to start categorizing and organizing my thoughts.

Things are terrible—horrible—the worst they've ever been. That's true. It's also true that all of my problems have a singular fix—one thing that will make all this disappear.

I think about my short conversation with Reggie. *Fuck that guy*. What kind of asshole tells someone they are a lock for a job and then pulls the rug out? Well, nothing in life worth having is easy to get. I will convince the board I'm the right man for the job. Sure, Aneel has his benefits, but just as Reggie said, I bring a lot to the table, too.

They're meeting this afternoon to decide, so I have just a few hours to make something happen.

I peel myself off the floor and climb to a standing position. I make my way unsteadily back through our bedroom and change my clothes. My stomach continues seizing up every thirty seconds, but thankfully, nothing is left down there.

As I pull on my shoes, the doorbell sounds through the house. I freeze. Is the cop back already? I pull on my jeans and a T-shirt and creep down the hallway, hugging the wall and trying to stay out of sight.

The first things I notice through the window are

the pencils quivering in her hair. Her face is pressed against the glass, her hands cupping over her giant glasses and her breath fogging up the window.

She backs up and rings the doorbell again—then again, then three more times, then twice more.

Jesus Christ.

I stalked to the front door and rip it open.

"What?" I yell.

She pushes her way past me into the house.

"This place is a wreck. What happened here?"

"What are you doing here?"

"You missed our appointment this morning."

"Did we have one set?"

"We need to finish. You've already taken two days off. We have to..."

She seems agitated in a way that I haven't seen before.

"No, no," I say, still holding the door open. "I don't have time for this today."

"You need to make time. This is important."

"Lori, you have no idea what's going on. My life is falling apart. My meetings with you haven't done anything to make things better. In fact, my life has only gotten worse since I started all of this with you."

"Things often have to get worse before they can get better."

"Well, they're definitely worse, so I must be on the right track. Please, just go. I'll call you to set a new appointment."

"You can't stop now."

"Yes, I can. Now get out."

Lori moves toward the door, and I hope I've convinced her to leave. Instead, she snatches the door from my hand and slams it shut.

"Eric," her voice has raised an octave. "Do you remember the last memory? What happened down there?"

Of course I remember—the dungeon, the guard, the whip, and the screaming. I've been able to mostly distract myself for the last couple of days. Still, the memory is constantly pushing just at the edge of my consciousness.

"You wanted to go back. To save him. Now's your only chance."

I sighed and checked the clock. It was 10:01 a.m.

"How long is this going to take?" I ask.

35

RED RIGHT HAND

I sit on my couch, the same one I watched the Premier League highlights from only a week before.

"Ready?" Lori asks.

But before I can answer, I am back in the pitch-black passageway to the torturous crypt's third door. I can sense Lori close by, and after my eyes adjust to the flickering flame light, her silhouetted face betrays worry, even with the forced smile she's presenting to me.

Now that I'm back, hearing the calling screams echoing through the halls, my memory of what happened before reemerges. The room. The soldier. The desperate child with ragged flesh.

At last, I answer, "I am. I have to rescue that boy."

Determined and sure, I move to hurry down the tunnel and return to that room, but Lori catches my shoulder and pulls me back to face her.

"Listen, Eric. These things," she shifts her feet uncomfortably and looks into the distance behind me. "They go sideways sometimes. But just trust the process. Trust yourself, okay? You'll get through it."

"It's okay, Lori. I've got this. I have to save him."

I pull away, but she holds me back a moment longer before letting go. I press into the darkness.

Once again, pain and agony, as if they've taken physical form, push in around me. As I pass, I hear pleas and moans escaping from behind the first two locked doors, but those aren't the room for me. Determined, I keep moving. There it is!

I recognize the piercing tenor of this scream as the one that stood out from the rest the last time. He's still stuck down here, alone with that sadistic beast thrashing him.

I trip and slide and stumble my way through the darkness, scraping my hands and knees along the way. I don't care. I have to get to the boy and rescue him.

Soon enough, the doorway appears with the light cracking through the entrance. I slam into the door, shoving it open. I see the boy, curled up, his back exposed and bleeding.

The giant soldier turns to face me, and I lunge at him before he can attack. I shove him backward, slamming him into the slick masonry wall and ramming my forearm under his chin. I press against his throat, cutting off his airway.

I momentarily look down at the confused boy and then turn back to his inquisitor.

His monstrous red eyes grow wide with fear, and he gurgles as he tries to speak. I release a bit of pressure so I can understand him.

"Sir?" his slick voice croaks. "What's wrong?"

Sir?

For the first time, I notice a bronze cuff secured around my wrist. Startled, I release the pressure more and look at myself. I have the same scaled armor and short sword as this man.

I let go of him completely, stumbling back to discover a red sash attached to my armor and splayed down my back.

The soldier coughs and clutches his throat but remains hunched over, watching me.

"You're doing it wrong," I hear myself say. "Give me the whip."

The soldier obeys, holding out the whip to me. I take it from his hand and slide the loop over my wrist.

"Now get out," I whisper.

"Sir? You—"

"Get the fuck out!" I scream. The soldier scurries, ducks out of the room, and savagely pulls the door closed behind him.

I take a step toward the boy.

"You filthy little shithead," I mutter.

The boy's whimpers reach my ears, and an unquenchable anger overcomes me.

I pull the whip back behind my head, turning my hips open to ensure I put all of my weight behind the swing. I lunge forward, snapping the whip down with all of my strength.

Thwack!

The boy screams louder than before, but it's still not loud enough. I feel blood splatter against my face.

I pull the whip back again, and the boy brings his face out from under his arms to look back at me.

It's my face. Six years old. Less than a year after the last time I saw him.

"Don't look at me!" I roar and swing the whip again.

The boy buries his face into his arms again and he lets out a longer, higher-pitched scream. More blood sprays across my face and chest.

Rage courses through my bloodstream. I shout every obscenity I can think of at the boy as I hit him again. And again.

Oh my god, oh my god, oh my god. Stop! A small voice pushes into my mind.

I fall back against the wall. I step toward the boy, wanting to comfort him, but the anger redoubles.

I have to get out of here. Run. Leave. I can't keep doing this.

I tear the door open, and the hulking soldier waits on the other side. I know he will just take up the beatings once I am gone, but I don't care. I can't be a part of this anymore.

"Get me out of here!" I scream as I run. I can hear the armor rattling as my feet pound the stone floor.

I enter the labyrinthine hallway and immediately trip and fall, slamming my face into something hard and cold. Stars explode in my vision, and I taste the metallic glint of blood in my mouth.

I scurry back up to my feet and keep running. Twice more, I trip and fall hard, but I keep moving.

As I run, I scream for Lori to come and get me. Save me! Take me out of here!

I trip a fourth time, slide out of the hallway into the room with the single torch, and collapse at Lori's feet. She squats down.

"Why are you back here?"

"Get me out of here. I can't do this."

"You need to go back to that boy," she says.

"No! I can't. The other guy works for me. I'm the one in charge. Hurting him more. I've got to leave! Right fucking now! I can't do this."

"Eric, you can't stop now. We have to—"

"No!" I push myself to my feet. I shove Lori, and she stumbles backward. "You get me the fuck out of here now," I roar, pointing in her face. "I'm done with whatever crazy game you're playing on me."

Lori's face goes cold. The pencils in her hair cease quivering as she tucks her hands inside her shawl.

"You know the rules. If you stop, I can't ever bring you back. I move on, and you'll never see me again."

"I don't care," I say, breathing hard. "All this shit has

done is fuck up my life more than it already is. I want out. Take me out."

"Okay," Lori says. "You're the boss."

I feel the armor drop off my shoulders.

"You were so close."

The words float away with her.

36

CAN'T LET GO

I come to racked with sobs, curled up on the floor by the couch. I know I'm back in the real world, thank God. Still, I can't pull myself together. Every time I start to calm down, my mind phases back down into the abyss. I hear the boy's howls and screams. I smell the rot and enveloping fecund mildew of that place. I feel the blood rush on my face and the satisfying way I could make the whip snap against the boy's back. Then the torment of my responsibility for his suffering begins anew.

How could I abandon the boy down there? Now, he is alone again with that soldier. But is it worse than being with me? I beat him harder. Hated him more. Even now, I can feel the anger and shame well up in me when I picture him.

What is wrong with me? How can I hate that boy so much?

Does it matter? What can I do? Lori said I could never go back. He's stuck down there. Forever?

And what does that even mean? None of it is real. It's all in my head, some sort of hypnotized hallucination from that crazy woman. I need to get back to Earth and deal with Earth problems, not schizo fantasies induced by a wacko therapist recommended by some random guy at work.

I struggle up from my prone position and then manage to stand. I catch sight of myself in one of the decorative mirrors by the television and am startled. My face is red, swollen, and puffy. My hair sticks out at odd angles, and I can still taste blood in my mouth.

My eyes roam the house.

What do I need to do?

What's next?

Again, my mind slips back into the void. I feel the armor's heaviness and the whip's rough texture in my hand. I start crying again as I look around wildly, wondering if that monstrous soldier with the red eyes is coming for me next.

"No!" I say out loud, clenching my fists. "Get it together. You have shit to do!"

I shake my head and slap my face hard before grabbing my phone and, without thinking, dialing Marie's number.

It rings its way to voicemail, and I dial again. She picks up on the first ring this time.

"Eric?" Only it isn't Marie. It's a man's voice.

"Hello?"

"I believe my daughter told you not to call." His stern voice hits me like a steel beam.

"I—uh, just—I wanted to talk to the boys."

"They're taking a nap."

"And Marie?"

"That's none of your damn business."

I swallow hard and clear my throat.

"Can you just tell her something for me?"

Silence.

"Tell her I miss her and I love her, and I will fix this. I can still fix this. I have—I'm going to—"

"Haven't you fucked this up enough, Eric? What else can you possibly do?"

"Sir, I know you hate me right now. If it's any consolation, I hate myself too. But I—"

He hangs up.

I swear the sound of him hanging up matches the snap of a whip.

"That's okay." Again, I'm talking to myself out loud. "Everyone's still mad. But it's not over. I really can fix this."

What now?

I find where I dropped my bags last night and dig through for the extra cell phone Ty sent me.

John answers on the first ring.

"Can you get me the numbers of the other board members? I talked to Reggie, but he was a dead end."

"Are you sure that is a good idea?"

"I have to get this job, John. Everything depends on it. Can you help me out?"

He sighs but shuffles around on his end for a few seconds before reading off their names and numbers.

"You did not get those from me," he says, then hangs up.

I call the first number, but no answer, so I call the second.

"Hello, Montgomery? This is Eric Bauer. I met you Saturday at the Phoenix. I did a presentation for the super PAC."

"How did you get this number?"

"I—uh—"

"It was John Smith. Wasn't it? That asshole—"

"I just wanted to chat with you about the super PAC ahead of your final meeting today."

"About what? You gave your presentation. And so did Mr. Banerjee. We're making our decision based on those."

"I understand. I'm wondering if I could answer any final questions."

"Don't you think we would have reached out ourselves if we had any questions?"

I don't answer right away. The words won't come. I snap my head around, looking over my shoulder. I could have sworn I heard a child scream behind me. It sounded like—

"Mr. Bauer?"

"Yes, I'm here." I clear my throat. "This role is vital

to me. I'm very excited to be a part of the congressman's campaign and help him get elected. I know I can do a great job for him and for you."

"I have to go," he says and hangs up.

I think of that line they used on those nineties sitcoms like *Friends*. I can hear my inner Chandler Bing saying, *That went well.*

I call the first number, which went to voicemail again, so I call the third.

A woman answered.

"Hello, yes, I'm looking for Ms. Cunningham."

"She's not currently available. May I take a message?"

"Yes—No, I mean. Yes, can you tell her Eric Bauer called?"

"Sure. Does she have your number?"

I'm not sure, so I give her my number.

"Do you know when she'll be free?" I ask.

"She has a pretty busy day. She often does her call returns in the evenings, so maybe then or tomorrow."

"There's no way I can talk to her in the next few hours?"

"No, sir, I'm sorry."

We hang up, and I sit, sullen and heavy, on the sofa.

I call the first number again. This time someone answers on the first ring.

"What?" Spencer's voice is gruff and angry. I freeze, unsure how to reply.

"This is the third time you've called me in five minutes. Who the fuck is this?"

I hang up.

My options have dwindled quickly. The board meets in just a few hours, and they'll give the job to Aneel. Reggie said the decision wasn't final, but he was just covering his ass. He wouldn't have told Ty about the change yesterday if we had any chance. Maybe Ty could do something. He's big, loud, and persuasive. Can he sway the board with all that bravado of his?

Even though it's midday, the room seems to darken around me, and I shiver against the cold. The white walls of my living room appear to shift into gray, hard stone. The flicker of torchlight catches my eye, but when I look around for it, everything snaps back into reality.

I stand, whipping my head around to clear the invading thoughts. I need to get out of here. Away from this house and the constant reminder that Marie left me.

It's been over two days since I showered. Two long days full of airports, heavy drinking, and vomiting. I need to wash the layers off my body and leave. I'll head to the office and give Ty a call to see if we can pull any last-minute Hail Marys to push this through.

37

ISOLATION

The shower feels great.

I let the water run hot for several minutes. Every thirty seconds, I bump it a little hotter until I can feel it scalding my skin. The pain keeps me in the here and now, which is where I need to be if I'm going to solve my problems. I've had enough of "not here" and "not now."

I take my time washing, forcing myself to stay under the scalding spray until I can't stand it anymore.

I read somewhere that when nothing is going right, you must do the little things to take care of yourself. So I take a extra few minutes to shave, fix my hair, put on a button-up instead of a T-shirt, and pull on my leather boots.

The doorbell interrupts my final check in the mirror.

My gut drops, and my anxiety spikes.

It could be just the UPS guy dropping off a package. Or a neighbor dropping off mis-delivered mail. Or somebody selling a magazine subscription? Or the Mormons?

I creep down the hallway until I have a line of sight on the front door, and sure enough, the deputy is back. He knocks, waits, and then rings the doorbell again. He then cups his hands and peers through the glass. I back up and lean against the wall out of his sight.

"Mr. Bauer," he shouts through the door in his thick Tennessee accent, "I know you're home. Your car's here, and I've talked to your wife. I just need to talk with you. Can you come out so we can have a conversation?"

He rings the doorbell again.

I wait, my eyes closed, fighting off the howling screams of pain that invade my mind in the darkness. I slide down the wall to a crouch, hugging my knees and praying for him to leave.

After a few moments of silence, I look up and let go of the breath I didn't realize I'd been holding.

He's gone.

I stand and slowly enter the kitchen, scanning through the front windows. The deputy's car still sits in the driveway, and he stands by his back bumper, out of sight with the trunk open.

I watch from behind the kitchen island so I can duck out of sight quickly.

A few seconds later, he closes the trunk and

emerges with a large triangular metal contraption in his hand with a large disc on one end and a hook on the other.

Oh shit.

He kneels by the back driver's side tire of my Tesla and starts applying the boot, which will make the car undrivable. After the deputy locks it in place, he rattles it a couple of times to make sure it's secure and then gets back into his patrol car and backs out of the driveway. I watch him through the window as he pulls away, but he doesn't turn toward the neighborhood entrance. Instead, he takes a left, eventually circling back in front of my house.

The boot isn't enough, apparently. He's going to patrol for me as well. Vitriol wells up in me at the thought. I live in Nashville. Theft, murders, drug deals, and unending homelessness happens all around us. Still, apparently, this deputy's most pressing duty is to chase down a guy behind on taxes.

Now what?

I can't drive anywhere, and if I so much as darken my front door, I run the risk of the deputy spotting me. As much as I don't want to get picked up by the police, I also know I don't have it in me to run if they spot me.

I just need a little bit more time. If I can get somewhere so I can work in peace and call Ty, maybe we could conference into the board's meeting or, I don't know… I'm out of ideas, but I know I need to get out of this house.

Back in the bedroom, I change into a ratty old pair of jeans, a T-shirt covered in paint splatter, and the shoes I use for yard work. Then I pack my nicer clothes in an old backpack and head out the back door.

My property backs up to a skinny track of wooded land. Beyond that fifty yards of woods, a steep drop-off leads to a small row of stores on a main thoroughfare. From there, I can order a car to pick me up.

I hug the wooden fence, staying low as I make my way through the yard. Then I climb over the back fence and push my way through the brush and trees. Once I scramble down the hill, I run into the *Five Below* store and change into my nicer clothes. I pull out my phone to order a car to come pick me up, but of course, it kicks back because my credit card on the account is at the limit.

I stay in the bathroom uncomfortably long since the ventilation does not meet *Neiman Marcus* standards. I'm trying to figure out what to do when somebody starts banging on the door.

"Someone's in here," I call out, but the person keeps knocking.

I yank the door open to find Bob standing on the other side.

"Eric!" he says.

"What are you doing here?"

"You okay? I've been waiting a while." He slips past me and unceremoniously begins to unfasten his trousers. "You want to grab a coffee or something? You seem kinda squirrely, like maybe you could use someone to talk to. What with the deputy looking for you and all?"

"No, Bob, I don't have time for that right now."

I escape, slinging my ragged backpack over my shoulder.

Out on the sidewalk, I start distancing myself from my house, unsure where I'm heading except *away from there*. I decided to call Ty, but as I began to dial, he calls first.

"What the fuck are you thinking?" Ty is already yelling when I pick up.

"Ty?" I looked around as if he had just watched me escape my own house.

"You're calling the board members?"

Oh, right. That.

"Yeah, I thought—"

"They've all called me bitching about you bothering them this morning. Are you fucking crazy? How do you think that is going to help us?"

"I don't know. I thought maybe I could reassure them we're who they want running the super PAC. Show I really care about getting the job."

"Well, it didn't fucking work. All you did was annoy them. Now, they definitely don't want to work with the guy who will randomly call them and ask them stupid questions. *Fuck,* Eric."

"I'm trying to do *something*," I say maniacally. "I've got the sheriff on my ass. Marie has left me. I need this job, Ty. I'm at the end of my rope here. If this doesn't come through, I'm fucked in every way possible."

"Jesus, Eric, stop playing the fucking victim."

"What are you talking about? I *am* the victim!"

Ty sighs and mutters, *"Fucking shithead,"* under his breath. I can picture him pulling the phone away from his head and rolling his eyes.

"You know exactly what you need to do to get this job."

I don't answer.

"I've gone way out on a limb for you here," Ty says. "Did you really think this would be easy? That you would just waltz through this with no problems? You swore to me that you would do what it takes, so now's the time to follow through on that promise. I need you to come through for me. Marie needs you to. Your boys need you to, too. This is real-world shit here, not fantasy land. So, man up, motherfucker. "

"What are you talking about?"

"You've known Aneel for a long time. And I know you've got something on him. Tell me what it is."

38

POSITIVELY 4TH STREET

I don't notice when Aneel's BMW pulls into the empty parking lot of Chuy's Tex-Mex restaurant. My body is waiting, squatted down on the curb with my back to the street, but my mind has been sucked back down into the void. I'm lost, struggling to find my way out.

He rolls down his window as he approaches.

"Eric? You okay?"

I snap back into reality and force out a laugh, nodding, as I struggle to my feet. I surreptitiously wipe the tears from my eyes and then slide into his passenger seat.

"Your office?" he asks.

I nod.

We pull onto the street.

Aneel is uncharacteristically silent as he navigates downtown. I keep glancing at him, wondering why he isn't filling the silence between us.

At that moment, I realize this is the dynamic, or more accurately, the one-way nature of our relationship. I rely on him to carry not just our conversations but the whole friendship. He is my only friend, and if it weren't for him texting, calling, and pursuing, we would have lost touch years ago.

He's always gone out of his way to be my friend? Why?

Look at me, I think. *I'm a disaster of a person, a real shithead. He's got his shit together. Yet, he still wants me in his life.* Was it some kind of masochistic game on his side?

Then I understand. More than likely, I'm a charity case. Being around me made him feel better about himself. He carries around some sort of survivor's guilt of the ubersuccessful, and I am his little project to help him sleep better.

Either way, I'm about to burn down the friendship once and for all. Where I'm heading, I can pick up friends like colds. Fuck him and his charity, I resolve.

He pulls into my office's parking lot and picks a space closest to the door, but neither of us makes a move.

After a full minute of silence, Aneel turns to look at me.

"Eric, I'm worried about you, man."

I keep looking ahead, not meeting his eyes, so he continued.

"Marie wasn't doing great yesterday. She kept

putting on a smile, but I could tell she'd been crying. And then a deputy showed up about something. What was that about?"

I turn and meet his eyes but don't say anything.

"Where were you yesterday?" he asks. "Why weren't you at David's party?"

"I missed my flight Saturday evening," I shoot back. "You know that."

"Yeah, but you still could have made it back. Buy a ticket on another flight. Rent a car and drive all night. Hell, bribe somebody at the gate to give you their seat."

"I don't have any money, Aneel!" I don't mean to yell, but that's what comes out. "I'm broke. In debt up to my fucking eyeballs. Flush out of money. I had fifty dollars in a Ziploc bag to my name at the airport and no room on the credit cards. What was I supposed to bribe people with?"

It's Aneel's turn not to respond.

"I've been struggling for years, Aneel. Barely making ends meet. In fact, in no way was I making ends meet. No matter how hard I worked, I just got further and further behind. Now it's all finally crashing down around me."

"Damn," is all he can get out.

"Don't act like you didn't know," I say, angrily looking away.

"I didn't! You asked for some work last week, but otherwise, you always told me your business was doing great. How could I possibly have known?"

"Well, it's not doing great. Never really has been, actually."

"I'm sorry, man. Can I do anything?"

I cut my eyes at him.

How can he ask me that question? He's competing with me on this life-changing job, and he's going to fucking win. Now he's sitting there asking me if he can do anything.

"You know how hard it is to constantly be around you? Success just falls in your lap. It's like you trip over it walking down the street. That's not how it works for most of us. For me. No matter what I do, it never seems enough, and when I do get a good opportunity, I manage to fuck it up somehow. I just..." The thought of the six-year-old in the dungeon slips into my mind and derails my train of thought. I can see him again getting the shit beaten out of him by that red-eyed monster.

"Eric?"

I look at Aneel, locking my eyes and forcing my mind back into the present.

"Remember that job you did for the lawyer down in Atlanta? Ten years ago?"

Aneel begins to fold in on himself.

"I just thought of it the other day. What happened again?"

"You know what happened."

"It was something with a lawyer. Right? Didn't he pay you, and didn't you accept that payment from a client's misappropriated funds?"

"Something like that."

"But you didn't know? Right?"

"Why are you bringing this up, Eric? Of course, I didn't know. I got roped into the case like I had something to do with the misappropriation. Turns out the asshole had stolen millions from his clients. I got deposed a couple of times and was on a list of people who could be charged, but he pleaded guilty, and they dropped everything else."

"Hm," I say.

"What?"

"You think the super PAC board members know about that? I wonder how much background they did on you."

He waits a beat before answering.

"Probably not. It was ten years ago, and most of it was never made public."

"What do you think they'd do if they found out? I mean, you'll be handling millions of dollars running the super PAC. I doubt they could risk hiring someone who had even a whiff of fund misappropriation in their history."

"What are you doing, Eric? Why are you bringing this up?"

I don't answer at first, letting the silence hang, but Aneel won't fill it.

"I really need this job, Aneel. I'm in a huge amount of tax debt, which was why the deputy was at my house, not to mention the credit card debt, car payments, David's school, and everything else. The signing bonus alone would get me close to even."

"You'll probably get the job, Eric. I heard you and Ty killed it in your meeting."

I shake my head.

"They're going to pick you. We got a heads-up from one of the board members. They're meeting in a couple of hours to finalize their decision, but it will be you."

"Okay. What do you want me to do?"

"I want you to call them and pull out of the running for the job. If you don't, Ty will tell them about what happened in Atlanta. That won't just ruin this job. You won't get another chance in this world again."

Aneel stares at me, and I hold his eyes. It's the least I can do. Some, like Ty, don't even do that. They get people like me to do it for them.

"Okay," he says, adding, "you know I would have backed out if you had just asked me."

I look at him long and hard and see, for the first time, he's just like me.

Full of shit.

39

LIFE'S WHAT YOU MAKE IT

I take a couple of steps into the foyer, where I know Aneel can't see me. He sits in his car staring after me for a minute and then dials and talks to someone on his phone.

When he drives away, I approach the door to watch him disappear, leaning my forehead against the plate glass door to steady myself. Add him to the list. Simply one more person I've left in my wake who is worse off for knowing me.

I should start warning people when they meet me. I seem like a nice guy. I'll try to do the right thing. But in the end, I'll fuck up your life, and you'll wish you'd never crossed paths with me.

"You doing alright over there, brother?"

Bob's voice rings through the lobby.

Of course, he's here.

"Sure, Bob," I say, turning to find him standing by

the elevators to the floors I can't afford, coffee in hand and a giant smile on his face. "It's just been a long day already."

He takes a gulp from his "Mondays… am I right?" mug, the long hairs from his mustache dipping into the brown liquid as he drinks. He swallows and sticks his bottom lip up to suck off the dangling drops.

"Wanna talk about it? I'm a great listener."

"No, Bob, I'm good."

"You get that mess sorted out with the deputy?"

"Yeah, just about. I need to get to my office and make a call."

He nods as I pass. When I look back, he has the same look John had at the Phoenix meeting, staring off into some distant landscape of his own.

Does the man ever work?

Once isolated in my office, I slouch into my chair. It's over. I have the job. Right? Only two bids were in the running, and Aneel is pulling out. That leaves me and Ty.

Why don't I feel better? Some sort of relief?

It's the ending to an explosively shitty couple of days. Marie and the boys are holed up with my asshole father-in-law. My car is booted in my driveway with a deputy patrolling the neighborhood. I just blackmailed my only friend, not to mention getting drunk off my ass in DC and being tased by an old geezer smoking at a cancer center.

I also still don't technically have the job. I won't be

able to take a deep breath until Ty gets the official call from the board, which will only last until I have paperwork in front of me, ready to sign for the job. Then I'll have to wait until the bonus check arrives. Only then will I be able to pay off the IRS and show Marie the proof that our debt is paid. If I beg and plead with enough vim and vigor, maybe, just maybe, she'll relent and come home with the boys. Then everything will be the way it was before.

My phone starts buzzing, and Ty's name pops up on the screen. For some reason, I let it ring several times before answering.

"Reggie just called with the news," Ty yells. "Aneel dropped out of the running! Good work, Eric. *Great* work!"

"So we got the job?"

"Yessir."

"Officially? They're sending over contracts?"

"Well, they still have to do an official vote at the meeting in a couple of hours, but we're the only ones they can hire, so it's looking that way."

I nod and wiped my face with my hand. For some reason, I start crying—not tears of joy or relief. I'm suddenly overcome with sadness and grief. I think of that poor boy trapped forever in the dungeon. I think of all the horrible things I said to him. Is that really what I thought? I imagined little David or Matthew down there. Would I abandon them the same way?

"Eric? Yo! You still there?"

I push the tears away with the heel of my hand.

"Yeah, I'm here."

"Okay, so I'm going to need you in DC on Friday."

I don't realize what he's said at first.

"Wait, what? *This* Friday?"

"Yeah, we have a tiny window between when the board makes their final decision and when we can't interact with Bryant anymore. He's got the morning open on Friday, so your and my asses need to be in chairs across his desk."

Can I leave while Marie is sitting tight with the boys at her father's house? She's made no mention of any divorce…yet…but me leaving town so soon wouldn't be much of a deterrent from her beginning that process. Leaving isn't a good idea. If I can get her to come home before that, which was a very big "if," leaving immediately after she does will be even worse.

"I'll line up meetings for us Friday afternoon as well. I can pull together some former super PAC members so you can pick their brains. Then we'll need to start working up a budget on Saturday. That's the first thing the board is going to want from us. We have to shoot big here. They need to know we're serious."

My mind struggles to keep up with what he's saying. I grab a pen and start jotting down notes.

"Okay, so I'll be gone Friday and Saturday? Fly home on Sunday?"

"Yeah, that's fine, but we'll need to hit the road again the week after. We'll start in South Dakota,

Bryant's home state. Meet with past donors—the guys who got him into Congress in the first place. Get their buy-in early on supporting the PAC. Have them pull in some of their rich buddies, too. It's all about the early buy-in. If we get some momentum going, we can start building that wave and everybody will want to be in. It's amazing how these rich assholes still care so much what everyone else thinks."

"And you'll need me with you?"

"Of course! You're my wunderkind! These guys like to see a youngster in the room. Makes them feel like we'll be cutting edge with all our marketing."

I'll be the youngster in my mid-thirties?

"You'll need to start building out your team too."

"My team?"

"Yeah, you can't handle the whole campaign yourself. You'll need ad buyers, consultants, developers, and I don't know, whoever the fuck else. This is why I want you to talk to the other PAC guys. They'll give you people to hire. It's going to ramp up fast. We're technically already behind schedule."

I nod, still taking notes, but don't say anything. I don't need to.

"You'll need to check in with John weekly. The Dicky has a penchant for changing his mind a lot, especially during a campaign. John will help you thread the needle to make sure we're pivoting to support without being obvious enough to be questioned."

I'm embarrassed how little this fazed me. At this

point, with me kissing another woman at a bar, hiding from the cops, and blackmailing my best friend, the idea of spending the next couple of years circumventing federal campaign finance laws that come with heavy fines and jail time seem—I don't know—par for the course? Who am I now?

Ty keeps rattling off to-dos. I keep a rough running total of the amount of time all of this will take.

When he finally pauses to take a breath, I jump in.

"Hey, Ty, I got to shoot straight with you. My life is in shambles at the moment."

"The IRS shit? We're gonna get that cleared up shortly."

"That. And Marie..." I choke on the next word. "She left last night after I got home. Took the kids and went to stay at her dad's place."

"That bitch," he mutters.

"Woah, Ty. Come on. That's my wife."

"And shouldn't she support you now instead of distracting and punishing you?"

"Well, you don't know the whole story. I've done a bunch of stuff, too."

"You fuck someone else?" he asks.

"What?"

"Did you stick your dick in another pussy?"

"Uh, no—"

"Then she should be by your side helping you make this happen. I know you, Eric. Anything you've done, you did for your family. Now, when you're right at the crest of something big happening, when it's the hardest for you, she gives you a swift kick to the dick and disappears. Fuck her."

Is he right? Here I am feeling ashamed and low because, obviously, if she's left, I've done something horrible and wrong. But is it true? What had I *really* done that was so bad? Plenty of guys keep money troubles from their wives. Other than that, what? What was so bad it was worth walking out and taking my kids?

"Listen, Ty, either way, shit's hit the fan here. I'm not sure what the next few weeks will look like for me."

"Eric, I'm with you. You do what you want to do with your personal life. But things are ramping up for us. This isn't some forty-hour-a-week, clock-in-clock-out, take your two fifteen-minute breaks bullshit. You get that. Right?"

I scan the giant list I've scrawled down. I end my running total somewhere north of seventy hours a week. He's right. This isn't a typical full-time job. It's *two* full-time jobs, probably more.

Even if my personal life wasn't teetering on the edge of an erupting volcano, I'm not sure how I would be able to pull this off while keeping my family intact. Maybe this is it for me and Marie. She obviously wanted me to stay small in my work and life. She's probably scared of me changing and turning from a nobody into a somebody.

Is that who I really want to be with?

40

BACK TO BLACK

Faye's face squinches and looks disgusted as I stop to sip my cold coffee. She cuts her eyes off to the side, staring off into the middle distance. The rims of her eyes are red.

"How could you blame *Marie* for this?" she bites at me in a low, strained voice. "What choice did she have? The way you spoke to David and Matthew. The lies. And that woman in DC. But it was all *her* fault? How could you say that?"

"Faye." I take a deep breath. "Would you agree that Marie attacking me when I was in the shower was not cool?"

"You had it coming."

"Okay, I see your point. So, correct me if I'm wrong here, but what if the roles were reversed? Let's say Marie had been responsible for the IRS debt. Then would I have been justified in attacking her when she was naked and vulnerable in the shower?"

She doesn't respond, so I go on.

"When a relationship hits a wall, two people, not just one, have a role in its crash." I probably shouldn't be such a smartass, holding up two fingers to make my argument.

I can tell Faye is at her breaking point. She looks like she's had just about enough of my saga. She begins to collect her things but stops herself. I can feel her fury.

She points a finger at my face. "Who the fuck do you think you are?" she shrills. "What did David fucking…" but she stops herself from finishing, sensing that the entire coffee shop is now very interested in our conversation.

I hold up my hands to calm her down.

Faye looks around and notices the tension in the room.

"And scene…" she waves her hands like Tina Fey and then addresses the concerned onlookers. "Nothing to worry about here, folks. My acting partner and I are just working on a scene for class."

I can feel the room breathe a collective sigh of relief as Faye returns to her chair and drinks from her water bottle.

"Okay, Eric, I'm stuck here now, so let's hear the rest," she says with a tight smile.

I spend the next hour organizing the to-do list in some sort of coherent order. Then I sketch a mind map of the support positions I will need to hire.

There's definitely room for Andre and Bethany to join me in the super PAC, but I worry whether they will want to, especially Bethany. She loves the pace and hours I provide for her, and I doubt those will translate well to running a campaign.

The presentation to the board contained the breakdown of my plan, so I start there. Some will be contractors, and others we will need full time. I have no idea what my budget will be, but I decide to plan out the perfect scenario. This will be a long, complicated process, and I have a lot to learn.

Once the board officially hires us, I will call Reggie and ask him about the stuff from Aneel's presentation that I had missed. Several times, I forgot what I had to give up to get this job, and the thought popped into my head to text Aneel for his ideas and input. Each of those times, I had to realize that I'd welded that door permanently shut.

Nevertheless, focusing on the work feels, if not "good," at least productive, like I'm getting somewhere instead of standing like a shithead in the wind hoping someone will come to save me.

For a few minutes, I even forget about the sheriff, the IRS, and the booted car sitting in my driveway. I don't think once about the little boy being brutalized in the dungeon and only intermittently about Marie, David, and Matthew.

That is, of course, until she calls. I lunge for the phone when I see her name on the caller ID.

"Marie?" I cringe at the desperation in my voice.

"Eric..." She stops for a moment. I open my mouth to fill the void, but my mind is blank, so the silence hangs instead.

"I probably should have planned more before I called, but I—Jesus, Eric, Aneel just called me."

That *fucker*. He doesn't get the job, so he calls my *wife* to tattle on me?

"He's worried about you, Eric. So am I."

"Why's he worried?"

"He wouldn't say exactly. He said you called to have him give you a lift to the office and that you were acting strange, but he wouldn't say anything else. So he called me thinking I would know something."

"Did you tell him that you left?"

Silence.

"You left me, Marie. That's a fact. When I needed you the most, you took David and Matthew and ran back to your father's house. It's no secret he never liked me, and now he never will. Now I'm stuck at that house alone and freaking out while I'm in the middle of trying to get a job that will secure our future. And now—whaddya know, this shithead actually got the job, Marie. I wanted to call you and tell you that, but I know you don't care because of how it will look to your friends with me working for a controversial politician. Our money and IRS problems will be cleared up this week. This job is going to *suck*. Sixty, seventy, eighty-hour weeks probably. But it's worth it. It's worth it if I fix all this so you'll come home."

"Don't act like you're doing this for me, David, and Matthew!"

"Are you fucking kidding me? Of course, I'm doing this for you. Why else would I take this job? Why else would I hock myself up to my eyeballs to get you the right house, the right car, and the right schooling for our kids?"

"Nice try, Eric, but you fucking did it for *you*. Because you have some sort of small man complex you're always trying to fix. That's why you bought me that Navigator and your Tesla and that *fucking* house you're now stuck in, and you spent money we didn't have, and you keep chasing these big-time jobs you think are going to—I don't know what. Make you happy?"

"Fuck happy. I'm just trying not to be such a loser, to have my wife and kids be proud of me. And here I am, finally getting there, and I don't even have your support. You choose the moment when I'm at my lowest to abandon me. And now, when I'm actually accomplishing what I set out to do, you keep kicking the shit out of me."

"That's not what I'm doing! Jesus, Eric, how can you not see that?"

"How else can I see it? You're the one who left. Not me."

"Why would I stay? All you've done is lie to me. Lie and lie and lie. And then you stole from us."

I roll my eyes.

"I can't steal money that is already mine. I earned that thousand bucks and stuck it in the safe for an emergency and, guess what, it was an emergency! So I used it for exactly what we agreed."

"If it's totally fine you took it, why didn't you tell me?"

"I don't have to run everything by you, Marie."

"How about not going to the meeting with the IRS? You didn't need to run that by me either? Even though you *told* me you were going to go. You promised me."

"I had to go to my therapy appointment. I didn't have time to do both. Remember? The therapy *you* told me to go to. Which, by the way, has obviously not made anything better."

She doesn't respond.

"Marie?"

"I'm not doing this anymore," she whispers.

"Doing what?"

"This. Having these same goddamned conversations over and over. Trying to get you to see what's going on. To get you to see… how you're destroying yourself."

"What am I not seeing?"

"I've already told you a thousand times."

"Then tell me again!"

"No! I'm sick of this. Sick of having to overexplain everything to you so you can pick it apart and tell me why I'm wrong so you can just stick to what you already think. You keep believing some fucked up story about yourself and about me and how I'm this awful, overbearing, she-beast. And you keep saying you're doing this for me and the boys, but it's all a lie. All of it. And I'm not cosigning on your bullshit anymore. If you want to take the job, take it. Go ahead. Pay off the debt. Get our finances in order. Fix everything. But don't think for a minute that I'll be coming home. I'm done, Eric."

"Done? So what are you going to do? Live off your daddy?"

"You think this was a rash decision I made, Eric? That I just got angry and decided to leave you? I've felt this coming for *weeks. Months.* I've already looked at apartments, talked to a realtor, and lined up a couple of jobs. I didn't want to do this, but the worse you got, I knew I needed a way to take care of myself and the boys when you couldn't anymore."

"You've been planning this for months? Now, who's the one lying?"

"Yeah, exactly, *I'm* the bad guy here. If that makes you feel better, I'm happy to play that role."

"And how can you say I can't take care of you and the boys? Have you not been listening? *I got the job*. I'll have the money to fix all of this in the next couple of days."

"Then what? You'll just put us right back in this position again, but somehow worse. And I'll never know if you're telling me the truth about what's going on. You always hide yourself and what you're doing from me until the hole is too deep and you're desperate to get out and freaking out."

"See. Even *you* think I'm a fuckup."

Marie lets out a frustrated growl.

"I'm going to go."

"Jesus, Marie, you can't do this. We made vows. We're married. You can't just leave me. What about the boys? What am I going to do?"

Again, she doesn't respond.

"Marie, please. Just come home. We can talk through this. I'll stop arguing. I'll hear you. Please don't leave me all alone."

"I'm hanging up now."

41

BLACK HOLE SUN

I sink to my knees, staring at the phone. Is this really happening? Is my marriage over? Am I now one of those guys who gets my kids every other weekend and half the holidays?

I did it. I actually did it. I managed to fuck up the only relationship in my life that really mattered to me. Marie is gone. I'm alone.

Alone.

I see the boy again, his back open and bleeding, cowering in the corner. Alone. Abandoned down there with that giant monster beating him.

The sobs come from deep inside me, somewhere more resounding than the physical realm. They erupt out.

I need help.

With shaky hands and several autocorrects, I managed to type out a message.

I need another session. Marie has left me. She took the boys. I'm freaking out.

My knuckles turn white as I grip the phone. I hold on like it's a lifeline, staring, waiting, hoping for that blessed bubble to pop up, indicating someone is typing out a reply.

Nothing.

I force myself to wait a full two minutes before I tried again.

I know I fucked up. I shouldn't have left when you told me I needed to stay. I shouldn't have pushed you. I'm sorry. I'm ready now. Please.

This time, I only wait a minute before I call the number. It rings four times before the voicemail picks up. It isn't Lori. Instead, a robotic voice reads out her number and says to leave a message after the beep.

As it speaks, I steel myself. I don't want to sound desperate and insane on the phone. I don't want to scare her away. I spin up a straightforward explanation of what's happening along with a plea to her sympathies. Surely, she wouldn't hold fast to the rule that if I stopped I could never go back. That was stupid rigid. No way to run a business. And Lori was running a business, after all.

And with what happened down there, what could she expect? But now, I feel it's more than I want or need to rescue that boy. Even though he isn't real—I mean seriously, how can a six-year-old version of me trapped in some dungeon be real?—and the whole thing is just some crazy-ass hallucination, I have a compulsion, a mission, that is clearer to me than anything has ever been before. I know if I don't go back and help that boy, I will die in some way. Maybe not literally die, but die inside.

The same robotic voice continues, "The mailbox is full and cannot accept new messages at this time. Goodbye."

The call disconnects.

"Fuck!" I scream and sling my phone across the room.

I punched the wall, and the drywall cracks underneath. The piercing pain feels good, so I punch it again and again until it gives way and crumbles, letting my fist pass through.

I slam my head into the wall and kicked at it, too, causing cracks to run through the white paint. I back up and punch it again, this time leaving a smear of blood from where my knuckles have opened up.

A scream escapes again, along with some intelligible gurgling this time. I kick the wall again, and my foot falls through. I yank it out, stumbling back into my desk and knocking my computer monitor over. I shove it off onto the floor, and it releases a satisfying crunch.

Next, I fling a stack of books to the floor and knock the whole bookshelf over.

The room seems to darken around me. My screams meld into the boy's screams in my head. Every time I break, throw, or smash something, it sounds like the snap of a whip.

Voices start crowding into the room, too. Whispers at first, they grow louder to match the chaos I'm creating around me.

You stupid fucking loser. Look at what you've done!

Marie's better off without you!

David and Matthew, too! All you would do is fuck them up like you do everything else.

I put my hands over my ears, screaming to drown them out.

I have to get out of here and find Lori. Get her to save me from all this.

I fling open the door, stumble into the dark hallway, and run through the lobby into the darkness of the setting sun.

My car is still booted at the house, so I'll walk the mile and a half to Lori's office.

I start at a run but immediately stumble and fall, ripping the knee out of one of my pant legs. I scramble back up but slow to a walk, trying to keep my bearings. This isn't the best part of Nashville, so I need to keep my wits about me.

Two blocks in, a homeless guy seems to coalesce from the shadows directly in my path. He holds a sign that reads, "Why lie? I need money for weed." I wave him off, shaking my head and muttering to myself.

In a few more blocks, I cower under the piercing noise of the Nashville Pedal Tavern as it rolls by, packed with a bachelorette party belting out an off-key rendition of "Man! I feel like a Woman!" by Shania Twain.

I keep moving. She'll be there. She has to be there. She can't abandon me like this. She has to help me find the boy and get him out of that dungeon.

My eyes stay on the sidewalk in front of me as I make it to the Gulch and the crowded sidewalks. Just a couple more blocks.

It's fully dark when I turn the corner onto 11th Avenue, and I'm openly sobbing as I walk the last block to Lori's building.

I scramble up the steps, rattle the locked handle, and mash the buzzer button, but nobody responds. I wait a few seconds and then try the handle again. This time, it opens, and I fall through.

The stairs seem to have an extra creak as I climb to the second floor, leaning heavily on the railing. I keep my hand on the wall as I make it down the hallway while the whole building seems to be tipping off to the side and threatening to send me to the floor.

Lori's office door sits cracked open, so I push on it.

"Lori?"

The door swings open to reveal an empty office. No rug. No therapist chair. No blood-red loveseat. Just bare wooden floors.

I move over to where the loveseat used to be and sink to my knees.

The darkness closes in around me.

“Eric?” a voice calls out.

My head snaps up like a cartoon character, looking around wildly.

The monster is here, searching. He’s coming for me now to punish me for abandoning that poor boy to his eternal fate. He’s brought the whip. He’ll open me up and then tear me apart.

Again, the voice calls my name, but I hear it as a sickening growl.

It’s out in the hallway.

I scramble to my feet and lunge for the door, slamming it shut and turning the little knob on the handle to lock it.

“Eric!”

I scream obscenities back, trying to scare away the monster on the other side of the door. The handle rattles again, and then something heavy hits the door, shaking it in its frame.

I cry out, backing away to the other side of the room. I hit the wall and scrunch down, gripping my legs and hiding behind my knees.

With the second impact on the door, something crunches under the lock. I beg the monster to leave me alone. On the third impact, the door gives way, an explosion of splinters as it slams back against the wall.

Bob stands breathing heavily in the doorway, looking somehow unnaturally impressive and large, as though he’s shining. He comes in and kneels beside me, his giant glasses half-fogged and sliding to the end of his nose. I cower away from him, still crying, still unsure if he was sent there to beat me for my sins.

"Eric? Can you hear me?"

I nod. I can hear him, but now, in my terror, I can barely see him.

"I think maybe you need to tell me what's going on."

I stare at Bob, unsure. My senses begin to come back online, and I mostly conclude that he isn't here as a representative of the dungeon. But to tell him what's going on? I barely know him. And how did he even know I was here? Did he follow me?

He holds my gaze, and I can see something shining through his eyes—something I hadn't seen before in our interactions—strength and kindness. I feel like he's peering into me, talking to those deep parts of me—the parts I've lost along the way.

He isn't asking about my IRS debt, the super PAC job, or even my marital problems. He's asking about the dark places I'd been—the underneath, the dungeon, and the boy.

"It's going to sound crazy," I mutter.

He stands and closes the door, wedging it back into place so it will hold against the broken jamb. Then he sits cross-legged in front of me and takes my hands in his.

"Why don't you try me?"

I hesitate at first, sharing bits about Lori, saving her

from the bus, and this odd little office. However, once I reach the cave, everything starts flowing out of me. I cry and cry as I relate the visit to the hospital on the day I was born and meeting Marie there with the baby. I told him about the deep caverns, facing down the snake, and finding the light in the giant baby. Then I share about the dark tendrils swallowing the boy's light.

When I get to the dungeon, I have to stop several times. I keep losing myself in the dark places, but each time, Bob squeezes my hands and coaxes me back into reality so I can keep going.

By the end, I'm exhausted, and my crying has stopped producing tears. Something about getting all of that out has made me feel both better and worse, like cleaning out a gaping, bleeding wound.

"I have to get back there. Save the boy. Rescue him. But I can't. I don't…there's no way…"

"I think that's the problem, Eric," Bob says softly. "I think in this one, you're not the rescuer."

I look up into his kind eyes and sniff hard.

"What do you mean?"

"All those voices you hear. Listen to them now."

"No, no, I can't!" I reply desperately.

He squeezes my hands again.

"I've got you. But it's time. Stop running. Just listen."

I nod and close my eyes with a death grip on poor Bob's hands.

The whispers immediately crowd back in.

You're broken and useless. Nobody can fix you.

You filthy little cunt.

You'll always be alone.

You're better off alone, actually. That way you stop fucking up everybody's life.

You have shit for brains, shithead.

I stop pushing against them and running from them and let them approach. They keep getting louder and more precise.

Fuck you, fuck you, fuck you.

David and Matthew hate you.

Everybody hates you.

You'll never, ever be anything but a fucking loser.

My eyes snap open.

The voice.

I know it.

"It's me," I say.

Bob doesn't respond. He doesn't have to.

My voice has been saying those awful things. I was beating that poor boy.

I close my eyes again and feel my heart wrenched apart by the understanding.

I'm no longer the rescuer.

I long ago took over the role of perpetrator.

It's not on me to rescue the boy.

Instead, I need to finish what I started.

The voices disappear.

The room grows cold.
I open my eyes.
I'm alone.
The room is brutally dark.
Except for a single flickering torch.

42

NEVER LET ME DOWN AGAIN

I push up to my feet and immediately feel the weight of the armor on my body. The piercing scream doesn't take long to find me, and I move headlong into the pitch-black labyrinth. Soon, I stand again at the third door.

I realize I've made it back all by myself and know what I must do, yet I hesitate.

A wet smack and a shriek escape from within.

I take a deep breath, swallow, and throw open the door.

My entry interrupts the monstrous soldier as he poises, readying another swing. I don't attack him this time. I simply hold out my hand.

He unloops the cat-o'-nine-tails from his wrist, hands it to me, and then exits, ducking through the doorway without a word before closing it behind him.

The rage returns. The shame floods. I feel bile sluice

its way into my throat as I tighten the whip against my wrist and step forward.

Repulsed, I want to run again from the powerful attraction. I feel the yank in my gut, but I resist. This is what I need to confront. This is where I belong, down here in this dark place doing these dark deeds.

I close in on the boy, pull the whip back, and open my hips wide, knowing how to perfectly turn them over. Then I release the most amount of damage I can muster.

Thwack!

The blood from the boy's torn back pops and sprays.

He lets out a long, wet scream.

"Shut up!" I yell. "You deserve this, you little piece of shit!"

I opened my hips again and—

"Stop!" Faye's breath catches as a sob heaves out of her chest. Wet streaks run down her face. "I can't—" she pushes back from the table and hurries to the back hallway toward the bathrooms, leaving her sunglasses and phone on the table.

A few people glance at me confusedly, so I hold up my notebook to indicate our "script." Relieved, they go back to their coffees and smoothies.

Several minutes later, Faye returns, her eyes still

wet and her fists clutching bunched-up brown paper towels. She eases back into her chair and dabs at her eyes.

"I'm not sure how much more of this I can take."

"I'm sorry," I say. "I forget how upsetting this is."

"I don't know how you can talk about this."

"I don't."

Faye doesn't respond right away. She stares at the table, her jaw working as her thoughts churn. She finally lifts her eyes to meet mine.

"And Marie didn't know?"

"How could she?"

"Why didn't you tell her?"

"I think it's better if I continue than try to answer that one."

Faye draws back, tears filling her eyes again.

"Eric, I don't think I can—"

"I'll skip ahead," I say. "But just so you know, it got—worse. You see, down in the underneath, there is no time. No ending. The beatings can go on uninterrupted. I didn't know that then, so I kept going, screaming every insult and obscenity I could conjure while inflicting as much pain as I could muster."

"Please," the boy speaks. "Just tell me what I did. I won't ever do it again. Just tell me. I'm so sorry."

"I don't know!" I roar at him.

I drop to my knees, sobbing, heaving, exhausted.

I remember seeing him first in the hospital room and how his little light had flickered to life there. Then I remember how it filled the cavern with the snake. Then I remember how the words of my parents, my sister, and all those other voices had called forth the tendrils to start hiding and stealing his light. Somewhere along the way, all of those voices highlighting the darkness had become my own.

The boy manages to turn his head toward me. As I catch my breath, he drags himself over to me, leaving a thick smear of dark blood across the rough cobblestones behind him.

When he reaches me, he takes my hand. The hand holding the whip.

"I'm so sorry," I say. "I don't want to do this anymore, but I don't know… how else to…"

He pulls himself a little closer to me and whispers.

I can't make out what he's saying, but he is looking and pointing at my middle.

"I see it," he whispers. "It's right there."

I look down and see the light. It's bright and white, peeking through the thick black tendrils.

My eyes return to the boy. His light is shining, too, growing brighter, stronger. Our lights join together to illuminate the cell, and the boy smiles.

I squeeze my eyes shut as the enormity overwhelms my senses. Something inside of me loosens and lets go. I open my eyes again.

I am still in the dungeon, but my scaley armor and whip are gone. I am barefoot, dressed in white, loose pants, and a T-shirt.

I look up to see the boy standing over me, whole and well and smiling.

He still has my hand in his.

“Come on!” he says excitedly. “Let’s go!”

He pulls me to the door.

“Wait. Where are we going?” I ask, standing as he tugs at me.

“I’ll show you! Come on. Come on. Come on!”

He lets me go and then rips the door open and darts out.

I run after him, following him through the now brightly lit tunnels. We reach the room with the single torch, now wholly lit up. With the fresh light, I can see a previously hidden stone staircase at the back of the room. The boy hits the first step at full speed, racing upward, and I struggle to keep up.

The stairs ascend story after story. Hundreds, no thousands of steps, but neither the boy nor I get tired on the race to the top.

Eventually, a wooden door appears at the precipice, and I see a white light streaming around the edges. As the boy reaches the top, he leaps, slamming his entire body into the door, which flies open under the impact.

He falls through the door out of sight, and I panic. When I reach the top, though, I find him rolling up to his feet in the lushest, greenest grass I have ever seen.

I shade my eyes to adjust to the brightness of the sun overhead, which hangs low in a cloudless aqua sky.

I hear laughter and shouting all around us.

Children of all ages are running and playing with adults who look vaguely like them. Everybody has bright lights emanating from them.

"Let's go!" my boy yells, running away. I take off again, following him through the grass and under trees until it opens onto a long field with a group of kids and adults chasing a soccer ball.

The boy skids to a halt, and I join him. He takes my hand.

"You wanna play?"

"I—"

"Come on. It won't be even teams if you don't play!"

I don't know what to say. I look around, and all I see is light and joy. I look down at the boy, and he is so happy. I realize he isn't just happy to be free of the dungeon and the pain. He is delighted to be with me. He trusts me. He now knows I will care for him and protect him. Even with all the pain I've caused, he sees me and loves me.

"Okay," I say. "Let's play."

43

WONDERING WHERE THE LIONS ARE

We play for ages, mainly soccer, but we also build mud dams in a creek we find while wandering through the woods, climb several trees until they swayed under our weight, and have a pine cone fight. By the end, my lily-white pants and shirt are covered in grass and mud stains.

Halfway through our fourth round of soccer, he wanders over to the edge and sits down in the grass, squinting up at the sun.

I join him, a bit concerned. It's the first time he's stopped moving since we arrived.

"You okay?" I ask.

He shrugs and digs his big toes into the turf.

"I'm getting kinda bored. You ready to go back?"

"Back?" I feel a burst of anxiety as I look over my shoulder toward the door that leads back into the dungeon. "Do we have to go back?"

"Yeah, don't you have stuff to do? Family, job. Grownup stuff?"

I do.

I think about Marie, David, and Matthew, and a longing wells up in me. I definitely have some things I need to handle.

"What about you?"

He pops up, wiping his hands on his pants.

"I'll come with you."

"Yeah?"

"Of course. Where else am I going to go?"

"You won't be bored?"

"Nah. Let's go!"

He takes my hand, and we both squint in the sunlight.

When I awake on the floor of Lori's office, I'm laughing at a joke I can't remember.

Bob is gone.

I push myself to my feet, a loopy grin stuck on my face.

I wander down the hall and staircase and step out into the morning sunlight. It's all the same, of course. Nothing has changed in the world. Yet everything has.

It takes me two blocks of walking to realize I have nowhere to go. No car. No money. My clothes are ripped and stained. And I have no way or reason to get home. And—I checked my phone—eight percent battery left.

I've done a fantastic job burning through all my options over the previous week.

I take a deep breath and dial.

Twenty-five minutes later, my dad's twenty-year-old burgundy Honda Accord rattles up to the curb. I can see his forlorn "For Sale" sign stuck to the rear window. The door crunches and scrapes as I open it, and I slide into the passenger seat.

"You've got to lift the handle and jiggle it a bit when you open it," he corrects me for about the thousandth time.

I carefully pull the door shut, and he starts driving.

"What are you doing here on a Tuesday morning?"

That's a tough one.

"Hard to explain."

He grunts in response. I wait for the next round of questioning, but it never comes. Instead, we drive silently the rest of the way to my parents' house. As soon as I step into the kitchen, I figure out why my dad has refrained from asking questions.

The interrogation will be formalized.

In my family, we don't yell. We don't fight. We don't scream.

Instead, the offended party calls a meeting with the other family members and is expected to come prepared with notes.

My mom is waiting at the kitchen table with her

yellow legal pad, crammed with writing from the top down and in the margins. My father sits beside her and motions for me to sit across from them.

He will sit quietly through most of the meeting, providing nonverbal but incontrovertible backup support and agreement with whatever she says.

I've been here before.

As soon as I settle in, my mom begins with an opening salvo she's rarely presented.

"We are very disappointed with you."

You would think there could be a lot worse things parents could say to their middle-aged son, but from my mother, this initial blow sank deep.

She continues, "We've known something was going on for a long time, but we couldn't figure it out. You kept saying everything was fine, and it's not our place to pry. So we let it go. We were very concerned, even outraged, when you didn't show up to David's party on Sunday. It was apparent Marie was upset, but she wouldn't say much other than you were *out of town working*. When the deputy arrived, honestly, I didn't know what to think. Marie still wouldn't give me much information, so now we were wondering if you were going to be arrested for something or—or, I don't even know what!"

She pauses to calm down and takes a sip of water.

"I called Marie yesterday, and she tried to tell me to call you. I knew you wouldn't tell me anything, so I kept asking. She finally broke down. She told me she was staying at her father's, and you two were separated. She talked about debt and lies and this job you're taking and—Eric, what is going on?"

She folds her hands over her legal pad and stares directly into my eyes.

I'm sure Marie said as little as possible. She knows how much I care about my parents' opinion of me, and even in this hellish mess, she would try to honor that as much as she could.

It's my turn to talk.

My mind immediately starts spinning and weaving a story that borders truth but keeps my reputation with my parents intact while getting their sympathy.

I don't make it far down this path before I feel a tug on my shirt tail. I look down to find the boy.

Why are you doing that? he asks.

Doing what? I respond.

Lying to them.

I look at my parents, waiting patiently for me to respond.

I can't tell them the truth.

Why?

Because then they'll know.

Know what?

The truth.

Of course, not just the truth about this situation. The *real* truth. The truth is their son is a fuckup loser. The truth is that I'm an awful, shameful shithead. The truth—

I ticked these off in my head out of habit, but something is different. Something's off. What is it?

I look back at the boy, and he has a grin.

We're not down there anymore, he says. *Just tell them.*

And so I do.

I leave out the whole bit about the boy and Lori because that isn't their concern. I don't think they're ready for that. I'm having a hard enough time with it. But I laid everything else out on the table.

I'm honest about my mishandling of the money for years. I admit to the lies I've told Marie and the lies I've told them. I tell them about the IRS, the job offer, the trip to DC, stealing the emergency money, getting drunk at the pub, and missing my flight. I even tell them about blackmailing Aneel, which Marie didn't even know about.

I cry a good bit as I tell them, and I apologize at various points, but I get it all out.

It hurts them. I can tell. My dad has to stand up and walk around the kitchen three times as I spill my guts. They don't say much, but a child knows.

"Why didn't you tell us?" My mom was dumbfounded.

"I was afraid you would be ashamed of me—ashamed that I'm your son."

"We could never think that of you," my mom says as my dad winces and then buries the palms of his hands into his temples. I've never seen him so tormented, like it's somehow all his fault.

What can I say to that?

The meeting fizzled out as a disciplinary device. What can you do when someone admits everything and accepts responsibility? I suppose you could heap some more verbal abuse on them, but that isn't my parents' style. It hasn't been in a very long time.

"What will you do about the job?" my dad asks. It's the first time he's spoken.

"What do you mean?"

"Are you still taking it?"

"That's the plan. I have to do something about this debt."

He nods, but I can't tell if it's in agreement. Then he stops himself from not offering any advice and says, "Can I make a suggestion? Why don't we walk through the numbers?"

"Okay," I say. I mean, why not. Right? My dad had run his own business for forever, at least as long I was alive, and he definitely knew how to stretch a dollar. We always had plenty of food on our table, and while I didn't have the most stylish clothes growing up, I always had exactly what I needed.

"What's the salary?"

"180,000 a year." He doesn't blink. He just runs his internal calculator.

"After all of the taxes are taken out, you'll clear about sixty-five percent, which is one hundred seventeen thousand dollars net or nine thousand seven hundred and fifty per month. What's your monthly mortgage on the house?"

"Twenty-nine hundred forty-eight dollars. I got it before the rates increased."

"Nice!" he's impressed. "Okay! So that's six thousand eight hundred and two dollars left. What are the car payments?"

"Fourteen hundred and eighty."

"Ugh. Not so nice. Now you're at five thousand three hundred and twenty-two."

"School payments? Cable? Internet? Telephone? Electricity? Gas for the house? Insurance? Gas for the cars? Food? Clothes? Credit card payments?"

After subtracting those, I had one hundred and seventy-three discretionary dollars a month left, which amounts to dinner for the four of us once every thirty days at Chick-fil-A.

"But, Dad, there's a hundred-thousand-dollar signing bonus!"

"They'll take twenty percent of that off the top for federal taxes, Eric, so it's really only eighty thousand dollars, and then you'll have to pay taxes on that money too, so it will end up as sixty-five thousand when it's all said and done. Rendering unto Caesar what is Caesar's is getting harder and harder that's for sure."

I can see that if anyone on the planet is sympathetic to my plight, it's my father.

"But I owe back taxes of $82,262.58!"

"So even with this new job and the big bonus,

you're right back where you started, maybe even worse, and you'll give up seeing your family because you'll be working eighty-hour weeks and traveling to every swing state in the country." Then my dad did something he had never done before. He told me what he honestly thought about me.

"Son, you're a brilliant person. Smarter than I ever was. And you aren't afraid to work hard, either. It's your decision, and your mother and I will do whatever we can to help you, Marie, David, and Matthew no matter what. But..."

And now I could see his old temper.

"Don't let those sons of bitches steal your life from you!"

My mother gasps at my dad's cursing.

"What about Marie?" she asks.

I sigh and run my hand over my face.

"I don't know."

"You have to get her back."

"Mom, you didn't hear her on the phone yesterday. She's lining up apartments and jobs already. I think it's too late. Besides, what am I asking her to come home to? Our whole life is in shambles because of me."

"Son..." My father is on a roll. "Do not let that woman go without a fight. You'll regret it for the rest of your life."

My phone buzzes. Calvert Struthers showed on the caller ID.

"Excuse me," I say, pushing back from the table. "I've got to take this."

I hustle out the front door onto the porch, answering as I step outside.

"You busy this afternoon?" he asks.

I almost laugh at the question. I feel like I have both nothing and everything to do.

"What you got for me?"

"First of all, Ty told me the good news about the super PAC—congrats, by the way!—and I realized it was time for me to introduce you to my brothers in the Pinnacle League. I called the director of the Nashville chapter, and he'd love to have you join for a meet-and-greet luncheon. It's today at 1:30. If you're busy, you could wait until the next one, but it won't be until next month."

Holy *shit*. It's already happening. This is where Cal met Ty in the first place. The connections I'll get in this club will be unbelievable.

"Yeah, absolutely. I'd love to go."

"Fantastic! I'll let them know to expect you. Make sure you wear a suit and get there a few minutes early so they can introduce you around before it starts. The director's name is Andy. Great guy. Ask for him. I'll text you the address."

"Thanks so much, Cal!"

"Of course! Knock 'em dead!"

I return to the kitchen with a big, stupid grin, which, under the circumstances, confuses my parents.

"Dad," I say, "can I borrow your car? And a suit?"

44

MR. JONES

I slow the ancient Accord as I approached the address. It indicates a brick, neoclassical building with intimidating columns nestled in the leafy, high-end part of town on the eastern edge of Nashville.

A valet stands out front guarding the only available parking.

I can't bring myself to be seen on the property in this ragged, rattling machinery, so I keep it rolling. The twenty-something valet looks up lazily from his phone as I coast by, probably assuming someone in this car in this neighborhood was lost.

Thankfully, I find some street parking two blocks away and hoof it back to the club. I tug and shimmy in my dad's Men's Wearhouse two-for-one special as I approach. At first glance, it fits mostly fine, but the material is wafer-thin and poorly cut. I'll have to be careful making any quick moves, or I'm likely to rip out the seams.

An older man in a red suit and white gloves guards the entrance. I give my name and offer Andy's name in lieu of a membership card. He reluctantly nods and allows me to enter, suggesting I check in at the front desk. A young college-aged woman smiles as I approach and agrees to take me to Andy.

We head down a hallway as she gives a de facto tour, referencing the steam room, multiple bars, smoking room, soundproof rooms for phone calls, conference rooms, and the second of two formal dining rooms. Everything is built out of dark mahogany and inlaid with gold.

More than thirty men chat, laugh, and back-slap in groups of three to five. I definitely bring the average age in the room down by a few years and, from the looks of things, bring the average yearly income down even more significantly.

The greeter takes me to Andy, a man in his mid-forties who looks older because of his full head of prematurely gray hair and a few extra wrinkles around his eyes.

"Outstanding! Outstanding to meet you!" he says, vigorously shaking my hand and nodding at the receptionist to leave. "Calvy said you'd be coming. We're very excited to have you. And Ty's a favorite around here, too, so any friend of his is a friend of ours."

I thank him and follow as he takes me around to introduce me to a few people. I meet a venture capitalist, three guys in various aspects of banking and finance, and one who owns many of the skyscrapers built in Nashville in the last decade.

Everyone is friendly and welcoming, shaking my hand and passing me business cards.

The responses I receive when Andy shares my new role with Congressman Bryant's super PAC are wide-eyed and impressed—except for one, a man whose age aligns with his gray head of hair. He shakes his head in recognition.

"Oof," he says, laughing. "So we won't be seeing you around here again for a couple of years?"

I match his smile but ask, "What do you mean?"

"I've known a couple of guys running these things, and the hours and travel are brutal. It gets worse the more successful you are. If you raise a ton of money, you have to work to spend it. You get plenty of off-time between campaigns, but during them..." He whistles. "It's a young man's game for sure. You don't have kids. Do you?"

I confirm I do, in fact, have two young boys.

"Well," he says, chuckling, "they'll go to great colleges, and you'll have plenty of money to cover the cost of them talking to their therapists about their absent father the rest of their lives."

The man's voice sounds like he's joking, and I do my best to laugh along with him, but something in his tone disturbs me.

Andy leads me away, talking low.

"Ignore Winston. He's a windbag. We would have kicked him out years ago, but..." He shrugged. "He keeps a steady supply of Gurkha Black Dragon cigars for all the members, so we end up letting most of his annoying habits slide. Lunch won't start for a few more minutes. Let me walk you around a bit."

He shows me a few rooms the receptionist had mentioned but goes deeper into the amenities. As a member, I would receive full access to the facilities. They include all of the events, such as this luncheon, along with access to club facilities in most major cities, which included DC, where, he assumes, I'll be spending a lot of time shortly. All drinks are on the house and scheduled events admissions too. The dining room is open to my guests and me. Breakfast, lunch, and dinner are served every day with both a buffet and formal seating. And if you've had occasion to have a tipple too much of single malt, the upstairs bedrooms are available to sleep off the effects. The rooms are also bookable for out-of-town guests, so you won't have them lurking around your house.

Around the lunch table, discussions range from various investments the members are making and tax shelters getting set up to comments on how the next election will affect their businesses.

If I have to rank the top five aggregate priorities of the men in the room, it would go something like money, cigars, tax shelters, financial status, and, finally, "capital," whatever that was.

I sit quietly, taking it all in and having nothing to add to most conversations. Besides a few blatant arrogant assholes, everyone seems nice enough.

Andy stands as the meal winds down, and we approached the end of our hour together. He thanks everyone for coming, makes a few short announcements about upcoming events, and then acknowledges the presence of a potential new member.

"Eric, why don't you introduce yourself?"

I quickly wipe my mouth and take a swig of water before standing.

"Hello, my name is Eric Bauer. I recently accepted the chief operations position with a super PAC for Congressman Ricky Bryant."

As I give a short spiel about my role and duties, I look around the room at the men I will be expected to spend time with as a member. I can see the loads of opportunities membership will provide. Salaries and money aren't the core of what these men focus on. They prefer leverage, tactics, and strategies to manage, grow, and protect their wealth along with all the privileges, status, and power that comes with it. It feels almost like a religious conviction each had taken up at birth or when they'd been recruited or invited into the club.

At this moment, I think about Aneel. He isn't a member of a group like this. Instead, he invites poor assholes like me to lunch. Or used to. Am I really going to replace him with these guys? Are any of them capable of actually caring about me? Aneel isn't perfect. Who is? He likes to play the role of the guy who accidentally wins every game he plays without having to try all that hard, but he's certainly more interesting to talk to than these guys.

My speech peters out as my eyes survey the room again. I realize I will be spending a lot of time in rooms like this with people like this, raising money for my candidate. These guys are actually the perfect target market.

I become aware of the boy at that moment. He doesn't like the room's vibe or the entire mansion. It's too stiff and doesn't have a game room to play foosball, either, just some big snooker table that obviously no one uses. I can feel his anxiety growing. When I mentally check on him about the source of his stress, I can tell he's looking around the room at all the men, except he sees *their* little ones.

I'm unsure where they all are, and I doubt I want to know, but I know they didn't spend much time in the grass and sunlight, climbing trees or playing soccer.

"Eric?" Andy whispers. He has a confused and embarrassed look on his face. "Are you okay?"

"Yeah, sorry," I sputter and then pause again. "I appreciate all of you having me today, but this isn't the place for me. I've… uh…" I check on my boy again, and he's already edging toward the door. "I've gotta go. Have a great rest of your day!"

I slide out from my space at the table, turn my back on the silent room, and hurry out of the dining room. I'm jogging by the time I pass the front desk and startle the white-gloved man as I shove through the large mahogany front door into the sunlight.

45

I'VE SEEN ALL GOOD PEOPLE

By the time I hit the sidewalk, the phone is to my ear, and the number I dialed is already ringing.

When Ty answers, I have to suppress the joy in my voice and replace it with a very serious tone.

"Hey, Ty, I'm really sorry to do this, but I've decided... Ty, I can't take the job."

Silence. The longest silence Ty has ever let hang, probably in his entire adult life.

"What are you playing at?"

"I know this is probably coming as a shock to you, but—"

"Eric, stop it. Stop fucking with me."

"I'm not fucking with you, Ty. I'm serious."

"What happened?"

"I just... It's hard to explain. Nothing really *happened* other than I realized there's no way I can do the job.

I've got my family to think about and my employees and my business and—"

"You mean that failing piece of shit business you told me about? The one I am saving you from? That's what you're going back to?"

I don't answer right away, so he keeps going.

"And what about the IRS debt? What are you going to do about that?"

"I don't know yet."

"You are such a fucking idiot. You know that? Opportunities like this don't simply come along. You're never going to get a chance like this again. You turn this down, and I guarantee you'll never get a seat at any powerful table. Hell, I'll make it my life's mission to bury you under so much propaganda that nobody I know or who knows anyone I know or knows anyone that knows them will ever want to work with you on anything ever again."

"I understand. I do. I know this must be frustrating."

"Frustrating doesn't begin to cover it. I stuck my neck out for you, shithead. I could have brought anyone in to do this job, and I plucked you out of obscurity because I thought you were ready to be something other than a small-time fucking loser."

At that moment, I feel the weirdest sensation—nothing.

If someone had said that to me at any other time in my adult life, especially someone like Ty, I would have melted through the floor. It would have pierced my soul. I would have immediately caved to whatever I needed to do to convince the other person and myself that it wasn't true.

But instead, at this moment, I almost laugh. I can't believe it. It feels like all the social bullets I've been worrying about my whole life have been spent from a gun, and the more-powerful-than-me assassin is pulling on an empty chamber.

Ty keeps talking, vacillating between threatening, cajoling, and belittling. He tells me Cal suggested me because I was so desperate to get out of my business I would do whatever was asked of me. He says if I'm stupid enough to turn down the job, any sane woman like Marie should definitely leave me. My kids will be better off if she does. Maybe she can find them a real man to be their father. And on he goes.

I make it back to my dad's car but stay out on the sidewalk, pacing as he drones on. Finally, when he stops to take a breath, I jump in.

"Look, Ty, I really appreciate you bringing me in for this. I do. I know I'm leaving you in a tight spot, and I'll do whatever I can to help you recover from it. But we both know the right man for this job is Aneel. He killed it in the meeting and will do a great job—better than we can."

"Oh fuck that. *Fuck* that. You think I'll let that towel-head son of a bitch get the job instead of me. No way. No fucking way. I won't just tell the board about his involvement in misappropriation. I'll get it printed in the *Washington-fucking-Post.*"

"You know that story is bullshit. He didn't do anything wrong, and he was cleared of any legal responsibility. He even returned the money that was wrongfully paid to him."

"You think I fucking care? If you don't take this job, Eric, I will not just burn you. I'm going to burn everyone you've ever known."

My anxiety comes crashing back. What have I done? How have I told Aneel's secret to anyone, let alone this asshole? For the first time, I falter. Maybe I should take the job after all, even if it's just to protect Aneel. I've already stabbed him in the back, but at least it hasn't hurt him beyond this one job. Something like that being published in the *Post* would be in the top results for any search for Aneel or his company for the next decade. Taking the job to stop that from happening would be worth it.

Or, even better, maybe I can find someone to take my place. Ty keeps saying he could have had his pick of guys. I'll help him find that guy and hand the reins off to him. I can give him my presentation, all the notes and plans I've made, along with all of the—

Ah! One of those lightbulb-above-the-head moments strike me.

Relief spreads from my head down to my toes like a warm bath. I hurriedly unlock the Accord and climb in, wrenching the door closed beside me for some privacy.

Bethany and her systems! Thank God I wasn't going to lose her.

"I don't, uh, I don't think you want to do that, Ty."

"Yeah? Why's that?" Ty snapped.

"You see, I record all of my phone calls. I usually use it to listen with more intent, take better notes, and remind myself of things I forget. But in this case, I have all the conversations you and I had about circumventing the federal campaign finance laws around this super PAC. I have the call with you and John, where we were clearly coordinating the campaign ahead of time. I have the calls from John, in which he gave me information clearly breaking the rules. I have the directions you gave me about coordinating with John after we were running the super PAC. I have all of it. Saved and backed up to the cloud and stored in offsite hard drives. Plus, I have the burner phone, too.

"I even have this very call where you are threatening and blackmailing me, planning to knowingly print lies to hurt someone else's reputation, which, I believe, is the textbook definition of libel. Which means you can be personally sued, and any reputable news outlet would never publish it.

"You might be thinking at this point that I would be just as liable if this all came out and that you could get me on illegally taping the calls, which is probably true, but you see, I don't have much to live for now. Whoever wants a piece of my sorry ass will have to line up behind the IRS and my wife… The question is: Who would want to take down Ricky the Dicky? Is it gonna be you?"

I clear my throat, letting some space hang to see if Ty will respond immediately. When he doesn't, I continue.

"Under the circumstances, the best thing for us to do is bow out of the job. When we get off the call, I'd like you to call the board and recommend they hire Aneel. I'll text him to make sure he knows it's safe to accept."

I wait for Ty to respond. I check my phone twice to make sure the call hasn't been disconnected.

"Ty?"

"What?"

"I need to know whether I should pull all my recordings together. Or are you going to take care of it. I'm going to need a verbal response here, buddy."

Another long silence.

"I'll take care of it," he says and hangs up.

I immediately text Aneel.

Hey Aneel, you're going to get a call from the super PAC offering you the job again. Please accept it. I've taken care of my end of things.

The bubbles pop up immediately and then go away. I wait a couple more minutes, but he never responds.

I get it.

What could he say? Thanks?

I lean back against the tattered cloth seat and take my first deep breath since that letter arrived from the IRS a week ago. I have no idea what will happen to me next, but I feel relaxed for the first time in as long as I can remember.

46

STRANGER IN A STRANGE LAND

It's time to go home.

A big part of me wants to avoid it. I could sleep at my parents' house, work from the office, and put off the inevitable revisiting of what had become a dark and lonely place.

But the boy following me around everywhere is having strange effects. If someone looks at my life logically, it's clear everything has gone horribly wrong. Nothing has actually changed in the last twenty-four hours. In truth, now that I have turned down the super PAC job and can't dig myself out of my financial cesspool, I'm in worse shape than ever.

Yet now I'm calm about it. I feel like the unending white noise of voices in my head has been, if not shut off, at least tempered to a quiet hum.

I pull into the driveway, park beside my booted Tesla, and head inside.

The disheveled relics of David's birthday party, which I'd failed to attend, are just as I left them. I cry fresh tears when I notice the remnants of the nondescript cake Marie must have hurriedly procured at the last minute. David hadn't had his father's attention, a well-considered present, or even a cake with his name on it for his birthday party.

Those are just facts.

I let the tears flow—this time, they're for David and not for me—as I pull out trash bags from under the counter and start gathering the trash: paper plates, Solo cups, and plasticware. Then I pull down the streamers and move the dishes that need washing to the sink. I toss out the leftover food.

I carefully wash the dishes, wipe down the counter, and sweep the floor, doing my best to get the kitchen in pristine order.

My cleaning then extends throughout the house. I straighten up the living room and pound the dust out of the decorative couch pillows before vacuuming. I run a couple of loads of laundry, make the boys' beds, and clean up the toys in their rooms, methodically putting the whole house back into the order Marie painstakingly kept.

Finally, I tie up the trash bags and head to the front door.

I stop short at the deputy's car sitting in the driveway. He stands beside my father's car, staring at it curiously. I drop the trash and back away from the door, ready to duck and crawl away if and when he heads toward the house.

Then I pause. I can sense the boy's misgivings with this response. I remember our conversation when I talked to my parents. It wasn't just about telling the truth, I remember. It was time to live it, too.

I retrieve the trash bags and open the front door, stepping out onto the stoop. The deputy turns at the sound.

I wave to him, open the trash can, and drop the bags inside.

"Hello, deputy, I'm guessing you're looking for me."

"Bauer, Eric?"

"I am." I reach out my hand. He takes it in his, returning a firm shake.

"You're a hard man to locate," he says sternly.

"Yeah, I'm sorry about that. I hear you've got a summons for me."

"I do."

"From the IRS, I'm assuming? Agent Alex Mason?"

"That's the one. Unfortunately, you've missed the summons date again and are on the verge of a warrant being issued for your arrest. I think we can get around that, but you'll need to come with me right now to the IRS office to check in with them."

"That works for me. Let me grab my coat." I'd removed the suit jacket as I cleaned. "I might as well look my best when I meet the executioner."

"You're not going to run off again. Are you?" He smiles a little, just a little.

"No sir, I'm done with that." He could tell I'm not bullshitting him.

I put on the jacket and check the mirror on the way out, straightening my tie and running my hands through my hair.

"Do I need to come with you, or can I drive?"

"Why don't you drive, and I'll just follow along? I have to make sure you actually show up to release the summons."

"What about uh—" I motion to the bright yellow boot on my Tesla.

"I'll come straight back here after you've checked in and pull that off. How's that sound?"

"Perfect. Thank you, deputy. Again, I'm sorry for the runaround I've given you over the last few days."

"I've dealt with worse."

I maneuver my dad's car downtown while the patrol car follows along. I find street parking, and he makes up his own parking spot right in front of the building. He escorts me all the way inside through the double doors of the IRS office. Then he watches as I check in with the receptionist who was guarding the giant room of gray cubicles.

I give him a thumbs-up as the receptionist calls back to Agent Mason, and the deputy waves and tips his hat to me before leaving.

A sudden urge to run off and skip the meeting wells

up inside of me—not from the fear of it but simply to play a joke on the kind deputy. Maybe sprint by him so we could have a good chase?

I realize this is the boy whispering his thoughts into my head. I close my eyes to check in with him and find a mischievous grin. I can tell he's mostly joking.

"Mr. Bauer!" a friendly voice.

"Hi, Ashley," I reply, turning toward the young man to shake his hand. "I'm sorry about missing my appointment last week."

"You'll need to contend with Agent Mason over that," he says. "Follow me."

We wind our way through the rows of cubicles, heading to one of the segregated offices in the back. To provide a reasonable degree of privacy, the floor-to-ceiling windows were frosted two-thirds of the way to the ceiling.

As we approach, I peered through the glass, trying to get a look at my federally-sanctioned hangman.

The first thing I see is a pencil sticking out of a messy brown hair bun. I must make a noise when I see it because Ashley shoots me a questioning look as he pushes open the door and holds it for me.

She pops up from her chair and comes around to shake my hand.

"Mr. Bauer! The man of the hour! You put my people through some work to get you in here."

I sit in the plush blue chair as Ashley backs out of the doorway and leaves us alone.

"Let's see here." She shuffles through several thick file folders on her desk until she comes across mine. She flips it open and ruffles through the papers until they're organized and ready. She retrieves the pencil from her hair and jots down a couple of notes.

"You've dug quite the hole for yourself here, Mr. Bauer."

"Yes, ma'am, I realize that, and look, I don't know what happens here, but I don't have the eighty-three thousand dollars I owe. I don't have any of it, really. I don't know what that will mean. Am I going to jail? Are you taking my house? My cars? Will you start garnishing my bank account?"

She holds up her hand to stop me.

"Slow down, Mr. Bauer. Slow down. Yes, eventually, all of those things can happen and would if you didn't come in to see me. But you're here now, and we can start working to fix it. We have to go over a lot of stuff today. I'll need you to pull together your records, and we'll need to get your tax returns up to date, but..." She pauses and glances around like someone might be listening and then leans across her desk. "Can I tell you two secrets about the IRS that almost nobody knows?"

I nod, leaning in, my mouth too dry to talk.

"First, we like to scare you with big numbers to get you to take us seriously. My guess is that once we actually get your taxes sorted, you won't owe anywhere near that much money. And two—this is the big one—we're happy if you're paying us *anything*. So many people simply don't pay that if you're sending us a little bit of money each month, we'll pretty much leave you alone."

She sits back, resuming her normal volume.

"Now, of course, you still have to deal with some interest and penalties, but you can usually get some of those waived if you're consistent with a payment plan. Okay..." She reshuffles some of the papers. "Let's get started."

For the next hour, she asks me questions about my business, personal income, and expenses. I spend a good amount of time on my phone looking up the answers from my bank account and other records as best as possible. Still, I mostly gave her estimates based on what I can remember.

After we get through all of her questions, she spends several minutes tapping away at her computer.

"Okay, Mr. Bauer, I'll still need your records to confirm what you're telling me. You'll need to work with your accountant to get your taxes revised and refiled, but I estimate you'll end up owing just under fifty thousand."

Of course, I felt some relief at having over thirty grand knocked off the bill, but that was still far more than I could hope to pay anytime soon.

"Now, the big question," she says. "How much do you think you can pay each month?"

She looks me in the eye, her pencil hovering above a small notepad.

"You're asking *me*? I thought you would give me the number."

"We want to work something out that you can actually stick to. It doesn't serve us to put you in a position where you literally can't pay. So what's the number?"

I think through my finances. I honestly have no idea. How much does a divorce cost? I'm sure I'd be paying alimony and child support on top of my own living expenses.

I also know I'll work to cut my expenses and put all I can into making my business more profitable.

"A thousand?"

"A month?"

"Yes, ma'am."

"Are you sure you can swing that?"

"Pretty sure."

"Okay, why don't we do this? Let's make it six hundred for now. If you're doing well and keeping up and want to pick up the pace to avoid some of that interest and penalties, we can address that in six months. How does that sound?"

I nod again, a lump forming in my throat. At this moment, I realize this poor woman I avoided and jerked around actually cares about me. From her side of the table, she could have easily labeled me a deadbeat tax evader and gone out of her way to make my life a worse version of the hell I was already living in. She had the backing of the federal government, for God's sake. I could have done nothing about it.

Instead, she's going out of her way to be kind to me and put me in a better situation than when I walked into her office.

I can't stop. The tears come. A man is permitted to cry on occasion in front of his wife and his mother, but not in front of anyone else, especially an IRS agent. And now I'm a blubbering mess.

The look of compassion on her face only makes me cry harder.

"What's wrong, Mr. Bauer?"

"Why are you being so nice to me?" I stutter out. "I've been such a shithead."

She shrugs. "You're not a shithead. You've been through a rough patch, fell in a hole, is all. And everybody needs to be thrown a rope every now and again to pull themselves out," she says, scooting the box of tissues on her desk closer to me.

I thank her profusely over the next few minutes as we wrapped up the meeting, and she gives me details on what will happen next. She stands, indicating it's time for me to leave, and I join her on my feet.

47

FADE INTO YOU

As promised, my Tesla is boot-free and drivable again when I return home. For the next two hours, I detail the car thoroughly, vacuuming, buffing, and beautifying it. I wash and wax it, getting it as close to brand new as possible.

I receive two offers within a few minutes of posting it for sale online. I let them stack up for the next twenty-four hours and then agree to a sale. The second highest offer is from a wife buying it for her husband's fortieth birthday. I can't say no to that.

After paying off what I owe, I have just over ten thousand in walking around money. I use it to pay the most pressing of the outstanding bills, the mortgage, the Navigator payment, and back utilities. I still have more than seven thousand in cash left.

My dad charged me $2,559.95 for his Accord. The

bluebook value was $2,500 but he'd just been to Jiffy Lube, which is where he was when I called him.

I deposit the rest in Marie's and my joint bank account and text her to let her know cash was available for anything she needs.

I don't receive a response.

Those first two days after meeting with the IRS, I spend all my spare time at my office, getting my business and finances back in working order as best I can. I call the credit card companies and start the process of transferring the debt to new cards with six months of no interest so I can start making up some ground.

I have conversations with Andre and Bethany, apologizing for my absence and general assholery. Then I review and work on all the open projects, getting them caught up or wrapped up wherever possible.

With Marie and the boys gone, I decide to work fourteen-plus-hour days to make as much progress as possible. I work the phones and emails, doing my best to generate fresh contracts. Nothing comes in immediately, so it's time to pound the pavement and drum up new business.

Toward the end of the second day, the building manager, Randy, shows up to fix the holes I put in the walls. I apologize profusely and offer to cover the additional cost, but he waves me off.

"You're the easiest tenant, Eric. Don't worry about

it. This will cost maybe fifty bucks to fix. Can I ask, though? What happened?"

"Bob didn't tell you?"

"Bob?"

"Yeah, actually, I haven't seen him around. I need to thank him for his help the other day. Maybe he's out of town?"

"Who is Bob?"

I cock my head. If anyone would know Bob and his deal, the building manager would.

"Bob…" I don't actually know his last name. "He's always hanging around here, coffee mug in hand. He's a tall guy with glasses, a bald spot, and a mustache."

Randy shakes his head.

"I know everyone in the building, and there's no Bob here or anyone who looks like that."

I stare at Randy. He gives no indication that he's joking. In fact, he shrugs and goes back to work, apparently forgetting his original question.

I push back from my desk and enter Andre and Bethany's office. I ask them both about Bob, and they respond the same way as Randy. I walk the hallways but don't find Bob. Then I check my phone log from Saturday when he called me about the sheriff showing up at the office. I dial the number and immediately receive an automatic recording that the number is disconnected and no longer in use.

Bob is—gone? Never existed? A figment of my imagination?

The picture of him standing in Lori's doorway like a fucking superhero will be forever burned in my memory. Odd.

What do you do in a situation like this? The only thing I can think of is to send a prayer of thanks out into the ether and hope it finds its way to him. It's no use driving myself crazy. I've already done that.

Randy has left my office, probably to get supplies. A phone starts ringing but not the one in my pocket. I dig through my dive bag to find the burner phone.

I hesitate but answer anyway.

"Ty told me what you did," John says with zero preamble.

John's voice is too deadpan for me to know how he feels about the subject.

"Yeah?"

"That was impressive," he says. "Judging by his reaction, nobody has ever turned the tables on him like that before. And using the recorded calls to blackmail him? You get a chef's kiss and a thumbs-up from me for that one."

"If I'm honest," I say. "I'm kinda proud of that one."

"You should be. You made the right call, kid. You do not want any part of this soulless quicksand."

"You getting out too?"

This is the first and only time I hear John laugh.

"I lost my soul ages ago."

It strikes me that John is not one for small talk, and

I doubt mightily he'd make a call just to congratulate me.

"Why're you calling John?"

"Those recordings you have—"

"Yeah?"

"You are going to keep those to yourself. I like you, Eric, but if those get out, just remember I'm a soulless man with many dark and soulless friends."

I gulp. "Understood."

"And get rid of this fucking phone."

He hangs up.

Later that night, I spend a half hour gathering all the recordings on my laptop and putting them under the heaviest encryption I can find. I then beat the shit out of the phone with a hammer and drop the remains in three different trash cans around town.

48

BUT THE WORLD GOES 'ROUND

After three nights of peaceful, empowering sleep, I realize the nightmares have relented. No dungeons. No monsters. No caves.

I lie in bed, awake again at 4:38 a.m., staring at the ceiling and thinking through the three big things on the to-do list for the day when I come up with a new code for 4:38. It doesn't mean "Fuck you, shithead," anymore. Now, it means "Love for yourself." A little cheesy, yes, but easy to remember.

A mix of emotions swirl through me—excitement, dread, hope, sorrow, love.

I spend the first several hours of the day on my laptop, returning to my prework routine but without the desperation. It's more like experimenting to see what will result rather than doubling down on super-important, make-or-break, all-or-nothing tactics like my previous work. I already have a couple of responses to my outreach and a few past clients who are interested in having my company do more work for them.

With my inbox cleared and tasks appropriately delegated, I get ready and leave the house at 7:45 a.m. so I can arrive at Whole Foods just a few minutes after 8:00 a.m.

I see Aneel sitting at the counter and slow to a stop. The guilt and sadness are on the surface of my consciousness, not buried and avoidable, but I push forward. He sees me coming from a few dozen feet away and pauses with his burrito halfway to his mouth.

He sets it down, wipes his hands on the brown napkins, and turns toward me as I approach.

"Catching me in public so I can't physically attack you?"

"Maybe," I say. "May I sit?"

He doesn't indicate a negative, so I take the seat.

"I'm not here to apologize."

Aneel's eyes harden.

"I know no version of 'I'm sorry' can cover what an awful person I've been. When someone goes as low as I went with you…" I clear my throat. "I'm actually here to thank you. You've been a good friend to me for so long. Constantly seeking me out and encouraging me. Offering to help and talking me through rough spots. I was always so caught up in myself that I couldn't see how you just wanted to be my friend."

"Not anymore, dude."

"I get it. I've been an asshole to you all along, so stuck on my own shame and inadequacy that I couldn't accept someone offering me true friendship. I think I feel the worst about that. So I guess I *am* here to apologize, not only for the fucked up stunt I pulled on you to get the super PAC job but for all the ways I've treated you since college. I know there's no way to come back from what I did, but I didn't want to let it go without saying something."

Silence.

"I was a very lucky man to have you as a friend. I wish I had realized that before I ruined it."

Aneel doesn't speak. He just looks through me like I'm not there.

I nod and slip off the stool to head back to the car. As I turn my back, Aneel finally speaks.

"So, what'd you do to get me the job?"

I look back.

"What do you mean?"

"From what I hear of Ty, he's not one to let something like this go easily. If he knew what happened to me, why didn't he use it?"

I shrug. "Does it matter?"

"Let's pretend it does."

"You don't have to worry. He won't say anything. I made sure of it."

Aneel holds my gaze. He won't let it go, so I spill it. I owe that to him.

"That's pretty slick, Eric. I would say I didn't think

you had it in you, but I now know that's not the case. Come on, sit down, have a burrito with me."

"Yeah?" I ask, the hopefulness thick in my voice.

"The way I see it, two blackmails make a right. We're good." He calls out to the kid behind the counter, "Atticus, get my friend here another one of your world-famous breakfast burritos."

The young hipster nods his fedora-clad head and turns back to the grill.

Over the next hour, I download the whole truth of the state of my business, finances, and marriage to Aneel. He listens with the proper amount of empathy and doesn't jump in with advice and directives. I can tell he's rocked the most by the current state of my marriage.

"You think it's over-over?" he asks.

I shake my head and shrug. I don't know yet.

It's getting close to ten, and I have another errand to run. So we hug it out and leave.

The Nashville Humane Society is half a mile from the house, so I head home. Last night I browsed their list of available dogs and want to be there at 10:00 a.m. when they open. Freddie, the little gray terrier mix puppy, is just three months old and is *very* happy to meet me.

An hour later, after my application is approved and I've paid the one-hundred-and-fifteen-dollar fee, I carry him out to the car. He rides in my lap down the street to the pet store. I give the young woman with the blue work vest and purple hair a two-hundred-dollar budget and leave with everything a new dog owner needs a half hour later. Freddie leaves with a half-dozen new friends.

Back home, I feed and water him. I clip the customized dog tag to his collar and slip it on him, receiving several licks for my effort. I can't believe I've waited so long to listen to David. Every time I look at this little guy's face, I understand how wonderful the world is.

A few minutes later, I pack Freddie's supplies back in the car, slip him into his new kennel in the back seat—according to the purple-haired girl, this is a much safer way for him to travel—and pull out of the driveway.

Two hours later, I arrive at my father-in-law's long driveway and park in front of the immaculately landscaped brick ranch. Before I can shut off the car, Marie's father emerges from the garage. He's thick and strong. Forty-something years earlier, he'd been an all-state football linebacker and still carries himself with the same swagger. His face is set in something just south of boiling rage.

"I believe my daughter told you to stay away, so you need to get back in that piece of shit you're driving and get the hell out of here."

I exit the car, my hands up as if surrendering, but hold my ground.

"It's been five days," I say. "I want to see my kids and talk to Marie."

"Neither of those things are going to happen. You hear me? I don't care if I have to stuff you in the trunk and drive you back to your bullshit palace myself, but you're not coming in here."

Before I can respond, two small voices ring out from the garage.

"Daddy!"

I look behind Marie's dad, and he whips around to see David and Matthew pounding the pavement in my direction.

I hustle around the front of the car and kneel down to meet them. They dive into my arms, knocking me onto my back on the pavement. I laugh, hugging them tightly. Tears stream out of my eyes as I wrestle them while Marie's father glares down at me.

After a bit, we all struggle back to our feet. They're jibber-jabbering at me about their week, and I nod at the giant run-on monologues.

Once they slow, I turn to David and speak to him man to man.

"David, I'm really sorry I missed your party Sunday. I have no excuse other than I put myself ahead of you and what you needed from me." I start to cry, and for the first time, I don't pretend I'm not in pain. He puts his arm on my shoulder and steadies my resolve. "And I want to thank you, too, for having the courage all these years to fight for a crucial addition to the family."

I open the back door and pull out the kennel.

David and Matthew squeal at the sight of Freddie. I opened the little door, and the gray fur ball bounds out and jumps on the boys. They laugh and roll around with him as he licks and skitters and barks.

"You think this is going to fix anything?" Marie's dad speaks again.

I don't answer. I just keep my eyes on the boys.

"She's not here," he says gruffly.

I turn back to him.

"Where is she? I need to talk to her."

"She went out for a run!" David yells out.

Her father's face hardens, and I move around to the driver's side door.

"Hey, boys, you think you can watch little Freddie while I talk to mommy?"

They scream their delighted agreement, and I slowly back out of the driveway. When I turn back, I see Freddie relieving himself on Marie's father's pristine hedgerow. I can't help but smile.

Marie's dad lives in a large, winding neighborhood that has been expanded over the decades. It's easy to get lost in all the twists, turns, and dead ends. The longer I search, the more desperate I become to find her.

I want to see her. Look at her. Feel her presence. I kept reminding myself that all of this is probably over. She may no longer be mine. It may very well be too late.

If that's the case, I know I will be okay. I'll pick up the pieces and live my life. I can still be a good dad and work to provide for my family.

But I also want Marie in my life. The idea that I may lose her now, when I finally had somewhat of a grip on myself, threatens to overwhelm me.

I coast by a short cul-de-sac road and slammed on the brakes. I strain to see over my shoulder, and, sure enough, her blonde head pokes above the rise in the street as she jogs my way.

When she sees me, she skids to a halt and even backs up a few steps. She's breathing hard, her hair in a ponytail, and her pink tank top darkened with sweat.

She's more beautiful than I remembered.

I slow to a walk and stop a couple dozen feet from her. She stares at me, waiting, her arms crossed and her head tilted to the right.

This is the part I haven't planned. I don't have a prepared speech, no grand argument for why she should take me back. I'm not thinking so much as feeling that she will somehow be able to tell what had happened to me.

"Well, here I am…"

"I see that."

I check with my inner boy, desperate for help on what to do next. He stares at Marie's knees and is as dumbstruck as I am.

At last, he says, *She's so scared. Can you see how frightened she is?*

I look back at Marie and see what my boy was looking at. A little pig-tailed blonde-haired girl who couldn't be more than four years old is tucked behind Marie's leg, clinging to it and peering out at me from behind it. She's shaking.

Sorrow and bracing understanding sweep over me. All the promises I haven't kept, all the times I've lied and told half-truths, all the times I've blamed Marie for my own fears, shame, and shortcomings—all of that has been felt by her little one.

When we first got together, Marie opened herself up to me. She let me see her hopes and dreams, and I convinced her it would be safe to do so. She trusted me with her little one, and then I wrecked through all of it.

I think through all the hurtful things she's said to me, all the times she attacked me verbally and even physically in the shower a few days before. All that anger wasn't just anger. I have always seen Marie as this strong woman, and she is, but hers is a protective strength. It's courage in the face of threats. The roots run deep through the anger and are anchored in fear. She's fragile—not like a flower, like a bomb.

I know she loves me, but she's scared of me too. For good reason.

"You have every right to be scared of me. I've hurt you so much. I can see that now. And I'm so sorry."

I take a step toward her.

"I can't make everything right. There's no way to gloss over everything I've done. And I can't make big, bold promises about the future because I've done that too many times and let you down."

A few more steps. She's just ten feet away now, holding her ground but not backing up. Her little one had poked her head out further from behind the leg and stopped shivering.

"All I can say is I see how hard it is for you now. I'm very sorry to admit that it's for the first time. And I want to let you see me."

I close the rest of the distance and wrap my arms around her. She relaxes her crossed arms but keeps them down by her side, not resisting the embrace but not joining me in it either.

We stand there like that for several minutes. Marie sniffles against my shoulder.

"Please come home," I whisper.

"Okay," she whispers back.

49

WONDERWALL

Freddie bounds down the trail in front of us. He'd doubled in size since I'd picked him up from the pound, but he still weighs under twenty pounds. David clutches his leash, making sure he doesn't run off, and Matthew trails behind them, swinging a giant stick wildly around his head.

Marie and I walk slowly and quietly, bringing up the rear, her arms crossed against the autumn cold and my hands deep in my coat pockets.

The leaves are in a transformational state of wildly colorful in their dissipation but still conservatively clinging to the branches. The sky is clear, and it will be one of those perfect days that starts out cold and ends warm.

It's been seven months since Marie came home with the boys.

I've had a semi-profitable streak in my business

since I recommitted to it. A large part is the fifty to sixty hours I pull weekly to ensure I'm prospecting for new business as much as completing active business. I had to cover the back and current taxes I had previously skipped paying. So, just putting in the hours had an impact. But I also have a renewed vigor for the work.

The old underlying bitterness for my lowly place in the status-obsessed world isn't entirely gone. Still, when it creeps back in and starts to take over, with the boy's help, I can put it back where it belongs, in the backseat of my consciousness. I feel a calm contentment with my work that I've never experienced before.

I'm by no means a big shot, but the one-on-one relationships I'm building with very dedicated searchers for meaning—be they searching for the perfect tomato cultivation or the perfect murder mystery—enthrall me like they never did before. In other words, I've discovered I can be a good friend to someone else instead of demanding they be one to me.

Aneel has offered me a couple of gigs on the campaign, but I've decided to steer clear for everyone's sanity. We're back to our every-other-week breakfast burritos, and my willingness to ask for and accept his advice has impacted the business, too. His desire to move on from my assholery is truly spectacular. I think he figured out that he had independence, and the leeway to make mistakes without worrying about dependents was a choice he'd made more than an "unlucky break." The grass is different on the other side of the fence. It isn't magical and better.

I even called my sister. When I apologized to her for stealing that money so many years ago, she didn't even remember.

I also acknowledged I hadn't been a great brother over the years. I knew it was hard for her to have me come along and get so much attention. She owned her part, too, and something like a friendship instead of a competition took root between us.

The boys are great. As far as they know, at least this is what I've told myself, Marie's dad's house visit was merely a fun family spur-of-the-moment check-in with Grandpa, during which mommy happened to cry a lot. Matthew has been blissfully unaware, but a few weeks after returning, David asked Marie why Daddy wasn't mad anymore.

Trust me, I still get plenty mad. But I now know what anger is, sorrow, sadness about plans not working out as anticipated, and that generating more grief and misery by dumping it on the people I care about most and who cared about me is no way to dissipate it. Burying the old plan and developing a new one is a much better course.

The "you're not good enough, and you'll never amount to anything" noise has stayed in the background for the most part. My mind has recalibrated into a quiet hum that only existed in the innocence of my boyhood. So spending more time in that arena with my inner boy resulted in the nightmares being fewer and farther between, too.

The boy is available to me now. He isn't locked up in some psychic basement. He isn't always content, but because he knows he has a seat at the table and a fair vote in any decision I make, he can sacrifice when called upon. He constantly picks up on things I'm missing and is an indispensable inner resource.

The trail widens as we walk through the woods, and Marie sidles up next to me. She loops her arm through my elbow so we can walk arm-in-arm.

The first month was hard on her. She'd had to emotionally steel herself to have the courage to leave me in the first place, so bringing the wall back down felt dangerous to her. What if nothing had changed? What if I slipped right back to the way I used to be? She constantly side-eyed me and questioned my motives.

That was more than fair, and as I'm now playing the long game, it doesn't bother me as much as it used to. I understand, so I don't store resentment, bottle it up, and do something stupid with the justification that "I don't have to tell her everything!" That's not to say I don't express frustration every now and then, but it isn't much, and it doesn't linger like it used to.

Any slight indication that I'm slipping back to my old ways sparks a quick, hot anger in her. Then I get sucked into the anger, frustrated that everything I'm doing isn't enough. Each time, though, the fights burn off quicker than before.

Mostly, I focus on giving her the affordances she needs to work through it, which honestly aren't all that unreasonable or difficult to do.

I'm grateful she came home. A lot of people wouldn't have.

Somewhere in the second month, she started laughing again. By the third month, we returned to the good parts of our old, easy rhythm. At that point, we had our first real talk. We laid everything on the table from both sides. I did some more apologizing, and so did she. We both had a lot of growing to do. Now we don't have to white knuckle alone.

And now, walking through the woods as a family, it's been a couple of months since we've had anything worse than a mild disagreement. We're content and building deeper connections and meaningful mutual understanding.

I still fuck up from time to time, of course. Everyone can be a shithead every now and then. But it's incredible how quickly and easily you can apologize and move on when you're not trying to fight against the underlying belief that you are a worthless shithead as opposed to a worthy one.

Now I know my worthiness. And that has made all the difference.

50

TO BEAT THE DEVIL

"Oh, my ride's here," I say.

Faye blinks, her eyes refocusing back into reality.

"Can I walk you out?"

She nods, gathers up her glasses and phone, and presses them into her palm.

"Eric," she says, stopping short. "I… What do I do now? Why did you tell me all of that?"

"I don't know what will happen with you, David, and the girls. I don't know enough of the details to have a strong opinion about what you should do. But I…" I cleared my throat. "I wasn't as good of a dad to him as I should have been, and I can see him doing some of the things I used to do…"

She stops me. "I understand."

I walk her to the doorway and hold it open for her. She dons her sunglasses as she steps out into the brightness.

A red Prius is parked out front, and Marie lowers the window as we approach.

“Hi, Fee,” she says. “Get in the car, Eric! Chop chop, we’ve got shit to do!”

I slide into the passenger seat and buckle up.

ACKNOWLEDGMENTS

Writing this book has been a long, arduous journey—one I thankfully did not have to travel alone.

To Shawn Coyne, my editor, business partner, and friend: I wouldn't have had the ability or courage to write a book like this without him. He signed on to help an amateur writer nine years ago and stuck with me through many trials and tribulations. I can't thank him enough for helping me achieve this dream I've had since I was a child.

To Candace, my wife of twenty-two years, who never wavered in her belief in me or her courage to let me tell this story. She is the one who insisted I tell the Truth above all else.

To my boys, Conner and Max, who are the reason I did the work and my foundation for believing in the goodness of humanity.

To my mom and dad, who have always chosen unconditional love for their boys above all else.

To Kary, my therapist, who led me to my deepest, darkest places and brought me safely home.

To Danielle Kiowski, for those months and months

of ridiculously long Friday calls, trying to help me understand how to write a sentence that didn't suck.

To the Story Grid Community—if you hadn't listened to the podcast and supported the process, this would never have happened.

ABOUT THE AUTHOR

Tim Grahl is the C.E.O. of Story Grid, a university and publishing house dedicated to teaching and publishing complex stories. He is the author of the bestselling book marketing methodology and protocol, *Your First Thousand Copies* and *The Book Launch Blueprint*. His memoir *Running Down a Dream,* a warts and all confession of the trials and tribulations of a contemporary small business owner, drew accolades from Ryan Holiday, Barbara Corcoran, Daniel H. Pink, Derek Sivers, and Steven Pressfield, who described it as "Indispensable." The writing of his first novel, a young adult science fiction coming of age action story, *The Threshing,* was the subject of the first three years of the Story Grid Podcast, a perennial chart topper on multiple podcast bestseller lists.

www.ingramcontent.com/pod-product-compliance
Lightning Source LLC
Chambersburg PA
CBHW060609310726
48982CB00003B/497